For Carabosse, as always.

ALEISTER BLAKE

1875

ONE

THE RAT'S DRY, BRISTLED tail shifted against my bare foot and I didn't hesitate.

Guided by years of practice, I lunged forward in the darkness and grabbed the furry body behind its head with my right hand, thumb and forefinger pincered for maximum strength. I had taken time to perfect this move. Too little force and the rat could bite me or escape; too much and its neck could snap, making it worthless for Sharpe. No one paid money for a rat's corpse.

The animal screeched as it wriggled to get free, but there was no chance of that now.

"You're wasting energy," I said and readjusted my grip.

This wasn't the safest way to catch rats, especially not when hunting for them inside walls that allowed only the flimsiest bits of dusty light in. But it was the quickest way if you were fast and sure, and I was both.

"Nora, did you die in there?" Peter's voice echoed down the narrow passage between the two walls.

"I've got the last one, I think," I called back.

"You better be surer than that, or Sharpe is going to board you up there until you catch the rest."

"Let him try," I muttered, and used my free hand and my legs to wriggle forward. Not for the first time, I gave thanks that Sharpe's greed allowed me to wear trousers. I would have been ready to commit bloody murder if I had to do this in a petticoat and skirt.

I inched up and around a corner created by one of the kitchen walls meeting the sitting room wall, rodent gripped in a two-fingered claw with the back of its body pressed against my chest. If I hadn't smelled like rat urine before, I did now.

The ragged patch of sunlight that marked the entrance and exit point Peter and I had made with a sledgehammer darkened as my brother's head appeared.

"Come on, Sharpe's done settling payment. Took you long enough. I thought the rest were going to chew their way through the bag."

"If you think you can do it faster, the next one is all yours," I said, shifting the last two feet to the hole in the wall.

Peter laughed. "Can't even fit through there, can I?"

I lifted the rat out of the hole as he opened the latest in a long line of potato sacks. I released the animal into the twitching bag. There were no holes yet, though, no dark snouts working their way out. It would hold until we got to the Lantern.

"How many is that, then?" Sharpe's smoke-soaked voice said.

"Eleven," I said and stepped out of the hole. "Six adults and five pups."

"That ain't right," he said. "There's more pups than that usually."

"I don't know if it's right or not, but it's the case today."

"Watch it, girl," Sharpe said. "I ain't paying you to mouth off."

I rolled my eyes as I brushed away dirt and rat droppings from my trousers. "Are we done here, then, or are we going to stand chatting? They must be waiting for us at the Lantern."

Fixing my gaze on Sharpe, I dared him to say something, anything else. He wouldn't.

With a sharp exhale, he turned and headed past the two servants in full livery who had drawn the short straws and had been ordered to watch us in case our fingers were lighter than expected. And they would have been if no one were watching.

"You don't have to rile him up every time, Nora," Peter said. He grabbed the sack and twisted it closed.

"You're right, I don't have to. I just enjoy it."

He shook his head but couldn't hide the smile fluttering at the corners of his mouth. "Let's go before these two have a fit," he said, nodding to the two men standing behind us.

I twirled my fingers at them and followed my brother out of the sitting room overflowing with gleaming furniture and into an equally grand reception area. Two girls in crisp aprons leapt to their feet from beside the fireplace and looked satisfyingly slack-jawed to see us. Me with my trousers and Peter with enough mud on his clothes that they could stand on their own.

Peter lifted the bag. "Just getting rid of some vermin," he said.

The girls' faces lost two shades of color, though it was difficult to tell whether that was because of the squirming rats or Peter's wink.

I laughed as I followed him toward the home's servant's entrance. Why we had to traipse through half the house when the front door was right there in the reception room was beyond me.

Our feet echoed through the glistening hallway. All of it was done in carved wood and plaster so that everywhere I turned, round angels smiled or sat playing the harp, flowers swooned under the weight of their heavy petals, and birds flew in perfect formations in a way that I had never seen them do in real life. London's pigeons were more likely to crash right into someone's face than maneuver gracefully through the sky, beak clasping beak.

The hallways thinned and darkened as we made our way to the back of the home. Sharp voices gave orders I couldn't quite make out to maids I couldn't see, all to keep the monstrosity of this home in order. Every time I stepped foot in the glittering homes of the rich, I grew a bit gladder I hadn't bothered to get into service. Not that the option had presented itself. An orphan raised on the streets by her brother could never reach the level of gentility the great lords and ladies required from the ones scrubbing their floors or making their meals. It was enough that the likes of Sharpe, Peter, and me had to be allowed in to crawl through their attics or walls to catch the rats that had developed a taste for fine cuisine.

We turned into the last hallway that would lead us to the kitchen and out into the street. A bit of glitter caught the corner of my eye.

On a corner table, someone, most likely a servant with too much to do, had left a man's shirt that needed laundering. And on that shirt sat a set of the largest cufflinks I had ever seen. They were out of place in this dark, bare part of the house, but I could remedy that.

With a swipe of my hand, I pocketed them.

"Nora," Peter hissed.

No matter how good I got, how quick my hands and smooth my gestures, he always saw me. Always caught me in the act. Not that surprising, since he had taught me all of my tricks, but one day I would manage to steal something right from under his nose without him noticing.

"They don't need them," I said.

"If they see that they're missing after we leave—"

I waved his words away. "They won't." I'd taken something from almost every home we'd been in since we started working for Sharpe and no one had ever complained. They had so much, they couldn't keep track of it all.

We crossed the kitchen's threshold and headed for the back door. I smiled at a woman with a bouquet of keys at her waist and pointed to the wriggling bag of rats. The scowl on her face never wavered.

Together, Peter and I stepped into the November air. It nipped at my face after hours indoors, its bite as refreshing as a splash of water. I breathed in deep to chase away the dust I'd inhaled while hunting between walls.

From across the street, Sharpe motioned for us.

"Let's get our pay," Peter said. He offered me his arm and I took it with a laugh.

Sharp sniffed and nodded to the sack when we reached him. "It's a meager haul, this. Won't fetch much at the Lantern."

I could almost mouth the words as he said them. At least once a week he tried to weasel out of paying us fully for our work, pulling any excuse out of his head. If Peter was alone with him when he started muttering about payment, we usually walked away with less than half of what we deserved for our work. My work, really, since I was the one who crawled inside cupboards, in-between walls, inside nooks in attics and cellars, and into anywhere else I could contort my body enough to fit inside.

Which was why I now made sure I was there when the bag of rats exchanged hands.

"The family paid for them, though," I said. "Handsomely, too."

"That ain't the point," he said.

"Really? Because what they paid you is more than enough to pay *us* what we've earned, especially since you're going to get something more for them at the Lantern." I shrugged and turned to Peter. "We could try to sell them directly ourselves, I guess."

Sharpe raised a hand. "Now, now, that's nonsense. The two of you wouldn't get a pence out of George." He cleared his throat and lifted his jacket enough to pull out a small bag from his waistcoat. The movement displayed the tears and holes in his shirt. "Five adults—"

"Six adults," I said.

Sharpe looked up at me. I smiled and batted my eyelashes.

"Right, six adults and five pups." He brought out a handful of coins and counted them. "A shilling for every adult rat, three pence for every pup." His thick lips moved as he counted. "That is...seven shillings and three pence left over."

Stashing the rest of the coins in the bag, he handed our pay to Peter in exchange for the sack.

I gritted my teeth together. All of that work, all of those hours crawling through dust and worse, for seven shillings while he took the rest of it on top of whatever he got for them at the Lantern, without doing a moment's worth of actual work.

As if he'd read my thoughts, Peter placed a hand on my arm to quiet the words that wanted to spill out of my mouth.

"Thank you, Sharpe," he said. "See you at the Lantern tonight, then."

"Maybe, maybe not. There ain't a good dog in the fight. 'Least not one I want to put money on." He straightened his coat and nodded to us before walking away, toward the pub a few streets down.

"God, I hate that man."

"Yes, I know," Peter said. "He knows; all of London probably knows, by now."

"He's robbing us and he has been for years. Why do we still need him?"

Peter sighed. "You know why. He's got a name, a reputation for reliable service that we don't."

"A reputation that he built on our backs."

"Yes, but what would you have us do? No one is going to let the two of us into their grand homes without someone vouching for us." He brought his hand up, the two cufflinks that had been in my pocket a second ago twinkling on his palm. "And with good reason."

I gasped. "Blast, how did you do that?"

"It's simple to steal from someone who's upset."

"I'll remember that," I said and tried to take the cufflinks back. Peter swept them into his other hand with ease.

He glanced down at them. "They should fetch a good price. Keep us under a roof for a few weeks. We'll have to talk to Stuart at the Lantern about them tonight."

I started to nod, but paused when I caught up with what he'd said. My eyes widened. "'We'?"

"I think it's about time you come see what all the fuss is about."

Words slipped away from me. An uncommon occurrence.

Peter shrugged. "If you don't want to, then I can—"

With a laugh, I leapt and wrapped my arms around his neck. "I can go? I can really go?"

"Neither one of us is going anywhere unless you let me breathe, Nora," he said in my ear.

I released my grip enough to look at him. "And I can stay as long as I want?"

"That sounds fair. As long as you promise to behave and not pinch everything with a bit of shine on it."

Standing on my toes, I planted a kiss on his rough cheek. "Deal," I said.

Peter smiled and tucked the cufflinks back into my pocket. "All right, that's enough nonsense. What do you say we get something to eat?"

"I say you have taken the words out of my mouth, good sir."

"Well, then, madam, I know just the place."

I took his offered hand just like I'd done since I could remember and followed him into the street.

The night, and all of its waiting secrets, could not arrive swiftly enough.

For what felt like the hundredth time in five minutes, I pulled back the ragged cloth that served as the curtain for our only window and peered out into the street.

The woman screaming about fresh fish was still there, holding up a limp silver thing that even a dog would hesitate to sniff, as were the two men Peter had told me in no uncertain terms to stay away from.

"They make girls disappear, Nora, do you understand? Never get close to them. If you see them around, you come into the house and lock the door."

I had heard the rumors spreading like smoke through the alleyways of our world. Three girls had disappeared this week, ripped right off their lives and our streets, but no, I didn't really understand the fuss. Half the people we lived among could make someone disappear if they felt like it. Hell, Peter and I found at least one corpse a week while hunting for rats in alleyways and in the docks and none of them had gotten there on their own. But if it made Peter feel better, I'd stay away from these men.

I looked past them, down along the street. Still no Peter. Where the bloody hell had he gone off to? We'd be late if he didn't hurry.

He hadn't so much as given me a clue to where he was going and I'd been too distracted by my preparations for tonight to needle him too much about it. Something which I now regretted.

With a sigh, I sat back down on my bed and fiddled with the cufflinks I'd stolen. Nothing I could do but wait.

Come on, Peter.

A small eternity passed before I heard the usual groan of the damp-swollen door as he shoved his shoulder against it to dislodge it.

"Finally!" I leapt up.

"I've been gone half an hour, Nora."

I crossed my arms over my chest. "You said you'd be right back. Where were you?"

"Honestly, can't I have any secrets?" he said as he looked out the window, his smile tightening at the sight of the two men.

"No, you can't."

He snorted and turned back to me. "You'll find out later, I promise."

My eyes narrowed.

"I promise! Now, do you want to keep arguing or can I change my shirt so we can head out?"

The flutter of excitement at what I'd be seeing tonight returned to my stomach at his words. What was I doing wasting time? He and I both knew I'd ferret out the truth about whatever he was hiding soon enough if he didn't tell me. Peter had never in his life been able to keep something from me for longer than a few hours.

But now we had to go.

Without another word, I tugged on the blanket that we'd hung from a clothesline years ago to divide the room in two, hiding him from view.

"How very kind of you to think of my modesty."

I smiled but did my best to sound as gruff as possible. "Nothing to do with your modesty. I just didn't want to see that ugly face of yours anymore."

He pulled the blanket to the side just enough for his head to be visible. "This face, you mean? This wonder of the world?"

Rolling my eyes, I tossed my pillow at him. "Just get dressed, wonder of the world. If we miss tonight, I might just strangle you."

TWO

THE LANTERN'S CELLAR OVERFLOWED with people.

Men of all ages pressed against all four walls and up along the scuffed wooden staircase leading up to the pub. These were the late comers, the ones who had nothing to spend but still wanted a glimpse at the pit.

Smoke from the old lamps hanging from the ceiling mixed with the smoke coming from the men's cigars to create a veil over the entire space, so that only the bright colors of the dresses the two or three women besides myself wore speckled the dimness. But neither the smoke nor the bitter, biting smell of cheap alcohol did much to dispel the pungent odor coming from the very center of the room, from the pit itself.

It was a square separated from the rest of the cellar by panels of thick wood that were almost tall enough to block my view entirely from the action. Blood-soaked sawdust and dirt covered the floor of this pit, which no one bothered to change until it became too slippery for the dogs. Or so Peter had told me the few times I had managed to pry any information out of him at all about these weekly dealings.

"Can you see?" Peter asked, elbowing his way to my side.

"Only just." Although we had been able to find spots close enough to touch the pit's wooden barriers, there was a row of men in front of us who were all taller than I was.

"And you're sure you *want* to see?"

I smiled. "I've been waiting for this a long time, Peter." I grabbed his arm and squeezed. "I thought you would never let me come with you."

He had refused for years now. "You're not old enough, Nora," he said each time I begged to be brought, pushing aside my whining and my anger as I reminded him he had been much younger when he came to the Lantern's cellar the first time himself.

"You're a girl. It's different."

I couldn't blame him for his refusals. Ever since our mother had disappeared twelve years ago, swept away from our lives like dirt off a stoop, and with no father to speak of, Peter had been saddled with me. With a girl. He'd been left to care for me, a five-year-old creature who bit and scratched and spat, who grabbed everything she could get her stained hands on, but who was still a girl. Someone more likely to be prey than predator. That simple fact had to have weighed on his nine-year-old mind that first night on our own, and that weight had only increased with each passing year. He had never said so, but I could sense that tension anywhere we went, felt the clenching of his muscles when a man came too close or spoke too roughly, the fear that I would one day be wrenched from him just as surely as our mother had been.

But perhaps that would change tonight. I had turned seventeen last week, after all, and here I was, safe and at his side.

"Look, they're bringing them in," Peter said, pointing to a man carrying a larger version of the sacks he and I used every day.

The hiss of claws against rough fabric brought an instant of silence to the room before the men around us broke into booming yells and cheers.

Peter turned to look at me, waiting for me to flinch and ready to pull me out if I did, but I only laughed and joined my own voice to the clamor.

The man lifted the bag high, letting it swing from side to side. "It's getting to be 'bout that time, gents!"

More yelling.

"What d'you say we get this event started? You best have all your bets placed!"

I whooped along with Peter and the men all around me, my heart speeding up as the man placed his hands at the bottom of the sack and lifted it even higher, until it was well over his head. A sharp movement of his hands, and the sack was suddenly upside down, raining rats onto the pit.

I had never seen so many of them in one place! All sizes and colors!

Thuds gave way to hissing and screeching as the rats scrambled over one another on the sawdust, their twisting bodies racing away from the pit's center and toward the outer walls.

"Bring 'em out!" the man yelled.

The words were still echoing when the yipping and baying started, cutting through the crowd's yells like blades. Two metal cages were brought out and lowered into the pit. Inside each one was a dog.

The man in front of me shifted, blocking my view.

"Bugger," I said and stood on my tiptoes, but there wasn't a chance I would be able to see over his full height. Instead, I searched for a gap.

"Do you want me to lift you on my shoulders?" Peter yelled beside me.

I waved his words away. I'd figure out a solution on my own.

There! I bent my knees and settled my gaze through a gap no larger than my fist between one man's shoulder and his neighbor's.

Just in time to see the cages slide open, releasing the small, snarling dogs into the pit. They rushed in opposite directions, skirting the wooden walls as if they had been trained to do so, and in the space of a heartbeat, each one had a rat in its mouth.

A cheer rose from the crowd almost in unison and I joined along, my high scream making the man on my right flinch.

One of the dogs shook its head forcefully once, twice, and dropped the rat to the sawdust before taking off after another scurrying body.

The rodent was immobile where it had been dropped. Limp on the sawdust.

My voice lost some of its strength, my eyes blinking at the abrupt draining of my excitement. I frowned.

I'd known what happened in these gatherings beneath the Lantern. Everyone, including the coppers who patrolled these streets, knew. And everyone waited for the next one, counting down days, speaking about which dogs would be in the pit and how many rats each one would have to kill to be the champion for a week. I listened to all of this for years, imagining myself at the cellar on the nights Peter left me on my own, dreaming of the thrill of being here, where I now was, cheering for each rat that fell and would never get up again.

What was happening in front of me was no surprise. So why did I suddenly have to muster up the energy to clap and cheer along with the rest of the crowd?

Next to me, Peter struck a fist into the air as more rats thudded against the floor. I forced my lips to smile when he turned to look at me.

"That's five for ol' Two-Tone!" a man called out.

The dogs continued their chase around the pit, tongues stained with blood hanging out of their mouths as they darted one way and another. Rats crawled over each other to avoid their fangs and used their tails to propel themselves forward, searching for any direction that might offer salvation.

Don't be daft. I rolled my eyes at my own thoughts. This was ridiculous. I'd never been a ninny and I wasn't about to start now. What did it matter to me if these rats, which obviously weren't smart enough or strong enough to climb out of the pit, died? They earned their deaths. Fair was fair. The weak died, the strong survived.

When one of the dogs, the one named Two-Tone, gripped another rat and shook it until it snapped its neck, I made my hands clap, made my voice rise to cheer it on, made my eyes turn away from the bleeding body. One of many.

"Get them, Two-Tone!" Peter yelled. His face was flushed, his excitement leaping out of his eyes as he gave my arm a quick squeeze.

This time, my smile was genuine.

The smaller of the two dogs lunged at a pile of rats that was forming at the opposite side of the pit, scattering them in all directions. My eyes locked on one of them, a larger rodent than the rest, and surprisingly agile for its size. It had begun to race straight down the middle, paying no mind to the corpses or blood in its path, never veering from its course, not even when Two-Tone snapped at it and missed its neck by the thickness of a fingernail. Its powerful legs propelled it onward and onward.

It was like an arrow of black ink heading straight toward us. My eyes widened when the rat didn't stop or slow down to calibrate as it neared the wall. It jumped without hesitation, sure of its aim. With a heavy thud, it landed on the barrier right in front of us. Its claws scrambled for purchase against the wood and found it, or enough of it to lift itself up onto the edge of the panel.

If anyone else noticed the animal, they gave no evidence of it.

The rat's black, glittering eyes cut through the smoke and haze and landed on my own dark ones. It stood there, panting, tail twitching, staring at me as intently as I stared at it. As if it recognized me. As if it had something to say.

I gave it a small nod. *Well done*, I silently said to it. Now this was a rat worth catching.

In an instant, one of the men in front of me raised his walking stick and struck the animal back into the pit with an everyday, casual twist of his wrist.

My gasp was lost in the sudden roar of the crowd.

I'd felt that strike in my gut.

It wasn't the violence but the unfairness of that action that finally managed to shake loose the fantasy of these evenings from my mind. My stomach plunged with the sudden understanding. The rat had almost made it to freedom. It had earned it. It had slipped through death's grasp with skill and strength, with courage, and had still been thrown back to die. And no one cared.

The hot pounding of blood was suddenly the only thing I could hear. I pulled back from my vantage point, allowing the bodies in front of me to block my view of the pit.

Yes, I'd known what happened every week in this cellar, but knowing and seeing had never been so different.

There was none of the fierce, violent beauty of battle to these gatherings that I had imagined, just plain death to feed our greedy amusement.

The force of the unjust cruelty occurring three feet away, one that had swiftly lost all reason and all appeal for me, rattled my insides, making the voices around me suddenly too loud. Even Peter's yells scraped against my skin.

The wet-coin smell of blood filled my nose and mouth. People pressed against me on all sides, the heat from their bodies making it impossible to draw air, to think. And all the while the screeches and thuds continued just out of view.

I needed to get out. Now.

Turning on my heels, I elbowed my way between the men behind us.

"Nora?" Peter called, but I didn't look back. All I could think about was getting out of this cellar, out of the Lantern, into the cold night air.

My heart felt as if it would tear a hole through my chest as I shoved and ducked through the roiling crowd toward the stairs. I forced my way up the first few steps, cursing at my decision to swap my trousers for these blasted skirts.

"Where are you goin' in such a 'urry, sweet'eart?" a man said, blocking my way up. "Stay 'ere and I'll protect you from the nasty rats." Laughter brushed me from all sides. Behind me, I could hear Peter calling.

The man made to touch my hair and I smacked his hand away.

That cut the merriment in half.

"Out of my way or you'll get a knee to the bollocks."

Whether it was the hiss in my voice or the actual words I uttered, the man eyed me over once more and shifted to the side. "Ain't no need to be so uppity. Just payin' you a compliment, like," he muttered as I passed him.

Was there any air left in the room? In the entirety of the Lantern? The bit of it I could manage to breathe in while shoving people to the side to climb out of that cellar locked in my chest, creating a knot of pressure. Sweat trickled down my face and neck, and into the collar of my shirt. Behind me, Peter's voice glinted off a background of shouts and animal shrieks.

I groaned at the sound. I shouldn't have come here tonight. How would I wipe the unfairness of what I'd seen from my head enough to do my job tomorrow and the day after?

At last at the top, I pushed open the door leading into the main room of the pub, hitting someone on the opposite side with the force of the movement.

"Watch it!" a woman said.

I took the length of the room as near a run as I could and lunged outside through the front doors.

The air was like a wet cloth against my fevered forehead. I gulped it in, hands pressed to my chest to still the pounding of my heart. My knees trembled, slippery with sweat under my petticoat's fabric, while I walked the few steps out of the pub's light and away from the clumps of people milling by the door, into the welcoming shadows of the nearby alleyway. The darkness closed over me.

"Nora!" Peter's voice, now sharp with fear, flew into the night.

It would have been nice to have had a minute or two on my own to steady my nerves, but there was nothing for it. If I didn't answer, he would have half the Lantern out searching for me.

"I'm here!" I called.

Seconds later, his silhouette appeared at the alleyway's mouth.

"Didn't you hear me calling before?" He ran to my side. "Are you all right?"

"I'm fine."

"I knew I shouldn't have brought you. I knew it. It was too rough." He placed his hands gently on my arms. "I'm sorry."

I couldn't tell him the truth, not when he looked a moment away from begging for my forgiveness on bended knees. Besides, these gatherings were the one thing he enjoyed, what he looked forward to as we spent hours trailing after rat droppings or listening for scratches, day after day, week after week. If I told him what I'd realized less than five minutes ago, he'd never step foot in that cellar again for my sake, even if he didn't feel the same way. He would see it as his duty. I couldn't do that to him. I would have to find some way to come to peace with all of it.

"Don't be daft, Peter. It was just ungodly stuffy in there. I'm not used to so many people together in one place."

He bent to look me fully in the face. "That was all?"

I sniffed and turned away. "Of course. Just got a bit dizzy."

He was silent for an instant, watching me, his hands still on my arms. For the first time in my life, I doubted my lying skills.

"Well," he said, "let's get you home, then. You're probably tired after today and—"

Raised voices and the slamming of a door stole the end of his sentence. The unmistakable sound of glass shattering on the street's cobblestones.

Peter's hands tightened.

"Where is 'e?" a man shouted into the night. "I saw 'im come out chasing after some skirt. 'E must be nearby."

There was a murmur too low from which to catch actual words followed by stomping footsteps heading toward the alley. Toward us.

"Peter, they don't mean you, do they?"

Peter frowned, his grip on my arms edging toward the painful.

"*Are* they looking for you? What do they want?"

He opened his mouth but closed it as a shadow fell over us, blocking the bit of light coming from the pub.

"Luke, 'e's 'ere!" the shadow called out.

More figures appeared, thickening the darkness in front of us.

"What is this?" I hissed at my brother, but if he heard me he gave no indication of it.

A slice of night separated itself from the rest and moved closer to us. Its steps were slow, relaxed, a man walking through his home instead of down a dark alley.

"Peter, son, we thought you'd left us," the man said.

My brother cleared his throat and released my arms. "Of course not, Luke."

"See, that's what I told 'em. I says 'That boy would never do that, would never run out on a debt. He's honorable, he is.'" He spread his hands open. "And I was right because here you are."

My breath snagged on that word. *A debt?*

The man, Luke, continued his measured walk toward us. "I'm afraid you've been a bit unlucky tonight. Two-Tone did not live up to his promise, which is most unfortunate for you." He sighed, a sound that twisted into a harsh hiss.

I turned to look at my brother. "You bet on a dog without telling me?"

The men still standing at the alley's mouth laughed.

Although I couldn't see Luke's face, I knew the moment his gaze landed on me. "Not only did he bet on a dog, darlin' girl, he bet us three shillings a piece for him." He motioned behind him. "Now, I've never been too good at 'rithmetic, but that comes out to...twelve shillings."

My eyes widened. Peter had bet on a dog or two before on Christmas or on his birthday, but never more than a shilling and never without consulting me. It was both of our hard-earned money. Was that what he'd been doing earlier? But what had possessed him to bet that much? More than we had?

I shook my head and turned to look at my brother. "Why—"

"He got a tip on poor ol' Two-Tone which, as it turned out, was not genuine. That's why my companions got a tad worried about him slippin' away like that after you." He came to a stop in front of us, close enough to smell. An onion-like pungency of unwashed clothes and sweat. "Though I can't say I blame you, son, for chasin' after this one," he continued. "She's a fine specimen. Wouldn't mind havin' a go at her, myself. Could even forgive you what you owe in exchange for her."

He reached out, faster than I expected, and touched my face with one clammy hand.

I flinched.

"Don't you touch her," Peter said, his voice clean of all expression.

"I know plenty of men who would pay a mighty nice price to own this soft skin."

I tried to twist away but Luke was quicker, digging his fingers into my cheeks to hold me in place.

"Get your hands off her!"

Peter shoved Luke away and moved in front of me, blocking me from him and the rest of the group.

"You leave her alone! She's got nothing to do with this."

Luke laughed. "Oh, you're givin' orders now? Fancy that." He held his silence for an instant. "We can resolve this easily, Peter. Give us our money and we'll be on our way."

"I'll have it in a few days."

The men at the alley's mouth stepped closer, moving as one entity. I peered behind us, at the rest of the alleyway, my eyes searching for an exit that did not exist.

"So, you don't have it now?" Luke said.

"Not all of it, no."

"Then hand the girl over and we'll forgive the debt. The fine gentlemen who buy from us would be happy to add her to their next shipment."

I frowned. *Shipment?* What was he talking about?

Peter's whole body tensed and he widened his stance, his arms rising to block anyone who tried to get closer to me. "Never, you hear? She's never going with you."

The man was silent, his figure as still as if he had been turned to marble. "That is," he began, "the wrong answer, son."

A nod of his head was all it took to get the three other men to swarm toward us. Peter pushed me backward, but there was no contest. In an instant, two of the shadowy figures had hold of him.

I lunged forward and gripped one of them, digging my nails into his torso with all the strength I could muster. He yelled and released a hand long enough to hit me across the mouth. The pain was swift and sharp like a blade.

Hands gripped my arms, pulling them back until I yelped in pain.

"Let go of her!" Peter screamed.

I struggled against whoever held me but it was like trying to make stone give way.

Luke moved toward Peter's, his steps just as slow and even as they had been a few minutes before.

"You should never bet money you don't have, Peter. Didn't anyone ever tell you that?"

I squinted, willing my eyes to pierce through the darkness around me.

"It's just not good business, son."

"We'll get it!" I yelled. "Give us a couple of days and we'll have your money."

"Ah, but you see, we ain't got time to wait, girl. We need our money now, as promised. As owed." He leaned over Peter. "How much do you have?"

"Seven shillings," Peter said.

The man sighed. "That...well...that's just not good enough."

He thrust one of his arms forward, into my brother's midsection. Peter groaned, a deep, wet sound that sent a shiver up my back. The men released him and his body sagged, slumping to his knees.

"Peter!"

I waited for him to shake off the punch and stand up again, to prove the icy fear raging through me wrong.

"Unfortunate," Luke said, and moved his hand, allowing a stray beam of light from the Lantern to bounce against something he held. Something gleaming.

"No," I whispered. "Please, no."

Peter pressed his hands to where Luke had hit him with another groan of pain and lifted them to his face. Even in the dim light I could see darkness staining them.

Blood.

"No!" I shrieked, pulling on the man who held me with so much force I thought my arms would snap off. "You stabbed him! You bastard!"

Panting with fear, I brought my foot down as hard as I could on one of my captor's, feeling bone give way. With a yelp, his hold on me slackened and I yanked myself free.

I ran toward Peter and sank in front of him.

"Nora," he said. An edge of fear lined my brother's voice.

Blood spread through his shirt, blooming like a dark flower. I ripped the fabric, revealing a large gash high on the right side of his torso that spewed more and more liquid as I watched.

"That bitch, she broke my toe!"

"Don't worry, I'll give 'er a beatin' she ain't never going to forget!" A hand grabbed my arm, ready to pull me away from Peter, but my sudden throat-tearing roar made the man take a step back.

"Let her be," Luke said. "Ain't worth the effort. We'll find some other skirt. One that ain't goin' to give us this much trouble or that'll wake half of London. She's too wild for our clients, at any rate."

Never taking my gaze off the four men, I pressed my shaking hands to the wound. Hot blood squelched against my skin. "Help! Someone help!" I screamed into the night, knowing all too well no one would come. Not in this part of the city.

"Choose your men better next time, love," Luke said, turning away. His companions broke into laughter.

"I'll skin you alive!" I screamed, spitting the words out at their retreating figures. Rage boiled through me, the heat of it threatening to burn me up from the inside.

A gurgle brought my eyes up to Peter's face. Blood trickled out of his mouth and down his chin. Whatever strength had kept him upright until now suddenly ran out and he collapsed forward, onto me. I jerked my hands up to his shoulders to avoid being pinned beneath him and shifted him so that he could lie on his back. Was that the right thing to do or would he choke on his own blood?

His hand reached out, flailing in my direction, and I took it in my soaked ones. His mouth opened but only more blood poured out.

"Don't try to talk," I said. I pressed my hands against the wound again, but I knew it was useless. This much blood could only come from something vital that had given way inside him.   He was dying. My brother, the only person I had, the only person I loved in this world, my mother and father, my best friend, my teacher and conscience, was slipping away from me in a filthy alleyway. For twelve shillings.

"Please, no. Please." I hissed the words into the night, clenching Peter's hand tightly. "Please, I'll do anything."

"Perhaps I might be of some assistance," a soft voice said from the mouth of the alley.

I gasped and looked up. A figure, tall and thin, somehow darker than the rest of the shadows but at the same time more visible, stood looking down on Peter and me.

"Are you a doctor?" I asked. My muscles tensed, ready to lunge at the figure if he tried to separate me from my brother.

"No, I am not. He is too far gone for a physician's help, in any case."

Peter's chest heaved to draw in breath, making him cough up more blood. His eyes rolled back, his eyelids fluttering.

"He is dying," the shadowed man said.

"I know that!" I screamed.

"I can help him. Save his life."

The words, so soft they were barely audible, trailed over my arms and the back of my neck like a warm breeze. I shivered.

"If a doctor can't save his life, how can you?"

"I have my methods."

Peter gasped for breath with a wet, gurgling sound. Blood poured out of his torso, ink-black and thick.

"Your brother's life ebbs away with each second you waste in doubt. Allow me to help him."

His words fluttered around my head. How did he know Peter was my brother? And how could he offer to save him? How could he undo the damage quickly enough? How—

I cut my thoughts at the root. It didn't matter, nothing mattered. If there was a chance this man could save Peter, faint as it was, unlikely as it was, I would take it.

"Yes, help him," I said.

"There is a condition."

I bit back a scream of frustration and fury. "What?"

"You must agree to work for me."

That was all? Catch rats for him? "Yes, I—"

"No," the voice sharpened. "You must listen carefully before you decide. Otherwise, the bargain does not count." He took a step closer. "You will come live with me and do as I command. You will leave your brother, your life, all of this behind. You will not have any contact with him or with anyone who knows you. Not for the rest of your days. In return, your brother will live a long and healthy life. Those are my terms. That is the bargain I offer."

I tightened my grip on Peter's hand, feeling his strength disappearing. His skin was already growing cooler against mine. He had moments left.

"Do you agree?"

The choice was obvious. If I did nothing, Peter would die. If I agreed to the man's terms and he could do as he promised, my brother would be alive and I would find some way of seeing him. There would be no keeping us apart. I had lied many times before and I could do it again now.

I nodded. "I agree."

My words were still echoing through the night when the man lifted his arm.

Peter's hand snapped away from mine, clenching at his side as his entire body stiffened, contorting with a ripple of pain. His back arched up and his mouth opened in a scream he had no means to voice.

"Wait! You're hurting him!"

"Patience is a virtue," the man said.

A fist-sized ball of light materialized under my brother's skin, illuminating his insides as if he had swallowed a candle's flame. His ribs became visible, expanding, fighting for breath.

The pulsing light grew, doubling then tripling in size, until it covered the large, bleeding wound completely. Its glow poured out of the sliced skin like melted wax.

I shook my head. I couldn't be seeing what I was seeing.

The blood plastered against Peter's pale torso, thick and black just a moment ago, started to fade, to seep back into his body. Each drop of it soaked up by the glowing light. The gaping wound, too, had begun to shrink, sewing itself up from the inside, the skin puckering and smoothing out in a continuous swell, until not even the smallest of scars was left.

My head felt like it was on fire. This was not happening. It couldn't be happening! Only magic or a miracle could work like this and I had left those childish beliefs behind me years ago. There were no miracles in lives like Peter's and mine. And yet—

My brother gasped and his body slackened, the glow inside him all at once disappearing. The darkness that the light had pushed back swarmed around us once more.

I held my breath.

"Nora?" He sounded as he did when he was half-asleep, but there was no pain in his voice. No weakness.

It took my mind a beat to realize what I was seeing. He was alive. The man still watching us had somehow healed him.

"Peter. My God, Peter!" I sprang forward, ready to wrap myself around him and, if at all possible, never release him. Damn the promise I had made to hell.

But my arms banged against the space between us, forcing me to a stop. I winced and narrowed my eyes to see what I could have possibly hit. There was nothing and no one in front of me but Peter.

I tried again, and again came up against the same unseen obstacle. A pin point of fear broke through the relief I felt.

"What is this?" I murmured. It was as if the very air had turned solid. "There's something blocking me, Peter."

I brought my hands up, laying my palms on the sudden barrier. It was as cold and slippery as glass and it kept me from reaching my brother.

"Nora?" he repeated.

"I'm here. It's all right." I stood and began to trace my hands up the barrier, looking for an edge. But an edge of what? There was nothing in front of me!

"Nora!" Fear turned his voice into a blade that cut through the alley. He leapt to his feet with his usual strength, as if he hadn't been a breath away from death just moments ago, as if the blood still staining my skirt belonged to someone else.

"Peter, I said it's all right, I'm right here!"

But his gaze brushed by me when he scanned the alleyway.

"He can't see or hear you, Nora," the shadow man said behind me, his voice wrapping around my name like coils. "Or me, for that matter."

I turned. "What?"

"This is what you agreed to."

The speck of fear expanded until I felt like there was a hole in my chest. I shook my head. "No."

"You gave your word you would not have any contact with your brother, and this is what that means. You will find the same if you try to communicate with anyone else who knows you."

I slammed my fist against the invisible divide between me and Peter. He didn't flinch or turn my way. "No! I didn't know it meant this!"

"I made the conditions very clear," the man said.

I kicked at the barrier with all the strength I had, hoping to hear the crackle of splintering glass, but there was no give. I tried again and again, as Peter called my name.

"You are wasting your energy," the man said. His voice was still soft, feathery, unperturbed by my fear and Peter's. "What separates you from your brother cannot be broken or surpassed unless I allow it to be so. If you spent an entire lifetime kicking at it, you would still find it unblemished. Now," he said, and motioned for me with his arm, "it is time we were leaving."

Peter suddenly took off past me and past the man, out of the alley and into the street that led to the Lantern. I chased after him. I couldn't lose him.

"Nora," the man called after me.

"No!" I stood in the middle of the street, halfway between him and my brother. "I can't just leave him!"

"I see," the man said, his voice a caress of sound. "Well, then, if that is the case, I have no need to keep my side of the bargain." He lifted his arm once again and pointed it at Peter's retreating figure.

My brother's knees buckled, his hand shooting out to the wall next to him for balance as his body lost its strength. I moaned when I heard the gurgle of blood filling his mouth once more.

The truth burned through me. Nothing could be worse than knowing Peter was dead. Nothing. Not being kept from him, not having to abandon everything I had ever known, not having to do the bidding of this man who could take and give life so easily. Nothing.

"Stop. Please, stop," I said. "I'll go with you."

The man, still encased in the shadow of the alley, said nothing.

"I swear. Please help him."

Although I couldn't see his eyes, I felt their weight.

"Very well." A flick of his hand was all it took for Peter to regain his footing, to spit out the blood that had stopped his breath. His body filled out with life again. His steps were sure as he ran away from where I stood, calling and calling my name.

Taking a breath that shook as much as my hands did, I turned away from my brother. One foot in front of the other, I forced myself to walk from the person who meant everything to me toward a man who meant nothing at all. Tears spilled out of my eyes. "He doesn't know what happened to me," I said. "He'll imagine those men took me."

"He will mourn for a bit, true, but his life will continue. He will go on to get married and have children. He will be happy."

"You can see that? You know that will happen?"

The man inclined his head. "I do. He will live a full life."

I swallowed the tight knot in my throat. "Without me."

"Without you."

He stepped out of the shadows for the first time. The street's gaslight seemed to seep into his form slowly, as if he were fading in reverse.

Whatever I had expected him to look like, this was not it. He couldn't be more than twenty-one, if that, though his voice had given the impression of many years lived. His face, too, looked out of place. It would have looked more at home gazing out of one of the paintings hanging at the National Gallery than staring back at me out of a dark alleyway. His features had been carefully chiseled and radiated intelligence, but there was no room for kindness in them. It was the face of a prince or a king, someone used to being obeyed.

Despite his height, his movements were graceful when he began walking toward me, every muscle working in concert. He was in full evening wear, but had no hat and carried no walking stick, as most gentlemen did. What had he been doing dressed like that in this part of the city? He could have been in the Lantern's cellar, true; it wasn't unheard of to have gentlemen place wagers on a promising dog, but I would have noticed him even in the crowd. It was impossible not to.

"Come, Nora. It is not a very long walk home."

Without waiting for a response, he started down the opposite street from the one Peter had taken.

Everything in me resisted following him, pulling me instead onto my brother's path, but I had already made my choice.

I half-ran down the length of the street to catch up with the man. I sidled up beside him and tried to stem the flow of tears with deep, steady breaths as he led us down one lamp-lit street after another.

There were so many questions I had, about this stranger next to me, about what I'd just seen him do, about what my future life would be, that they tangled into knots in my head so that I couldn't choose a single one. But it was the pressing sadness I felt at leaving Peter behind that kept me from opening my mouth. I feared if I did, a scream would be the only sound I'd be able to make.

Peter and I had never been apart for more than a few hours at a time throughout the entirety of my life and now I was expected to go on day after day without him. The months and years to come stretched before me like the city's black, foggy streets, only this darkness would not be swept away by day's arrival.

I wiped at my tears with fury. There was no point in crying over this. Now I would have to concentrate on whatever waited for me at this man's house. After seeing the unnatural powers he had, I was sure my work would not involve rat-catching.

I knew what a normal man would want with someone like me. I overheard enough stories from the girls who stopped by the Lantern dressed in garish bodices and half-ripped skirts to know how this all worked. But if that was what he wanted, surely he could choose women better suited for the task. I had a pleasant-enough face, but there was no polish to me. I wasn't amusing, or kind, or even civil most of the time.

But the figure beside me was not a normal man, if a man at all. What he'd been able to do... my mind bucked from the memory of it, despite my own eyes' testimony.

"Bad night, eh?" a harsh voice said and yanked me out of my own head.

I turned to find a man staring at me, a wide smile on his lips. He laughed, a sound as rough as the pavement beneath me, and tipped a bottle to lips that were almost black with soot and dirt before walking away. But he wasn't the only one looking in our direction. The eyes of women and men widened with alarm as they caught sight of us, or of me, since they barely glanced up at the stranger at my side.

It took me a moment and a glance down at my hands to realize why I had captured their attention. They, as well as my bodice and skirt, were still covered in Peter's blood. It was drying into dull stains, but there was no mistaking it for what it was.

"Pay no mind to them," the man said. They were the first words he had uttered since we'd started walking.

I lowered my eyes to the street. It wasn't the easiest task not to mind now that I was aware of their stares, but he was right. What could their gazes or laughter possibly do to me?

At least I had clear proof that I hadn't hallucinated the entire episode. That I hadn't just given up my life for nothing. The blood on my clothes offered me my strongest grip on reality and on what I had sacrificed.

I turned my eyes from the pedestrians still on the streets at this hour and walked on toward my new life.

THREE

THE MAN HAD SAID his home wasn't far, but it felt like centuries since we had started off from the Lantern. My feet had begun to rub painfully against my shoes, the best ones I had, and I was afraid I would have to take them off if we didn't get to our destination soon.

As if he had read my thoughts, the man came to an abrupt stop.

"Here we are, then," he said. "My home, and now yours as well."

I followed his gaze.

The building in front of us stood at a street's corner. Its exterior was crisply white, with a dark and ornate door in stark contrast. The property was divided from the similar one next to it by an extending bit of wall that rose above the second-story windows to the height of the chimneys protruding from the roof.

This was where I would live from now on, then.

The man walked up the few steps to the front door and turned to look at me. His face held no emotion in it at all.

I wanted to run. Just take off into the night. Anything but go into that house.

Instead, I clenched my hands and followed him up to the landing. He brought out no keys, but only pressed the handle down gently and the door opened.

The first thing, the only thing, I noticed was that it was darker inside than outside. If there were any lights on in the residence, their glow did not make it to the entryway or anywhere near it.

The man stepped through the threshold, slipping into the gloom easily.

I'd never been afraid of the dark, not even as a young girl. Rats lived in the darkness, they thrived in it. If my mind had contained any trace of the almost instinctive fear of not being able to see, it had been wiped away by necessity as soon as our mother had left Peter and me to fend for ourselves.

Still, walking into a strange building with a man I didn't know was nothing like what I was used to. Rats were predictable. They were animals that wouldn't harm just because they could. The same could not be said of humans. If that was even what this man was.

Not that I had much choice in the matter.

I forced myself to take the few steps into the house. I was so sure of an impending ambush of some sort that I flinched when the door closed behind me with a click. At almost the same time, a light began to bloom above me, the glow gaining strength bit by bit until I saw what was creating it: a chandelier the size of which I had never seen.

"Electricity is a marvelous invention, isn't it?" the man said.

I blinked to wipe away the imprint of the light in my eyes and searched for him, following his voice.

One by one identical chandeliers came to life throughout the room, pushing back shadows and revealing where I was.

Never in my dreams had I pictured standing in a place like this one. The room, if it could be called such a thing, was so long I could barely see the end of it. Not if he had bought three houses together could this amount of space have been possible in this area of the city. Or in any area, unless you were Queen Victoria.

The walls were solid cream stone, their smoothness only broken up by brushstroke swirls of what glittered like liquid gold. Huge columns of veined marble that matched the gleaming floors had been carefully spaced on both sides of the room, leading toward its horizon. But it was the ceiling which caught and held my eyes, my mouth dropping open like a child's.

It curved over us, as lofty as a cathedral's, much taller and wider than it could possibly be. Shades of blues and creams created an expanse of sky that covered the entire length of the room, with the crystal chandeliers hanging from lengths of carved gold that looked like they had been made from captured rays of sunlight.

"It is something to behold," the man said.

I pulled my eyes from the ceiling and found him stepping out from behind one of the columns, as if he had wanted me to take in the entire room without his presence.

"From the exterior, the home is just as it was before I purchased it, but the interior has a few special touches," he said, as if tripling or quadrupling a building at his personal whim were no more taxing than adding new curtains. "I enjoy having substantial space. Gives my thoughts room to expand."

I blinked.

The man lifted a hand to stop the words that were about to leap out of my mouth. "I understand you have questions, and I will answer them in time, but not tonight."

"Why not?"

"It is not the right moment. When you are ready, you will know all."

I hadn't the slightest idea what that meant. I was bound to him already, what could he possibly reveal that would make a difference, whether I was ready or not? But I supposed that if he didn't want to tell me, I had no leverage with which to demand the truth. None at all.

There was one more thing, though. "At least tell me your name. Since you know mine, it seems only fair."

The man lifted an eyebrow. "Fair." He said the word as if his mouth wasn't used to shaping it. "Yes, perhaps it would be."

He was silent. His gaze dimmed like a shadow had fallen over it and he lowered it to the floor. Even when he lifted his eyes back to mine a moment later, he had to blink to bring them back to their full brilliance.

"Aleister Blake," he said.

That was a lie if I had ever heard one. I crossed my arms over my chest. "Is that your real name?"

"It's what you may call me."

Although his stance hadn't changed, his voice hadn't risen or lowered, these words had an edge of frost around them. And something else, something darker. They were an animal's hiss of warning. The beat before the bite.

I pressed my lips into silence and held my breath. Anything could happen now.

Like a peculiar fog, however, the change in the air around us wisped away, dissipating almost at once. Aleister, if that was what he wanted to be called, cleared his throat.

"Let me show you the house," he said, his voice as calm and still as it had been until seconds before. He motioned for me to follow him down the length of the room.

Bloody hell, just do as he says, I told myself.

Each one of my steps echoed against the marble and stone, but as I reached him and began walking beside him, I noticed his didn't. Aleister moved in complete silence. Like I was walking next to the dead.

The hairs on the back of my neck and along my arms rose.

There were no other sounds in the house, either. Surely there were servants who took care of a place this large, or vermin of one sort or another scrabbling up the walls as night wore on. But no, there were just my footsteps assuring me I hadn't gone deaf.

It was only as we reached the room's center that the three doors at the opposite end became visible.

"Through there," he said, and pointed to the large door on the left, "is the dining room and kitchen. The pantry and larder are stocked with the finest of everything you could possibly want, but if there is anything I have missed, advise me of it and I will provide it. You will find two meals prepared and waiting in the dining room at noon and at seven each day and evening, but you can cook your own or eat out in the city if you prefer."

The shock of his words brought me to a stop. "I can go out?"

Aleister turned to look at me and smiled for the first time. A colorless gesture that never reached his gleaming eyes. "Of course, Nora. You are not a prisoner. You may come and go as you please, without having to ask for my permission or even having to inform me of your trips. I will provide a generous allowance which you may spend as you like and" —he reached into his evening jacket and brought out a key so polished it caught the light from the chandeliers in its carved length— "your own key, so that there are no restrictions at all."

He held it out to me and I took it, careful not to touch him in the process.

The key was heavier than it looked, solid like one of the silver knives I'd stolen a few months before from a rat-infested restaurant.

"So, you see, you are not in any way prevented from doing what you like, when you like."

But that also meant... "Could I see my brother?"

I expected his face to tighten with annoyance, a denial already on his lips, but he only shrugged. "If you wish. You could see him again tonight, even, though I am not too sure what that would accomplish."

No, maybe he couldn't realize what good it did, but the knowledge that I would be allowed to at least check on Peter whenever I liked was enough to give me some level of peace in the madness this night had brought.

"Through there," Aleister said, pointing to the door on the far right, "are your chambers. You will find a comfortable sitting room, bedroom, bathroom, and the like. They are fully furnished but if you find them disagreeable, you may redecorate as you see fit."

He spoke as if I were used to sleeping on goose-down pillows instead of having shared a room with my brother for as long as I could remember in a rickety building that smelled of sewers on the best of days. I knew about as much of decorating as I did of parliamentary rule.

"And that door leads to my chambers," he continued with a nod to the center entrance.

"Which I may not cross, I assume," I said.

Aleister flicked a wrist in its direction and the door swung open with a violent bang. I gasped, taking a step back, and then felt like a dim-witted child. I had seen him pull someone back from death's threshold and was astounded when he opened a door from a distance?

"You may explore the entirety of the house, including my chambers. My secrets, such as they are, keep themselves." He turned to look at me once more, his sharp eyes cutting right into me. "Is there anything I have missed? Any question you need answered, apart from who I am and how I do the things I do?"

Oh, I was rich in questions, but there was one that demanded attention above all others. One that had started pulsing behind my temples from the moment I had realized he had no wife, or at least not one who lived with him. A young man without attachments, bringing someone like me into his life? This had to be the kind of "buying" that Luke had spoken about tonight. Well, it made the situation clearer, if not any less frightful.

I held his gaze even while I felt my cheeks warm. I would not be cowed by this. "Will you be visiting my bedroom in a regular manner?"

Not a muscle twitched in his face. His eyes were as hard and still as the crystals dangling above us. He watched me in silence, forcing me to draw on every fiber of strength I still had within me to not look away.

"You may rest easy on that front. That is not part of our agreement," he said. "You are safe within these walls, and that includes being safe from me. I will not disturb you." His voice held no anger or amusement. Not even the easy indignation of the insulted upper class. No expression at all. "Anything else you'd like to know?"

The relief his words brought seemed to snatch all other thoughts away because the myriad of things I had wanted to ask just moments before suddenly vanished from my mind. "No, I...I don't think so. That is, not right now."

"Then I will bid you goodnight, Nora." He nodded his head so slightly I could have easily imagined it, and started down the room, towards the door that led to his chambers.

The air seemed to part around him as he walked. I saw him take each step and waited for their sound but there was nothing. Not even a whisper of leather sole against marble.

"Oh, one more thing," he said when he reached the ornate golden door. "There's a meal waiting for you in the kitchen. I had it prepared in case you were hungry."

Before I could say another word, and without turning around, Aleister walked into his wing of the house.

The door slammed shut behind him without his having even touched it. I flinched.

Silence crowded swiftly around me. The force of it pressed against my ears. I held my breath, listening for any sounds. But I only heard the slight buzz of electricity from the chandeliers above me, and even that seemed to augment the quiet, not part it.

The silence cracked the thin layer of shock that had protected me until now.

My stomach clenched as if someone had punched it, and I found I couldn't catch my breath. The room was all at once too bright, the size of it adding to the emptiness yawning open inside me.

Thoughts as stinging as nettles flooded my head. I would never again embrace Peter. I would never again laugh with him, chase rats with him, complain about Sharpe with him. He was lost to me.

When my fingertips started tingling, I realized I was breathing too quickly. My entire body shook under the strain of making sense of what had happened tonight and I knew, as much as I wanted to, I wouldn't make it back to the room I'd shared with Peter in this state. I'd end up collapsing in the streets. In fact, I wasn't sure I could make it to the room Aleister had assigned me in this very house.

But I refused to faint in the middle of this grand foyer.

Feeling my muscles stiffening, knotting up, I started for the door that led to my wing of the house. I flung it open, more lit chandeliers blinding me with their cold sparkle, and raced to the first room on my left.

I barely registered it was a sitting room before heading to the next one, a study or library.

Tears sprung to my eyes. My hands felt like they were asleep and my teeth were chattering as I crossed the corridor and opened the last door. The warm light of a fireplace revealed a bed.

Gasping, I stepped inside and slammed the door shut, only just managing to turn the key that was already inserted in the lock. As if it had been waiting for me. My shaking legs buckled.

Slow your breathing, Nora.

I heard Peter's voice in my ears, and though I knew it wasn't him, it would never again be him, I listened to it. As I always had.

I took a breath and held it for as long as I could before exhaling. I did it again and again, tears trickling down my cheeks.

By miniscule degrees, the pressure in my chest eased and my muscles unknotted. The panic I'd felt receded, leaving me drained, a husk of myself.

I opened my eyes.

The bedroom's only light came from the fireplace across from the bed, its warm glow a relief after the harsh electric light.

It took immense effort to turn my head and take in the rest of the room.

The bed was a monstrosity. It could have fit at least six people comfortably, but it wasn't its size so much as its style that made it a horror to look at. Wooden figures swarmed along its posts and edges, leaning over to look in on whoever slept in it. I couldn't tell what they were from where I stood, but I was sure they didn't represent beings entirely human.

At the far wall was an armoire done in a similar, overly carved style, and glittering as if it had just been polished. Beside it was one of two large windows, both uncovered.

My head ached with unanswered questions but it was my heart, which throbbed with loss, that was the most painful as I stood on wobbly legs and walked to the bed.

The fire's warmth rolled over me. It began to pull on my rapidly mounting exhaustion and I didn't fight it. I needed to escape all of this, if only for a few hours.

I placed my hand on the wine-colored coverlet, ready to draw it back and sink into the bed, and groaned.

My hands and clothes were stained the same dark color, the fabric matted with Peter's blood.

The sudden need to get the blood off of me urged me into action.

I undid my bodice's buttons and unclasped my skirt, allowing them both to fall to the floor at my feet. Blood had seeped into my corset and undershirt, soaked up by the fabric, and the stains were still wet to the touch. I hurried across the room to the only door I had left to open in this part of the house.

It revealed what I had expected: a bathroom. A real bathroom, with a gold-footed white bathtub and two basins.

On a screen embroidered with red silk flowers behind which hid the toilet, an actual one and not the type of privy Peter and I had shared with six other people, hung a white nightgown. A nightgown that looked to be my exact size. One that looked as if it had been left there *for me.*

"Bloody hell," I murmured.

Shaking my head, I realized I just couldn't think about any of this any longer. Not tonight. My head would roll right off my shoulders if I did.

I walked to one of the ceramic basins. The sooner I washed this blood away, the sooner I could sleep. And, with any luck, wake up to find all of this part of a fever-induced dream. I didn't think I would, but hope cost nothing.

I turned the golden handle labeled "hot." Less than a second later, water poured out of the gleaming faucet and plumes of steam rose to my face. Though the water stung my hands, I shoved them fully under the constant stream and kept them there, rubbing at them with one of the many washcloths that rested in a pile beside each basin. I rubbed until every dried flake of blood disappeared. Then I did the same with my face.

There was no chance the bloodstains would come out of my corset or undershirt, however, no matter how much I scrubbed. There was nothing for it but to wear the nightgown.

I unfastened the laces at the front of my corset and removed it, followed by the thin undershirt, which I had to peel away from my skin in the spots most saturated with blood. Pushing the bloodied heap of clothing to one corner of the bathroom, I reached for the nightgown.

As I'd expected, it fit as if it had been tailored to me. Perfect sleeve length, neck width, a hem that just brushed the tops of my feet. My mind again reared up to ask for an explanation, but I just shrugged and walked out of the bathroom. Tomorrow, answers. Tonight, sleep.

The fireplace's warmth enveloped me once more.

I'd started walking to the bed, my swollen eyes already half-closed, when my foot landed on something hard. I sucked in a breath of surprise and dull pain and glanced down. It took me a moment to recognize what the twinkle at my feet was.

The cufflinks I had taken from the house earlier today. I had put them in my skirt's pocket to see if Stuart would give us a good price for them after the dog fight. I'd forgotten all about them.

I could have given them to Luke. They had to be worth twelve shillings, at the very least. I could have avoided all of this if I'd just remembered.

Feeling the tears I had thought exhausted start to roll down my cheeks again, I bent and picked them up. They seemed to burn as I closed my hand around them, squeezing until I felt them carve their shapes into my flesh.

FOUR

PEOPLE. SO MANY PEOPLE.

Hordes of them shifting, moving against me, shoving me forward. An elbow against my side, robbing me of breath. A hand tangling in my hair.

"It's pandemonium in here. It's pandemonium, Nora," Peter said from somewhere behind me, but I couldn't turn around to see him. I had to see him, I had to tell him something, but the roiling mass of bodies pressed closer and closer until I couldn't do anything but move forward with it.

"Peter!" I called out. My voice stuck to my throat and was covered completely by the cries and wails sprouting from the crowd. "Peter!"

A sound, strident like glass shattering, forced the people to speed up around me, so that I could hardly keep up. My bare feet brushed the ground without really touching it and I managed to stay upright only because there was no room for me to fall.

"Pandemonium!" my brother screamed behind me.

Sweat as salty as tears rolled down my face and into my mouth and down the back of my legs under my skirts.

"Peter!" I called again and tried to turn my head with no success.

That was when I felt the first skittering claws brushing my feet. I gasped and pulled away from the touch, but it was too late. Whatever it was had latched on to my skirts, had started crawling up, up, up, to my waist, as another set of claws grabbed on to the back of my bodice.

I opened my mouth to scream, to call for my brother, but no sound came out, only sweat pouring in like tears. Like blood—

With a muffled shriek I sat up.

My heart thudded against the back of my throat and in my temples as I tried to make sense of where I was.

A fire crackled in front of me, lighting up the carved figures on the mantle and on the frame of wood that made up the bed in which I lay.

That was enough to bring everything back to me with the force of a slap.

Aleister Blake. Peter. My promise.

I closed my eyes. All I'd done was just wake from one nightmare right into another.

With a shaking breath, I shoved the heavy bedcovers away, revealing a soaked nightgown that clung to my sweaty skin. The sheets beneath me as well as the pillow at my back were also drenched, my body's outline darkening the fabric that had been white when I laid down.

It hadn't been just the nightmare, either, I realized. The room was stifling.

Tepid morning light poured in through the uncovered windows, which meant it had been hours since I'd given over to sleep. Yet the fire in front of me still burned with as much vigor as when I'd first stepped into the room. As if someone had tended to it while I slept.

I wiped sweat from my forehead with my arm. Never mind the fire. What I had to do now was get dressed and go find Peter, ensure he was still all right. I would think of what to do about all of this later, once I'd had some fresh air.

Yes, that was exactly what I needed to do. Get some fresh air.

Riding that thought, I hurried to the bathroom to perform my morning ablutions, all of them much easier now with water that came at my bidding, at the turn of a knob.

It was when I walked back into the bedroom a few minutes later that I felt my heart leap up to my throat in fear.

My bloodied clothes, which had been on the floor when I rose, now hung from the dresser door. They had been carefully arranged, every wrinkle pressed away, the hem of my skirt starched solid. Beside my old clothes was another set, a brand new day dress, a pristine corset, and the whitest of undershirts.

I swallowed. None of this had been there when I woke. I was sure of it. The dresser's front had been bare and my clothes had been in a pile by the bed. Nothing else had been disturbed, at least that I could see. The cufflinks I'd clenched for so long last night they had cut grooves into my palms were on the night-table, where I'd left them.

Someone had to have come in while I was washing and done this.

I made myself walk to the dresser. A soft floral scent rose from my stained clothes as I ran my hand over the fabric. It had been cleaned and ironed. There was no mistaking the crisp feel of the skirt, the perfectly pleated bodice. They looked just as they had when I'd bought them two years ago. Well, with the added and rather unbecoming blood stains splattered through the cotton. The only things missing were my corset and undershirt. I peered back into the bathroom where I'd left them the night before, but they had disappeared.

There was sudden and swift movement from somewhere on my right, where the door was. With a gasp, I turned, fully expecting to see a maid or at the very least a large rat running for cover, but there was nothing there. Nothing and no one.

The hairs on the back of my neck rose. A shiver scurried through me despite the room's warmth. Yes, it was about time I got out of this house.

I reached for my skirt a second before I realized I couldn't possibly walk out into broad daylight wearing it. The bloodstains might have drawn stares last night, but those would be nothing compared to the ones I would get now. In this part of the city, I might even attract attention from the coppers.

Which meant the only other option I had if I wanted to find Peter was to wear the new set of clothes hanging on the dresser door.

"Fine," I said, nodding. I would have preferred my own things, but getting arrested or being thrown into the madhouse was not what I had in mind for today.

I took off the nightgown and slipped the undershirt on. The corset came next. It was heavier than the one I had worn for three years, with its lining done in gleaming cream satin instead of rough cotton and laces that were not frayed or stained. It was a work of art, but as beautiful as it was, there was something about it not quite right.

I wrapped it around my torso, but it didn't mold to my body the way it should have. It was almost as if it had been created backwards.

Oh, of course.

Peter would have called me a simpleton for taking so long to understand. The corsets I was used to were those made for women without maids to help them dress; they had laces at the front for easy tying. This one was not one of those.

With a sigh, I walked to the tall wood-framed mirror near the bathroom door and turned the corset around. The stays settled under my ribs as they should. Wonderful, but how in heaven's name was I supposed to tie the laces on my own?

I reached back with one hand, letting the other one hold the contraption in place, but although I could grasp the soft laces, I couldn't pull back enough to tighten them.

"Blooming hell," I said.

Perhaps I could tie the corset as I would my regular one and then turn it around, but that would mean it would not be tight enough for me to fit into the miniscule skirt and bodice. That was obvious just from looking at the pieces. Without shedding a few inches off my waist, nothing would fit.

I looked at my reflection in the mirror. "Now what?"

Darkness suddenly swarmed around me. Shadowed shapes I half-saw clutched at my shoulders, their claws digging into my skin, the instant before a violent tug nearly toppled me backward. I gasped as the fabric around my torso contracted, the stays digging into my ribs, the laces tightening all along my back.

My eyes widened.

Hands had started to pull on the corset, tugging the laces this way and that with so much force their ends slapped against my bare legs like thin whips. It didn't take long for the pressure against my chest to pass the point of comfort and dip into pain.

The darkness that had taken over the room spread. The mirror revealed nothing more than the bed and the night table, but even the fire's glow was losing its strength as whatever monstrousness had a hold of me pulled and pulled. It was squeezing the breath out of me.

And I was letting it.

That thought broke whatever shock had frozen me in place. I jerked to the side, my elbow hitting the glass in my frantic effort to get loose. But it was no good. The force continued to pull and pull, the pressure never slacking, the corset creaking with tension.

The fabric will split, my mind screamed. *It has to or my ribs will crack!*

I tried to twist around enough so that I could kick out at my adversary, but its grip was too strong. I couldn't do more than roll my shoulders and fling my fists behind me in a pointless effort to hit what I couldn't see.

An edge of black began to stain my vision with each gasp that brought no relief. I had never seen anyone drown or suffocate, but it didn't take a scholar to know I didn't have much time left to do anything but lose consciousness. And death, I was sure, would come swiftly on its heels.

"Stop!" I hissed with the last puff of air in my chest.

The pressure disappeared as suddenly as it had started.

My own force, now unopposed, propelled me forward so that I had to grip the mirror to keep from falling. I sucked in the largest gulp of air my lungs could manage, the darkness in my eyes increasing for a moment before dissolving. A cough scratched up my throat so violently I fully expected blood to spew out. But that didn't matter. The only thing that did was that I had to get out of here. Now.

Before I could recover my balance, the corset laces jerked and tightened once more. Bright panic flushed through me as I waited for the nightmare to start again, casting my mind about for anything that might save me now that I still had breath with which to think.

But the laces fell with a limp tap against the fabric. The unseen horror released me and the shadows that had filled the room retreated.

I didn't stop to wonder why. With a swallowed shriek, I grabbed the bodice, the skirt, and my shoes, and lunged for the door.

Cool air encircled me the instant I stepped into the hallway. Sweat dripped from my forehead and down the back of my legs, bringing back the dream I'd woken from only minutes before.

Every bone in my body seemed to be shaking with the kind of fear I hadn't known existed until last night. I took a step back, then another, until the hot air coming out of the opened bedroom door couldn't reach me anymore.

My hands scrambled over the corset, still expecting it to contract like a cramping muscle against my ribs, but it fit just right, squeezing my waist but allowing my chest to rise and fall with each breath. It was no more painful or dangerous than my old one.

I stepped into the skirt and slipped my arms into the matching jacket-style bodice, buttoning and snapping the perfectly fitting fabric into place just enough so that it wouldn't slide off me, before hurrying down the corridor. I clutched my shoes tightly with one hand and shoved open the wooden door that led out to the house's entrance hall with the other.

I didn't stop until I had crossed the entire floor and reached the front door, and I wouldn't have stopped even then if I hadn't seen a small bag and a piece of paper on a wooden table next to the entrance.

My back tingled with the expectation of a hand landing on me, trying to squeeze my neck or shove me forward, but none of that occurred. I grabbed the note and shook it open.

Nora,

I have been called away on some business this morning. Most unfortunate, since I wanted to be there to greet you and to speak with you about the specifics of what honoring your half of our bargain will entail. Alas, work cannot be avoided even for one such as I. We will touch on that matter tomorrow.

In the purse, you will find what I hope are sufficient funds to get you through the day. I look forward to hearing if you spent a comfortable night in your quarters.

Aleister Blake

I could almost hear the mockery rising from the page.

Bastard.

Crumpling the piece of paper in my fist, I flung it across the hall. With a swipe that sent the table teetering, I took the purse and shoved my way out into the brightening London morning.

I found Peter in front of the Lantern, accosting anyone foolish enough to walk too close to him.

Although I had just turned the corner and was still across the street, fighting with skirts much heavier and longer than I was used to, despair gave my brother's voice wings and brought it straight to my ears.

"Excuse me, miss, I'm looking for my sister. Perhaps you've seen her," he said to a girl about my age. "She's small, has brown hair with thick curls and brown eyes."

"That's 'alf of London!" the girl said.

Peter took a step closer to her. "But she's wearing a gray wool skirt with a...a lace trim and a matching jacket. Her name is Nora."

The girl waved him away and walked on. Without a pause, Peter turned to the next person he saw and repeated the inquiry to no better results.

I picked my skirts up higher than was probably decent and crossed the muddied streets to stand by his side.

I didn't expect anything to have changed since last night, but the way his eyes swept over me without recognition, without seeing anything but empty air where I stood, twisted my heart. The flashing panic I saw within them didn't make things any easier, either. Despite everything, at least I knew he was fine, but he hadn't the slightest idea whether I was alive or dead. One moment I had been beside him and the next I had vanished. He had to be imagining Luke had taken me, that he had sold me or done whatever bloody awful thing he'd had in mind.

He turned from one person to another, his voice repeating the same description. He had no likeness of me to show anyone. We'd never been able to afford a photograph let alone a daguerreotype, so he had nothing but his words to bring me to life for other people. And that is what he used, time and time again.

It was only when people caught on enough to begin avoiding the sidewalk in front of the Lantern that he moved on, first walking to the mouth of the alleyway where last night he had regained his life and I had lost mine. He stared into the gloom that even the morning couldn't chase away as if he expected me to step out from behind a clump of bricks, crawling out of the wall like I had thousands of times before.

It was natural that he was worried about me, but as Aleister had said, that would change. Even grief had to have a way of passing. He would go on to have a life and he would be happy. I had to hold on to that knowledge.

I followed him down the street, tracing the steps I'd watched him take last night without being able to go after him.

As I followed Peter, traces of last night's nightmare, in turn, followed me. They'd resurfaced throughout the morning and I hadn't been able to shake them off. I could practically taste the fear I'd felt, the fear which had saturated that one word Peter had repeated and which hounded me now. Pandemonium. Where had that word come from?

When the sun began to dip behind the taller buildings, Peter started to lead us down very familiar streets. His steps grew surer, his pace faster as we walked to the rank hole in the wall Sharpe called his office. The despair that had begun to close around him like a vice throughout the day slackened just enough to make me wince. He still hoped I would appear at our employer's. A hope that would be crushed in a matter of minutes and I would be right there to see it happen.

My steps became heavier the closer we got to Sharpe's.

Peter walked past the building and its filthy stoop, and headed for the back entrance through the alleyway. It was more conveniently located for access to Sharpe's room and had prevented me from cursing and kicking at the bloody urchins that crowded the front door every time we visited.

Rats skittered away into the garbage that piled on both sides of the door as soon as they heard us. Only one of them didn't bother to run for rotting cover. It sat still, its tail curled around its body like a cat's, watching us pass. Or rather, watching me pass, for its black beaded eyes weighed on me. Perhaps it was my tired mind, but I could have sworn it was the same large rat that had scrambled up the wall at the Lantern last night and had been shoved back to its death. It couldn't be, of course. After seeing what those events were like, I doubted the animals would be set free if they survived their ordeal. And yet the intensity behind its eyes, as if it needed to say something, was the same that I'd experienced last night before my world shattered into pieces.

I opened my mouth, unsure of what would come out of it or what I meant to accomplish, but the rat ran off.

Of course it did. It's just a regular rodent going about its life. It has nothing to say to me or anyone else. Despite everything that had happened last night, a London rat was still only a London rat.

I turned back to Peter, who had slipped into the building.

Sharpe's room was the first one on the right. Its open door spilled a rectangle of light onto the stained and warped floorboards.

"Peter!" Sharpe called out as we neared the door. "Get in 'ere."

He was at his termite palace of a desk, a bottle of something so strong I could smell it from where I stood open in front of him. At least the alcohol managed to mask the usual odor of the place: the mildewed sheets on the bed behind the gaudy false-Chinese screen that divided the room, the residue of cigar smoke, and other, less savory scents I had never cared to categorize.

"Found that sister of yours yet?" There was an edge of laughter in his voice as he sat back in his chair.

Peter's body seemed to collapse into itself at the casual words that snuffed out his last bit of hope. He shook his head.

"She'll appear soon enough," Sharpe said. "Probably with some lad, havin' a go at it."

I could have punched him in the jaw for that. If the barrier between us weren't ready to break my hand at any such attempt, I would have. That man had known me since I was six years old and he still thought me just another girl ready to lift her skirts in the back of an alley at the slightest display of male attention.

From the tightening of my brother's mouth, the thought of laying hands on Sharpe also crossed his mind. "She would never disappear without a word. Not if she had a choice about it. They took her, I just know it. I told you Luke and his friends attacked us last night." He ran a hand through his hair. "If I had known they were involved with those shipments, I would never have made a bet with him. Not ever."

The shipments again.

"But I must have hit my head," he continued, "because I don't remember what happened. One moment Nora was there and the next she had vanished. I do know she was crying, I remember that much. I can hear her voice, her screams, begging...begging..." His hands clenched into fists. "She needs my help!" His voice cracked open into a ragged sob.

The sound made my hands shake. Never had I imagined I'd be able to cause him such harm and still be alive to see it.

"Calm yourself, son," Sharpe said. "If Luke did take 'er, ain't nothin' you can do about it. You won't find 'er." He raised a hand when Peter tried to speak. "But I'm sure that ain't what 'appened. Sit down and 'ave a mouthful of this. It'll set you right in no time." He nudged the dark bottle in my brother's direction.

"No—"

"It ain't a suggestion. What use are you to anyone in that state?" He nodded. "Go on. It'll do you a world of good."

My mouth opened to tell Sharpe where he could shove that bottle before I remembered my limitations.

Peter hesitated. Both of us knew alcohol for the poison it was, for the way it had compelled our mother to take off chasing after it, never to return. Through the years, we had refused all offers of pints during birthdays and even on Christmas, when the entire neighborhood was deep into its cups. Alcohol was not welcomed in our lives.

But those lives, such as they used to be, had fallen apart.

Peter took the bottle and brought it up to his mouth quickly, as if allowing himself no second thoughts. He swallowed deeply and winced.

Sharpe let out a wheezing laugh. "That'll take the sting out of anythin'."

Peter sat down on the only other empty chair in the room, and lowered his face into his hands. "I don't know what to do."

"Ain't nothin' you can do now, son, but wait. Don't trouble yourself thinkin' the worst. One hour with Nora and Luke would 'ave tossed 'er right back in the street just to be free of 'er yellin'. She'll come back in a bit, 'er dress in a state, and that'll be that. Mark my words."

I gritted my teeth.

Sharpe tapped the desk with a fist. "Actually, it's mighty fortunate that you stopped by. I 'ave a letter that needs writin', if you're up to the task. Just some business corr'spondence."

"I don't—"

"It'll take your mind off all this nonsense." He smiled and nodded to the bottle. "'Ave another swallow and 'elp your old pal do this. It's a very quick note, I promise you."

That manipulative bastard. A quick note. What he needed was a quick kick to the groin.

Peter did as he was told and took another long drink from the dark caramel-colored bottle. He recoiled less from the taste this time, reaching up to wipe his face with hands that had stopped shaking. His shoulders had slackened and his body no longer looked like it would tear itself into shreds with worry as he rubbed his swollen eyes. That slight relief, at least, was something I could thank alcohol for this one instance.

He breathed deeply, a flush of color rising to his face, and his lips twitched into a small smile. "Of course I'll help you," he said.

"That's my boy!" Sharpe said. "We'll get this written in no time so you can 'ead 'ome to Nora. I'd wager she's on 'er way to your rooms as we speak."

He had no shame. Not a spot of decency in that ball of blubber he called a body. "You wanker."

Peter nodded and reached for a piece of paper from the stack Sharpe kept on the desk for display. He, like the rest of the neighborhood, didn't even know how to write his name.

My brother and I were the only people we knew who could read and write. And it hadn't come easy, the learning of it. It had meant months of staring at senseless figures, mouths moving in silence to try to work out the sounds that made up words. I would have given up after a week of it, but my brother had forced me to learn.

It was one more thing I owed to Peter.

My eyes widened with a realization that struck me like a slap. How could I not have thought of this before? I was such a simpleton! I would write to him. I would send him a note telling him...well, telling him something. Not to worry about me, for one. The details would come later.

But I had no paper or pencil on me, and Sharpe was leaning his entire body on the stack of blank sheets on the desk. Besides, I needed time to think of what I could write that would convince Peter I was all right and that he should stop looking for me. I couldn't do it right here, right now. I would most likely end up writing something so nonsensical my brother would head straight to Bethlem Royal Hospital to look for me.

There was a desk back in my wing of Aleister's house. In the study. I hadn't specifically looked for writing tools, but I was sure there would be some. Why else have a desk in a home like that but to write thank you notes and invitations to grand meals?

Now that the idea had bloomed in my head, I couldn't stay in that smelly little room a moment longer. Not if there was a chance this would work.

With a last look at my brother, who had put pen to paper already and was waiting for Sharpe to begin dictating, I hurried out of the room and back to that horrid house where I hoped the solution to all of this lay.

FIVE

I PICKED UP MY skirts and ran up the few steps to the front door. I'd had a moment of doubt leaving Sharpe's room of whether I would even remember how to get back here, but my feet seemed to know the way without needing to consult my memory. Another of Aleister's tricks, surely.

As I was about to insert the key into the lock, the door opened forcefully enough to yank the handle right out of my hand. I took a step back in surprise and my heel caught on the long hem of my skirt, my foot slipping on the edge of the step. With a gasp, I felt myself tip backward.

An arm snaked out of the darkness of the doorway and a hand closed tightly around my wrist. The strength in the grip stopped my fall, allowing me to regain my balance in an instant.

"That could have been painful," Aleister said as he stepped fully out of the house and into the afternoon sunlight.

After a flick of his eyes to ensure that I was not about to splatter against the pavement, he released my wrist.

"I'm fine," I said. Perhaps I should have thanked him, but I couldn't bring myself to say the words. They would have sounded as false as they'd have felt.

"Yes, I can see that." He gave me another quick glance, his voice edging on distaste. "You must have something very important to do, Nora, to be racing to the house with such speed." He stepped to one side of the stoop, allowing me access to the entrance. "But will you be able to accomplish it, I wonder?"

The blasted man. All he seemed to speak in was riddles. All he seemed to do was to laugh at me. It would have been satisfying to land a punch in that curling smile of his.

One of Aleister's eyebrows rose slightly. It was almost like he had heard my thoughts, which come to think of it, I wasn't sure he couldn't do.

"Right," he said. "I'll be off, then. I hope your evening is...fruitful." He touched his hat's brim in a gesture that would have looked courteous if anyone else had done it, but which he managed to make ironic.

I walked the few steps into the house. "Actually, stop," I said, turning back around. "This morning, something happ—"

Aleister was gone. He was not on the stoop or on either side of the street.

A ribbon of cold fluttered down my spine.

For the hundredth time since last night, I rummaged inside my head for the slightest sign that I had taken leave of my senses and came back to the same conclusion I had all of those times before. If I were hallucinating or mad, my delusions were as convincing as my life until now had ever been.

Shaking the chill of fear from my body, I closed the door behind me. The house's silence enveloped me, the ringing nothingness of the entrance hall muffling even my footsteps. As beautiful as it was, how could anyone live in this tomb-like place?

I hurried to the study in my wing of the house, feeling the weight of unseen eyes on me with every step I took, and sat down at the ornate desk. The room was ablaze with the sunlight that poured in through the curtain-less windows, but I could sense the waiting darkness. Every patch of shadows could be hiding one of the creatures that had attacked me earlier and I wouldn't know it until it was a beat too late.

Right, well, fear wasn't going to solve anything.

I turned to the task at hand. There had to be paper and writing utensils in one of the half-dozen drawers. If not, I would rip up a page from one of the books on the cases covering the walls all around me and write on that.

Quickly, I began searching. Most of the drawers were empty, the musty and sweet scent of old wood wafting up to my nose, while one contained a few stray ribbons in a variety of colors and another a handful of coins. Just a day ago I would have stashed them into a pocket without a second thought.

Finally, in the last drawer on the left I found what I was looking for: a stack of paper, a steel-nibbed pen, and a massive inkwell in the shape of a perching cormorant. I placed everything on the desktop, the words I was about to write already unspooling in my head, and opened the ink pot. The black liquid glittered.

I dipped the pen just enough to wet the nib and began.

Peter, I am alive! You will not belie—

But that was as far as I got. "No," I murmured, my eyes widening.

The words I'd just written had started to disappear, one letter at a time, fading into the paper as if they had never existed. As if I hadn't watched my own hand write them.

My heart pounded in my ears.

"No." With a shake of my head, I dipped the pen and started once more, this time further down the page. Those words, too, vanished, leaving nothing but a blank sheet.

"No!"

I shoved that piece of paper aside and grabbed another, with no better results. I left out Peter's name, next, and dipped my own finger into the ink to try to write with it instead of the pen. I even addressed the letter to the first random name that came into my head, but it was of no use. There was no fooling whatever power was preventing me from communicating with my brother. It knew my intentions and it forbade them.

Heat boiled up to my face and I yelled in frustration. My hands turned to fists around the pieces of paper, crushing them.

This had been my one remaining option and it was now gone.

With a yell, I flung the pen away. Its steel nib tapped the window pane before it clattered to the floor.

"Damn it," I said and brought my fist down on the wooden desk. A maw of blackness seemed to open in my mind, darkening everything within it. Swallowing the pinprick of light I had chased all the way here. Was that it? Did I not have any more options left to let my brother know I was all right?

A sudden tinkling of cups against saucers and the jangle of a heavy tray pulled me from the avalanche of thoughts. I frowned.

The sounds were coming from the sitting room, which was supposed to be empty.

I listened to the soft thumping and shifting of porcelain, my breath locked in my chest.

My impulse was to take off, to run out of the house and find a room anywhere else. But I'd seen and heard too much unexplained nonsense today to cower away so easily. If this was my life from now on, I had to face it and all of its horrors.

I stood and left the study.

A fire burned in the sitting room, its flames crackling in tandem with those blazing in the bedroom. A fire that had not been there when I'd walked into the wing. The fireplace was visible from the corridor and I had seen nothing before I stepped into the study. I was certain of it.

On a low table in front of the dark yellow sofa, something else rested that had not been there before: a white tea set edged in gold. Steam rose from the teapot's mouth. Beside it was a matching three-tiered tray on which finger sandwiches of all varieties, crumpets, biscuits, small cakes, and pieces of sliced fruit had been carefully arranged.

Swift movement caught my eyes, making me turn away from the tray. A shadow slid across one wall and out the door with impossible speed. Fright returned to me fully. I stood as still as I knew how, waiting for that creature to come back while I scrambled to think of anything that could be used as a weapon against a being that seemed to have no real body.

But minutes passed and it didn't return. I stood immobile, hardly daring to breathe. Waiting for an attack that never came.

Slowly, eyes flicking to every wall and every corner, I allowed my shoulders to relax, my hands to unclench. Whatever that shadow was, it seemed to be gone now.

With a sharp sigh of relief, I turned back to the tray of food. Not even the fright I'd felt a moment ago could keep my mouth from watering. No real surprise there when I realized I hadn't eaten anything since before heading to the Lantern with Peter last night.

As if they had a mind of their own, my feet took me to the sofa. I sat and grabbed one of the teacakes. I sniffed it, looking for peculiar smells, rotten or medicinal scents that might give away rat poison or arsenic, even a heavy dose of laudanum. But it only smelled of sweet icing and dough. And why would Aleister poison me, anyway? There would be little point in going to all that trouble to help my brother to go ahead and kill me the day after acquiring me. Still, that didn't exactly explain my brush with death this morning.

I took a breath and allowed myself only a heartbeat more of hesitation before I bit down into the teacake. Spongy sweetness filled my mouth. If there were anything dangerous baked into its flavors, it had been hidden incredibly well. The sandwiches I tried next were just as rich, as were the biscuits and crumpets I slathered with raspberry jam. I ate and drank until I patched up the hole that grown in my stomach. And nothing, not one piece of food or sip of drink, tasted strange.

The fire licked at the mounting gloom in the sitting room when I leaned back in the sofa, the exhaustion after all the hours of tension and grief growing now that my huger was satisfied.

It would soon be nighttime. I had to think of where I would spend the night, because I would have rather slept in an alleyway or in the sewers than in the bedroom Aleister had given me. Come to think of it, this sofa was not the worst choice for a bed. The fire made it unnecessary to grab even a bedsheet, and I could sleep just as I was. Only an idiot would attempt to take off this blasted corset and risk the same attack I'd had this morning. No. I'd remedy the undergarment issue soon enough, but for tonight, what I wore would be my nightgown. Uncomfortable, but I could handle that for one night.

Moving as little as I could get away with and still get the job done, as if afraid to dislodge another brick of sadness, I undid my shoes' laces and kicked them off. A world of improvement. I grabbed two sofa cushions, smacked them with my palms until they felt less stiff, and placed them under my head.

Not ideal, but I had certainly slept on worse.

Turning on my side and bringing my knees up to my chest as high as the corset would allow, I closed my eyes. Within minutes, sleep as warm as the flames that crackled across the room overtook me, pulling me down into the darkness where the nightmare waited. That one awful word crouched and ready to spring.

I opened the door that led out of my wing and into the hall the next morning, ready to leave the house in search of my brother once more, and found myself staring not at the marble-covered room I expected but at the bathroom's walls.

Gasping, I turned. Everything was just as I'd left it a minute ago when I'd rushed through my morning wash, my eyes casting all about me for signs of the shadows.

Something had moved me or had moved the house around me in the second it had taken to step through the doorway. Something had stopped me from leaving the wing.

I felt my stomach twist. Was a horror like I'd experienced yesterday going to happen every morning in this house? Was this what I would wake to from now on?

My feet seemed to become rooted to the tiled floor. What my body wanted to do, tired and frightened after another endless night of nightmares, was to curl into itself under this fresh onslaught of fear, to crouch down and make itself as small as possible.

And become prey to whatever those shadowed creatures were.

That thought snapped my paralysis in two.

I swallowed back the fright and forced myself to move, racing out of the bathroom and the bedroom, down the corridor, to the door leading out to the hall. I plunged through it.

Once again, the bathroom's tiles appeared beneath my feet.

I repeated it all one more time, though the truth of my situation had already descended on me.

Aleister had changed his mind. He wasn't going to let me leave. Not today.

Did he know I'd tried to defy his orders and write to my brother? Was this punishment for my disobedience?

With shaking hands, I tried the windows next, but none of them would open, not a single one, not in any of the rooms. Nothing I threw at them did one bit of good, either, bouncing harmlessly to the floor.

I was a prisoner. I would be locked in this wing until he decided to release me. Trapped just like an animal.

My hands clenched. "He wants an animal? I'll give him one."

Running out into the corridor again, I lunged into the sitting room, grabbing anything at hand. A vase, a ceramic figurine of a black dog of some sort, a set of china which I could only hope was horribly expensive, beautifully bound books, a spindly chair that looked older than the queen. Everything I found, I dragged out into the hallway.

I started with the vase.

With every bit of strength I had, I threw it at the door, the sound of it shattering cutting through the silence that encased the entire house. The china came next, plate after plate, teacup after teacup, followed by a hand mirror which gave a satisfying thud against the wood before glass shards shot out every which way.

"Let me out! You can't keep me prisoner!" I yelled. "Let. Me. Out!" I punctuated each word with a flung book.

The door opened the second after the dog figurine crashed against it.

Aleister glanced down at where its head rolled on the floor before he looked up at me. His face was unreadable, as cold as the ceramic had been.

"What exactly is the problem?" he asked.

"You've locked me in here, that's the problem."

His eyes glittered. "I've done no such thing."

"Really? Then why is it that every time I try to go through that damn door, I end up back in the bathroom? Why can't I open any of the windows?"

He cocked his head and watched me as if I were an organ-grinder's monkey. "I admit that is peculiar."

The brittle mockery in his voice was worse than any shouts or any orders he could have thrown my way. He was amused by my anger and fear. Was there any bit of humanity in him at all?

"Let me out," I said again, though my voice snagged on the last word. Because I realized something was happening to the corridor.

The chandeliers and sconces that lit it had started to dim. Though no, that wasn't right. The lights weren't dimming as much as they were being slowly smothered by a pooling darkness that appeared to seep out from the man in front of me.

As I watched, unable to do more than stand with my mouth half-open, his eyes grew brighter and brighter. Like he was drinking the light in.

I felt myself begin to shrink away from whoever and whatever Aleister was, preparing to flee.

That stopped me. Because even if I could think of some way to escape, would I risk my brother's life again just because I was afraid?

Never.

Clenching my jaw tightly, I stood up straighter and held Aleister's gleaming gaze.

Beat after beat of silence passed between us.

"Hmm," he finally said and blinked. The lights returned to their full strength in an instant, the darkness retreating back into him. "I think you'll find, Nora, that you will have no further inconveniences trying to leave."

I forced my voice up from where it had gone to hide. "I...I don't believe you."

"That is not my concern." He glanced back down at the floor, taking in the destruction with a tight smile. "Come with me."

The way he said it, like a command that I should not even think of ignoring, swept away some of the fear, replacing it with the desire to land a good punch somewhere soft.

"Why?"

"As I mentioned in my note yesterday, I rather think it was time we spoke of your part of our bargain, don't you agree?" His eyes still had a grain of that strange gleam within their pale depths, as if he were waiting for an opportunity to lash out again. "This should only take a few minutes of your time."

Sweeping an arm outward toward his wing of the house, he cocked his head. "Shall we?"

My heart broke into a trot. Was he inviting me into his chambers? He'd said sharing his bed wasn't part of the deal we'd made, I knew that, but I also knew there wasn't much I could do about it if he'd changed his mind the way he'd changed it about allowing me out.

He lifted an eyebrow at my hesitation. "You have no need to worry, Nora. I stated I wouldn't request anything untoward and I intend to honor my words."

Swallowing back the dryness in my throat, I started down the hallway, feeling his presence behind me although he didn't make a sound. I expected him to perform his little trick of flinging the doors open without so much as nearing them, but he opened them just like any other person in this world did.

"The first room on the left," he said.

Feeling more relief than I cared to admit, I realized he was leading us into a study. It was similar to mine, except this one had a large, chocolate-colored leather sofa sitting in front of a fireplace roaring with flames. The windows, like all the others I'd seen so far in the house, were uncovered.

"Have a seat," Aleister said, nodding toward the leather sofa as he walked to a nearby armchair.

I crossed my arms over my chest. "I thought this was only going to take a few minutes."

"And I thought you would like to spend those minutes in comfort," he said, his voice growing even colder. "But you may do as you prefer, of course."

He sat.

The words bubbled up my throat before I even knew it. "What the bloody hell was all of that back there? Are you going to let me leave or are you going to hold me prisoner whenever you feel like it?"

His smile was thin and none too reassuring. "You are not a prisoner, Nora. That was just a small test I devised, and one you passed admirably, I must say."

"A test?"

"Something to ensure that I have chosen the right person for what I require. That was all. I wouldn't want to waste my time with someone who would end up failing me."

I frowned. "And what would you have done if I hadn't passed? Would you have tossed me out into the streets? Broken our bargain?"

He shrugged. "Perhaps. But you have no need to worry; you did not fail."

The bloody tosser. He would have taken his powers back, then, allowing Peter to die wherever he was right now. Without even warning me.

"How do you find your rooms?"

"They're fine," I bit out. *If you consider almost being killed with my own corset by invisible creatures fine. Or had that been just another test, as well?*

I almost flung the words at him, but I found that my desire to not be in his presence a moment longer than was absolutely necessary was stronger than that impulse. I would deal with those creatures myself. Now I just wanted him to get on with what he wanted to say so I could leave.

"And your stay so far, have you found it satisfactory?"

"No, but it is what it is."

I held his gaze and waited.

After a few heartbeats of silence that almost crackled with tension, Aleister spoke again.

"How much do you know of the slave trade?"

The words were so unexpected, so abrupt, that I couldn't think of what to say for an instant. "I don't...The slave trade?"

Keeping his eyes fixed on me in a way that made my skin prickle, Aleister continued. "There are people in this world who buy and sell other people like chattel, claiming ownership of what should never be owned. Surely you must be aware of that."

His words dug like claws into me. What I'd heard Peter say yesterday, his fear that Luke would take me, his bright panic at what might have happened to me. It all flashed through my mind. How had it taken me this long to work it out?

"The missing girls," I said.

He watched me in silence for a moment before nodding. "You do know about them, then."

"No, I've heard about girls who have disappeared, but I don't know anything else." I shook my head. "They're being sold as slaves?"

"Yes. They are sold and shipped across the world for purposes too dark to speak of, but which I am sure you will have no trouble guessing."

I felt as if all of the blood in my body had sunk to my feet. The shipments. This was what they were, then. This was what would have happened to me two nights ago and what *was* happening to innocent girls right now.

I should have known people were capable of anything, but even with my natural mistrust of humanity, I hadn't imagined this horror was possible.

"Now," Aleister continued, "I am in possession of some information about one such shipment of girls that will be leaving our shores soon. What I require from you, Nora, is your assistance in finding out when the ship that carries this dreadful cargo will leave port."

I frowned, his words cracking through the shell of disgust that had encased me. "My help? You'd have more luck recruiting someone in Parliament. Or a copper, even." Though, god knew, they'd never done me any good. More of a nuisance than anything.

"Ah, that's where this becomes more complicated," Aleister said, leaning forward. "The leader of the slave trade based out of London is actually a man who makes his living blackmailing members of Parliament. He has a knack for getting wealthy people to reveal their secrets, it seems, promising them his expert help in getting rid of mistresses and the like and then extorting them for it. He's embroiled quite a few in this terrible business of his, threatening to reveal all if they refused to help him. He's even managed to get the prime minister under his thumb. A fortunate thing for him, since it allowed him to get the man's signature on the inspection papers for the ship so that no one will be able to see what it carries before it sets sail." He sighed. "So, you see, we can't depend on any assistance from official quarters."

I shook my head again. "But why? Why would anyone do this?"

"It's a lucrative business, the slave trade." His eyes glittered in the fire's light. "Who knows how much they can sell each of those girls for."

A sour taste rose to my mouth. Someone had actually decided what those lives were worth. Someone like Luke had put a price on their freedom.

"I'm afraid I don't know much else about the ship but its name, which is not all that helpful since there is no official record of it in all of Great Britain. I've looked."

"What is its name?"

"*Pandemonium.*"

My stomach clenched and I gasped in surprise.

"What?"

"That word!"

His eyes narrowed. "What about it?"

I hesitated. I didn't want to tell him anything, to share anything, but the nightmares had been just as vivid and awful last night. Full of violence, always ending with Peter screaming "pandemonium" and with me waking to find it echoing in my head like a bell's toll. If bringing them to an end required me to tell Aleister about them, then it might not be a bad idea to do so.

As succinctly as I could manage, I told him about the nightmares.

If I'd blinked I would have missed the swift contraction of surprise on Aleister's face. "That's unexpected," he said. "And you're sure it's that word, that exact one, that your brother screams?"

"Yes."

He looked away. "Perhaps you picked up on my preoccupation without realizing it. Because of my special...abilities, it can sometimes happen that more perceptive people can be influenced by them if I am not careful. Not severely, but enough to notice. I'll be more vigilant in the future."

I lifted an eyebrow. "And you think I'm perceptive?"

"I do, yes."

If he thought he would win me over with a compliment, as feeble as that one was, he was wrong. "Keep your preoccupations to yourself, then. I don't need nightmares, on top of everything else." I crossed my arms. "What I don't understand is how you know all of this. If it is all so secret, if there isn't even a record of the ship, how do you know it exists, let alone what its name is?"

Aleister sat back in the armchair. The fire's light flicked over his face and, in spite of everything, I couldn't help admiring the perfect beauty of his features.

He gave me a tight, mocking smile. "One of the most useful abilities I possess is that I can hear people's thoughts."

My breath knotted.

I knew it. I'd suspected it from the start.

"Well, perhaps I should explain that I can hear thoughts some of the time. When they are very loud, magnified by fear or anger, or any other strong emotion, I can receive exact phrases. Otherwise, I only get simple impressions, nothing detailed or vivid. Just a few scattered words here and there."

I'd experienced plenty of "strong emotions" since I'd met him, which meant he could have listened into my head any number of times. Wonderful.

My cheeks warmed.

"Does that make you uncomfortable?" Aleister asked.

"Not at all. Why would someone listening in on my private thoughts make me uncomfortable? Pure madness!"

His smile curled. "Well, if it puts you a bit more at ease, there are not very many thoughts that could shock me. I've heard them all."

"What would *really* put me at ease is if you left my head alone."

"It bothers you that much?"

"Yes, of course it does."

He shrugged. "All right. I give you my word I won't listen in on your thoughts. Not that you would be able to tell if I did."

I had to bite the inside of my cheeks to keep from spewing a few choice words. Damn him for finding me so endlessly entertaining.

"There are many people involved in this business, but most of them don't know very much," he continued. "I have done what I can, however, to follow the trail up to the blackmailer and leader, a man named Jonathan Geary. That is how I know everything I have told you, from his own thoughts, but try as I may, I cannot learn when the ship is actually departing. That piece of information continues to elude me."

I crossed my arms. "And why exactly do you care? Do you know any of the girls or are you trying to help them out of the goodness of your heart?"

His eyes appeared transparent when he glanced up at me.

Fear rippled up my spine. There was nothing human, nothing remotely recognizable, in his face.

An instant later, and just as suddenly as it had fled, expression flooded back into his features.

"No, I am not acquainted with any of them and it has nothing to do with my goodness. It may surprise you to know that, like you, I have the opportunity of reclaiming something very dear to me that I lost years ago. I recently learned that it will be departing aboard *Pandemonium*, as well, and the only chance I have of getting it back is to find the ship before it leaves. That is why I became interested in all of this. Why I bothered to search out *Pandemonium* in the first place. There is nothing selfless about my actions."

I kept my eyes on him, watching for signs that he meant me harm. But he once again looked like any other young upper-class gentleman waiting for his afternoon tea. All poise and manners.

As if attempting to complete that impression, he smiled and laced his hands together. "It's a cleverly named ship, isn't it?"

I swallowed back the remnants of fear.

"Because although people use 'pandemonium' these days in a casual manner, its original meaning is much more sinister."

As much as I hated to admit it, I began to feel the faintest twinge of curiosity. "What does it mean?"

"Many demons. 'Pan' means many, and '*demonium*' is obviously demons. It comes from this book." He stretched an arm toward the side table next to him and picked up a heavy tome. "*Paradise Lost*. Have you read it?"

He watched me carefully.

"What makes you think I can read?"

Aleister chuckled. "Oh, Nora. I know a great deal about you."

There was an edge of a threat in his voice despite his smile and his relaxed posture. A taunt for me to contradict him rippled across his eyes.

I looked away. I wouldn't be goaded again. "No, I've never read it."

"I highly recommend it, if you are looking to entertain yourself for a few hours. It was Milton who coined the word 'pandemonium.' He introduces it as the name of a location in hell. Satan's palace, if you will."

My eyes widened.

"Can you think of a more fitting name with which to christen a slave ship?" His jaw tightened and he looked away from me.

Silence so hard and cold it felt like it could cut me at my slightest move filled the room. Even with the blazing fire in front of me, I shivered.

After what felt like an eternity, Aleister breathed in deeply. "This is what you are here for, Nora. To help me with this."

"But what is it that you want to get back?"

"That is not something you need to know."

Of course not. Why would I need to know anything about anything when it was much more exciting to keep me in suspense? The bastard.

"Fine, but can't you just use your...?" I waved a hand vaguely in his direction as I searched for the right word.

"My abilities?"

"Yes, can't you use them to get the man involved in all of this to tell you when the ship is leaving?"

"You vastly overestimate my powers. I can do very little to affect people's lives without explicit permission, and I certainly can't force anyone to do anything if they do not want to."

"You need the kind of permission I gave you to save Peter's life, then."

His smile was a blade. "Exactly. And I need it every time, no matter how minor an intervention on my part. It's a bore, really."

"I'm sure the rest of the world would disagree."

"Oh, but I am quite benign."

Benign was the last thing he looked, watching me like a cat deciding whether the mouse in front of him was worth his effort.

"All right, but what if I just give you permission to bewitch the man in charge, the blackmailer? If I was able to allow you to interfere in Peter's life, I should be able to do the same with him."

"Clever, Nora. Alas, it does not work in that fashion. You share no blood with him, no connection at all. Your words wouldn't count."

"You're sure?"

"Of course. It's one of those pesky rules I must abide by."

My curiosity to know more about his talents and who had made all of those rules battled with my desire to be as unhelpful as possible. The latter won. I held my tongue.

After a few seconds of silence, Aleister continued. "It's become clear that I can't find the ship on my own. Which is why I need a smart, resourceful person like you to help me."

I scoffed. "You may be mistaken there, though, because I haven't the slightest idea how I could."

"That's simple. You are going to get the blackmailer to invite you into his home. Then you're going to find and steal the papers that detail the date and location of the ship's departure, as well as the inspection waiver the prime minister signed. Without that paper, the ship will not be able to depart and take with it what by right belongs to me."

He had lost his blooming mind. Either that or he was finding pleasure in confusing me. "Easy as that, is it? I'll just magically get invited inside for long enough to find what you need. I think you're forgetting *I* have no special abilities." I frowned as another possibility crossed my mind. "Unless you're asking me to seduce him. Not that I have any skills in that area, either."

He waved the words away. "Don't be crass, Nora. That will not be necessary."

"Well, unless he is out of his home for enough hours to allow me to ransack it, I don't see how I can do any of this."

"That's not a possibility. It is a rather large house, I'm afraid, and it is full of servants." Aleister's eyes glittered, boring right into me. "No. What I have in mind requires your considerable skills at deception more than your skills at lock-picking. Though the latter will come in handy, as well."

He stood and walked to one of the uncovered windows.

The silence and speed of his movements caught me by surprise again, making me flinch.

"Jonathan Geary is having a ball at his estate in a few weeks," he said, "and we have to be among the guests. It's the perfect opportunity. It will get us into the house at a time when we can be sure the servants will be busy, allowing me the chance to distract Geary without arousing suspicion while you find and take the papers we need."

I watched him stare out the window, his pale profile as sharp as if it were chiseled out of the marble he seemed to so love if the style of his home was to be trusted. His eyes pierced into the darkness outside, but I had the sudden sensation that he had somehow slipped out of the room. He was somewhere else entirely.

This is what he wanted, then. Perhaps it would have made a difference, made him less frightening, if he were holding me captive in order to save girls from a future I had almost shared, but he wasn't. He was doing it for selfish reasons. To earn back whatever blasted thing he had lost.

Well, it didn't matter. I had to do as he said, anyway. Might as well do some good while I was at it.

I nodded to myself and sighed. "How do we get invited to that ball? I'm certain you already have some sort of plan, so you might as well tell me."

"Yes, I do. And that plan, Nora, requires the perfect bait." With a biting smile, Aleister turned. "You."

Right. Of course it did.

Six

"YOU'RE FIDGETING," ALEISTER SAID, and took a sip of coffee.

"It's this dress." It poked and prodded me in all manner of places. Even the sleeves were itchy. And it was heavier than the other ones he'd bought for me.

Shifting in my seat, I tugged on one of the cream ribbons fashioned into rosettes that perched on my left hip. It wouldn't stay straight.

"You look perfectly lovely. Stop fussing," he said.

I glanced up at his words, ready to tell him where he should shove his compliments, but he had his eyes on the street corner in front of him, where Jonathan Geary, our blackmailer, would soon appear.

I held the elaborate collar away from my neck and slipped in a finger to scratch a patch of skin.

In truth, it wasn't just the dress. I could have been wearing the most comfortable of nightgowns and still felt like I wouldn't be able to sit still on penalty of death, and I didn't know why. Yes, we were about to put the first part of Aleister's plan into action, but I'd done similar things before. I'd once bolted in front of a carriage, spooking the horses enough to make them rear back, and pretended to have broken an arm just to squeeze four or five shillings out of the wealthy lady riding inside. I hadn't even been nervous then, and I could have been injured.

So why all this fluttering in my stomach and the inability to swallow the tea growing cooler in front of me?

Maybe it was because this was the first time I was doing something like this without Peter nearby to help if I ran into trouble. I supposed Aleister would try to keep me somewhat safe if he truly wanted back whatever he'd lost, but it wasn't the most comforting of thoughts that I wouldn't have anyone else helping me.

I glanced up at Aleister. For someone who depended on a stranger to help him, he looked entirely relaxed. As if he had complete confidence in my skills.

As I watched him, he leaned forward to pick up his coffee cup again. The movement dislodged something inside his coat, shifting it so an edge of it peeked out. It took me a moment to realize it was a feather. A gray feather.

He followed my gaze and his lips tightened into a thin line. With the most careful of movements, he tucked the feather back into his coat.

I frowned. Why was he carrying that around?

"Remember to speak normally," Aleister said abruptly, returning his gaze to the street across from us. "Don't try to listen for the change in your voice because you won't hear it."

"Yes, I remember."

That was one of the many things that had worried me when Aleister had shared his plan. The way I spoke would give me away the moment I opened my mouth. Because of Peter's obsession with my pronouncing every initial "h" and final "g," I did speak better than Sharpe and the other people I'd been raised among, but I still wouldn't pass as a lady of society. Not even close to it.

Aleister had suggested using his powers to modify my voice so that everyone but the two of us heard a different intonation, a higher-class accent, and I'd had no other real choice but to give him permission to do so. I still had to watch myself, however, because there was nothing he could do to correct my word choices. That meant "bloody," "bugger," "damn," and all the other juicy and satisfying words in the English language were out of bounds.

"All right, Nora, there he is," he said.

Another twinge of nerves thrummed through me as I turned carefully in my seat and peered over the manicured hedge behind me. Aleister had chosen this outdoor table at Café Verrey's because it put us in prime position to see Geary without running too much of a risk of being seen. It wouldn't do to be spotted before I was able to make my move.

"Which one is he?"

"The man in the striped waistcoat."

I turned my gaze from one figure to another.

Him? I narrowed my eyes. He was the unlikeliest candidate for a blackmailer I had ever seen!

He looked like a butcher in a dress coat. There was none of the sleekness and oily elegance I had expected, no sign of shrewdness in his flushed, round face. Not even his clothes were very refined, which they should have been with all of the money he was making exploiting secrets and selling human beings.

It was hard to believe this was the man who was manipulating quite a number of members of Parliament as well as the prime minister.

No. There was nothing to be nervous about, not anymore. Worse came to worse, I could outrun him in seconds.

As we watched, Geary strolled down the street toward a store about halfway to the next corner, the green and brown striped waistcoat that was stretched to snapping point around his bulging stomach leading the way.

"He'll be in there for about ten minutes, speaking with the shop's owner while his tobacco order is being prepared, and then he'll walk back the way he came. He's done it without fail every Tuesday for months."

I nodded and waited to stand up until Geary was far enough down the street that he would have to turn his entire body to see me.

"I'll be here the entire time," Aleister said. "If everything goes well, we'll meet back at the house," he said.

I nodded again and looked toward the street. The blackmailer had just slipped into the tobacco shop, so there was no more time to dawdle. "Aren't you going to wish me luck?"

"You don't need it, Nora."

Rolling my eyes at him and biting back a harsh word or two, I left the café and crossed the street busy with carriages and people. I pinched my cheeks as I walked, making myself appear as flustered as possible, and did my best to get as much mud on my skirts as I could to complete the look.

Aleister's gaze was a pressure on my back.

A moment after I'd started toward the tobacco store, I heard a sound my ears were attuned to noticing no matter where I was. The patter of rodent feet.

I glanced around and caught sight of the large black rat again, the one I was sure I'd seen that night at the Lantern and outside Sharpe's office. My impulse was to kick out at it, to shoo it away with a clap or hissed curse, but I had to remember who I was pretending to be. A lady would never do that. She'd do something useless like swoon or scream.

Fighting my instincts, I ignored the rat as I walked past a haberdasher's establishment, followed by a milliner's, and then a perfumer's. I stopped next to the tobacco store and turned to face the shops across the street. Just as Aleister had told me, the windows opposite from me reflected the tobacco shop's door perfectly. I'd be able to see Geary stepping out with enough time to make my move.

So I waited. Each minute passing like an age, the seconds stretching out so much that I could have been standing there for hours, for all I knew.

Finally, Geary's stout reflection appeared in the window.

I had to time this carefully. If I didn't, the whole thing would look forced and that would surely give me away.

I waited, watching the window, until the last possible second before turning toward the tobacco shop and breaking into a frantic walk. Geary was so focused on the cloth bag in his hands that I was able to keep my eyes on him until I overtook him.

Gritting my teeth, I slammed into the man.

"Oh!" he exclaimed, the bag with his order of tobacco falling to the floor when his hands grabbed on to my shoulders to steady me.

Perfection.

I gasped and clutched at my skirts in as good an imitation of high society horror as I could create. "Oh, sir, I do apologize!" I made my voice waver as I glanced down at the bag on the floor. "I'm so terribly sorry. Let...me...help." Without further warning, I broke into a lady's sob, all soft whimpering and delicate hiccupping, all the while keeping a half-lidded but sharp eye on the pink-cheeked man in front of me.

"Miss," he started, "please, there is no need to spill tears, I assure you." He bent down with a grunt of effort and grabbed the bag. "See? No damage done."

"Oh, I'm so foolish!" I said before whimpering again.

"Nonsense."

"I am! I thought I could manage on my own, but I've gotten completely lost in this city and now I've gone and made you drop what you were carrying. It has just been an awful day!"

He placed a thick hand lightly on my arm. "I'm sure it's not as bad as all that. Come, let us go into this shop here so you can calm yourself."

I bit my lips to keep from smiling as he led me inside. This was going perfectly.

The man behind the tobacco shop's counter left his post as soon as he saw us. "Can I be of assistance?"

"The lady has had a fright, would it be possible for her to rest here a moment and maybe get a glass of water?" Geary asked, guiding me to one of the two leather armchairs in the store.

"Certainly, sir. Right away. Would you like me to fetch a doctor, as well?"

Were ladies really considered this damn fragile? "Please, don't trouble yourself," I said as I sat. "I'm quite all right. I just need a few moments to catch my breath, that is all."

The shop owner nodded, but looked at Geary as if he had the last word on this. Like I needed a man to speak for me.

"Are you sure, miss?" Geary asked. "It would be no trouble at all."

"I'm sure, thank you." I made my voice as assertive as I could while still sounding breathless and delicate. I wasn't at all certain I succeeded.

"All right."

Geary nodded to the shop owner, who bowed his head and hurried off toward a door behind the large wooden counter.

I sniffled a bit, looking down at my clasped gloved hands resting on my silken lap. "I am most grateful, sir, for your assistance. I know I am drawing you away from very important things with my foolishness."

"It's Jonathan Geary, miss, and no, there is nothing very pressing I need to attend to, I assure you." He smiled widely, revealing lots of teeth.

It suddenly struck me that although he said all of the right things, all of the polite things that were expected in the higher tiers of society, there was something...off about the way he spoke. As if he were manufacturing the words, smoothing out the imperfections. His enunciation was a bit too perfect, his accent too polished. Like a cheap jewel that blinded with its false glitter.

I made myself smile and extended my hand. "I'm Lady Nora Blake."

He lowered his head to it and brushed his lips against the cream glove. His palm felt moist even through the fabric. I fought the urge to yank my hand back and wipe it against my skirts.

"Perhaps you know my husband, Lord Aleister Blake?" I continued. The words came out much more smoothly than I expected. As if I said them all the time.

There was only the slightest of hesitations. "I believe I know *of* him, madam, though I haven't had the pleasure of making his acquaintance in person."

I had to admit, he was close to being as good a liar as I was.

The tobacco shop's owner walked back into the store's front room with a glass of water on a gleaming platter. He maneuvered past the counter, careful not to spill a drop, and presented it to me.

"Thank you," I said, and took the glass.

"Madam." The man bowed and slipped out of the room again.

Geary watched me as I drank, I could sense it, and his gaze made my skin twitch. Knowing he was perfectly willing to steal girls right off our streets, that he wouldn't have hesitated to do it to me if given a chance, soured the water in my mouth.

Swift, sudden movement on the street caught my attention. Under the guise of adjusting my dress's train, I turned slightly and flicked my eyes toward the shop's door. It was the black rat, peering in through the glass. What was it doing?

Concentrate, Nora! I told myself.

"You said you were new to the city, madam?" Geary asked, drawing my eyes back to him.

"Yes. I've been here once before, when I was presented at court, but I never felt the need to return."

"That's unusual," he said with another of his harsh smiles. "Most ladies love London."

"I've just never enjoyed large cities. I tend to get horribly lost, as you witnessed today." I made myself giggle without too much effort. Nora Smith, lost in London? That *was* worth a laugh.

"Perhaps I can help you find wherever you want to go."

"That is so kind, but I'm afraid there are thousands of errands I have to attend to. We had to leave our home in Devon in such a hurry that we couldn't bring most of our things with us. We weren't able to pack more than a case each and—" I stopped, cutting my voice off as if with a knife.

I risked a glance at Geary and caught the glint of hungry interest in his eyes. I had him.

"In a hurry?" he asked.

"Oh, listen to me, talking and talking." I fussed with my dress's folds and batted my eyelashes like my head was stuffed full of silk ribbons instead of with a brain. "My husband always tells me I should chatter less and allow other people a chance to speak."

"Not at all, madam. It's delightful."

Yes, I'm sure it is. I sighed delicately. "It drives him to distraction to hear me prattle on, but it is so difficult when he is the only person I know in the city. I left all of my friends behind, you see, and it is not easy making new ones with...well, with everything that has happened. I just have no one to talk to." I bit my lips and looked down at my hands.

I felt his eyes travel over me again, taking in the quality and newness of my gown, the jeweled earrings I wore, the crispness of my gloves. Considering all the signs of wealth Aleister had put on display to convince him I was a bait worth taking.

I took another sip of water while he made up his mind.

Finally, he cleared his throat. "Madam, if you'll allow me to be so bold, no lady should be without friends in London."

With a small sniffle, I nodded.

"But that is easily remedied. I'm having a luncheon with my two sisters next week at *Rules* and I'd be delighted if you could join us."

It was hard to keep the grin from my face. This was too easy! "Oh, I couldn't impose in that fashion."

"It's not an imposition at all. It would honor us to have the distinguished Lady Blake with us."

"Are you certain, Mr. Geary? Your sisters wouldn't mind?"

If he smiled any wider, his lips were sure to crack. He nodded. "They would be delighted to have your company, madam, and they know the city so well they can easily help you with all of your errands."

"Oh, how wonderful!" I exclaimed, clapping my hands together and trying not to wince at the shrillness in my voice. "I can hardly wait! You don't know how difficult it has been, not knowing anyone in the city."

"Madam, I am very glad I've been able to help." He eyed me again. "Are you feeling more like yourself now? Would you like me to hail you a cab to take you home?"

"Would you? That would be lovely. I'm much too tired now to continue with my errands."

"With pleasure."

He stood and offered his arm to help me rise, which I took with a smile.

"It is a pleasant day, isn't it?" I said brightly as Geary opened the door. Rapid movement from the corner of my eye told me the black rat had managed to scurry away.

"Made infinitely more pleasant by our acquaintance."

His voice was so cloyingly sweet I was shocked he didn't choke on it. Was it even appropriate to speak like that to a married woman?

No matter. I was outside now. This would soon be over for today.

Geary lifted his hand at a passing hansom cab, and the driver immediately tugged the horses to the street curb.

"Where to?"

"Belgravia, please," I said, shifting my eyes quickly to catch Geary's expression. If he had rubbed his hands together in anticipation, he would have looked less greedy than he did now. The fool.

He helped me up into the cab, which was a good thing because I had never attempted to get into one with a bustle as large as this dress had and I would have ended up giving myself a good smack against the carriage's floor on my own.

"We'll say noon at *Rules* next week, Friday, then," he said when I had settled in.

"Yes. I can't wait to meet your sisters! And thank you so very much, Mr. Geary, for your invaluable assistance today."

"You are most welcome, Lady Blake. Good afternoon," he said, closing the cab's door. He tipped his hat to me as the driver got the horses moving.

I held on to my smile until I was sure we had left Geary behind and then slid over to the opposite side of the cab to look out the window.

Aleister still sat at the café's table. His gaze met mine as the carriage passed by, that peculiar expressionlessness that robbed him of any hint of humanity on his face.

After the blackmailer's oozing falseness, I was surprised to find it was like a crisp breeze on the hottest of days.

SEVEN

I TOLD ALEISTER ABOUT the invitation to *Rules* and headed back out into the city, trying not to think too much about why I almost smiled when he congratulated me on a job well done, despite the hint of mockery in his voice as he did so. I was just pleased with myself; that was all. Glad that I was a bit closer to helping the girls who would be shipped to a life I couldn't begin to imagine and that I'd almost shared. I didn't blooming care what he thought.

I went to see Peter.

Nothing could have prepared me to witness what he was about to do. Because that afternoon, my brother walked into the Lantern and sat down at the bar.

I could only watch, my hands pressed against my chest, fingernails digging into the bodice's fabric until I could feel the stays of the new corset I'd bought to replace the one that had almost killed me. All of me hoping he'd order something to eat or a glass of juice or milk, knowing he wouldn't.

It started as just a couple of pints in the afternoon, drunk alone at the bar with his eyes fixed on the wooden board beneath the glass full of amber poison, but it soon progressed to stronger options. Just two days after his first pint, I watched from one corner of the pub as he tipped back shot after shot of whiskey. I saw his eyes lose all focus, his mouth slacken with the relief of not having to care about anything for just a little while.

Then it was not enough to only drink in the afternoon.

Peter began stopping at the Lantern at noon, not leaving until his tongue tangled on my name, until he could barely remember if my eyes were brown or blue. He would weave through the people on the street for the hours it took the alcohol to wear off and then he'd return to the pub for more.

Darkness had opened up before him and he'd leapt in.

The knowledge that I couldn't do anything to help him when I had done this to him was like a wound that would not stop bleeding. Not only had I caused him the harm of utterly disappearing from his life, but I had also given him the means with which to destroy himself. Because every drink he bought, he did so with the coins Aleister left for me and which I slid under our door for my brother each morning.

If I had been sure Peter could have lifted himself out of the pit he was in, I would have stopped leaving the money. But I wasn't. If I didn't leave those coins and he continued to drink, he would be destitute in a matter of days. On the street. I would battle with every demon in hell before I allowed my brother to end up like our mother had.

But what could I possibly do to stop him?

I was asking myself that for the thousandth time when I saw Sharpe again.

I was outside the Lantern, my back pressed against one of its walls, watching the large black rat while it, in turn, watched me.

I had dipped my hand into a coat pocket to pull out some of the toasted almonds I'd bought earlier and was getting ready to lure the rat closer, for a distraction if nothing else, when I saw our old employer nearing the pub.

His face was mottled with anger.

He shoved the Lantern's door open and lunged inside. I turned to one of the windows, narrowing my eyes to see into the darkened interior, and saw Sharpe grab Peter by the arm, practically lifting him off the stool. My brother lost his balance and leaned against the bar to keep from falling. But Sharpe didn't allow him a moment of respite, instead taking his arm again and dragging him through the handful of afternoon drinkers out into the chilled November air.

"What are you doing?" Peter said. He sounded as if his tongue had turned to stone.

"What am I doin'?" Sharpe said. "You must be completely corned if you can ask me that with a straight face." He jabbed a finger right at my brother's chest. "You just cost me a job. A well-payin' one, too. You were supposed to be at my office two hours ago, two bloomin' hours ago!"

Peter blinked and opened his mouth, but Sharpe spoke over him.

"I stopped by the 'ouse and the client 'ad already 'ired someone else. MacDonald. The man couldn't catch a rat if it was tied to a post but 'e's got my money in 'is pocket because of you."

"Sharpe—"

"You keep your mouth shut, boy. I ain't done."

I stepped closer, my hands clenching into fists with which I knew I could do nothing.

"I been watchin' you, son, the way you've dived right into a whiskey bottle and 'aven't surfaced for breath. Still, I gave you this job. For old time's sake. Because the two of us both know it was Nora who had the talent, not you. Without 'er, your skills are replaceable. Ain't that right?"

"No, that's not true," I hissed, but Peter nodded and looked away from Sharpe's face.

"I was tryin' to be generous and 'elp you through this difficult time and all, but 'ow 'as my generosity been repaid? By you goin' and getting' so drunk you can 'ardly stand. And on my time!" He shook his head. "Sorry, son, but this won't do. There are plenty of people who'd be 'appy to take your place, and until you get your 'ead right, I'll 'ave to turn to one of them for assistance."

The unbelievable bastard. We'd worked for him, allowed ourselves to be gouged by him and his rates, for eleven years. We'd spent hours in filthy places, hot in the summer and cold in the winter, cramped into tiny crevices or dangling from rooftops looking for rat nests while he sat on his backside, and he dared to speak like that to my brother.

"Don't let him do this to you, Peter," I said. "Fight back."

But Sharpe was already turning away.

"You tosser!" I yelled, knowing full well he couldn't hear me but not being able to stop myself. I chased after his retreating figure, curses bubbling in my head.

A sudden wail of pain and anger brought me to a stop as surely as if my feet had been nailed to the pavement. It was a sound unlike any I'd heard before, an animal's cry using a human's voice. I turned back just as Peter's legs collapsed under him and he slumped to the filthy floor in front of the Lantern. He lowered his head into his hands, his shoulders shaking so violently he looked like he would split apart.

Forgetting all about Sharpe, I hurried back to my brother's side.

"Peter," I murmured, kneeling beside him.

He slammed his fist against the stones beneath us, another groan of pain clawing its way out of him.

I brought my hands up and pressed them against the barrier that separated us. "I'm here. I know you can't tell, but I'm right here."

There was no comfort I could offer. He had lost everything he had ever cared about the night I'd given up my old life. His world had collapsed around him and it continued to do so.

I'd been thinking only of myself and my own pain when I made that bargain with Aleister, blinded by the fear of how I could possibly live without Peter. But I realized now that I'd forced the fate I'd wanted to avoid on him.

The worst thing, however, the most selfish thing, was the knowledge that if given the chance again, I would choose for him to live. No matter what consequences it brought. I just couldn't be part of a world where he was no longer alive.

I closed my eyes and laid my forehead against the unseen wall between us. "I'm sorry," I said. "I didn't know what to do. I still don't. All I could think about was saving your life." My fingers pressed against the barrier. "Please forgive me."

Sobs were his only answer.

"Hello, Nora."

I flinched at Aleister's voice. Of all the days for him to be here when I arrived, he'd had to choose this one.

Sniffing and wiping my eyes with one hand, I closed the front door and turned to face him. "Hello."

His crystalline eyes flicked over me and the light, shallow smile on his thin lips faded. "Is something wrong?"

I shook my head. "I'm perfectly fine."

Aleister cocked his head to the side like a bird, his eyes never leaving my face. "And yet, you're not."

"I said I'm fine."

"And I say you're lying."

I sighed and rubbed my eyes. "Why do you care, anyway? It's not like it'll make a difference. Whether I'm fine or not won't change anything in our arrangement."

"You must have a very poor opinion of me, Nora, if you think that your happiness or lack thereof has no impact on me. I don't want you to suffer if there's something I can do about it."

I shook my head, ready to tell him I didn't need his sympathy, when he lifted a hand to stop me.

"I realize I am not your choice of company, but there is no one else with whom you can speak who knows you, is there?"

When I said nothing, he sighed and motioned to the door on the left side of the room. "I have had a long, tiresome day myself and I am famished. Let us go into the dining room, where I am certain a glorious meal waits for us. Over a glass of wine, we can discuss what is worrying you so."

I was about to refuse but I realized I couldn't stand the fear I was sure to feel in a few minutes. The shadows, the tea tray that would invariably appear on its own in the sitting room, the noises without apparent cause, the nightgown which would be waiting for me, pressed and freshly washed. It was too much for me to deal with today after everything.

And he might be able to help. If he could cheat death, he could surely do something for Peter. He might want something in exchange, true, but he'd already taken my life. What else did I have to lose?

Aleister noticed my hesitation and smiled thinly. "I'm sure between the two of us we can come up with a solution in no time at all."

Goddamn it. "Fine," I said.

He motioned for me to follow him into the dining room.

I hadn't bothered to go in there before now, so I wasn't prepared for the size of the space. It was almost as large as my sitting room and study put together. A table that could have sat fifty people or more stood at the center, with a large carved chair done in what looked to be solid gold waiting like a throne at one end.

"I assume that one is yours," I said with a roll of my eyes.

Aleister chuckled. It was a dark, biting sound. "It is, though you are free to use it, if you'd like."

"I think not." I wasn't completely sure I was tall enough to climb onto it, let alone sit comfortably in that monstrosity.

"You haven't been in here before, then?"

I shrugged. "There's always a tray in my sitting room and—" I bit my lip. "In *the* sitting room."

He waved that aside. "It is yours. That entire wing is. No one else has ever used it." Silently, he walked across the marble floors to the table and nodded to the chair on the left side of his own, where another place was set.

I would have preferred to sit on the opposite end, but there was no chance of that now. Not without seriously offending him, and that wasn't wise if I wanted his help.

"Come, Nora," he said. "Before everything cools."

Tightening my hands into fists, I walked to the table.

Aleister had been right. A feast awaited us.

Platters of sliced meat bubbling in their own juices lay next to potatoes done in a variety of ways, while vegetables I had never seen before stewed in white and glistening cream sauces. Rolls of freshly baked bread waited next to a thick slab of slowly melting butter as a crystal decanter glittered nearby, its belly full of dark wine.

Hunger opened its jaws inside me.

I had never in my entire life been offered food of this kind. No, not even five years ago when the rat population tripled in one summer and Peter and I had made enough money for a few good meals.

Peter. His name was like the flick of a whip inside me.

I'd left him back in the Lantern chasing one shot of whiskey with another, and here I was, living the high life. God help me, what kind of person was I?

Aleister reached for the decanter.

I leaned forward to grab one of the serving ladles, but he stopped me with a nod at the chair beside me.

"Sit. You are my guest."

Now *that* was quite a stretch of the truth.

Aleister poured me a generous glass of wine and went on to fill his, as well. I could smell the biting alcohol from where I sat, and I had to clasp my hands together to keep from flinging the crystals across the room. I would never taste that vileness.

With swift and sure movements, he began placing slices of meat on my plate, along with the creamy vegetables and the four different types of potatoes.

"Is that satisfactory?" he said. His face was impossible to read.

I nodded.

He repeated the movements with his own plate, though serving himself smaller portions than mine, before sitting down. "So," he said and brought the wineglass to his lips, "tell me all about what is worrying you."

I forced myself to start and once I did, I found I couldn't stop, couldn't keep back the worry. I told him everything, from the first day I'd started to follow Peter until this afternoon with Sharpe. I told him about the money, *his* money, that I'd been leaving under the door, and about my despair at watching how it was spent. Shame burned in my face as I spoke but there was no point in hiding anything, not if I wanted his help.

Through it all, Aleister watched me, his eyes never leaving my face even when I wished with everything within me that they would. He didn't touch his food but only took occasional sips of wine as he listened.

When I ran out of words, he leaned forward, placed the glass down on the table and laced his hands together. "There is a solution, there usually is, but it will not be an easy one for you."

"I don't care. I just don't want him to suffer like this anymore."

"A noble sentiment, but does it translate into everyday reality?" He took up his fork, skewered a piece of roasted potato, and brought it to his mouth.

"What does that mean?"

"It means that I am not certain if you will be able to cope with the results."

"I'm pretty sure that is up to me to decide."

He sighed. "Yes, I suppose so." He tapped his fingers lightly against the table, once, twice, three times. "All right, here it is. The only way to help your brother is to erase all memory of you from his head."

If someone had taken a blade to my insides it would have hurt less than his words did.

"Not only from his head, either, but from everyone's who ever knew you, Nora. Otherwise, it would just confuse matters. It has to be as if you never existed."

Never existed. The words echoed in my head, bruising everything they touched. "And that...that will stop this?"

"From everything you've said, the reason your brother is suffering is because of his love for you, a love which is built on years of memories and mutual experiences. I carve all of that out and the suffering goes with it."

"Couldn't you just stop him from drinking? Take the urge away or something?"

Aleister shrugged. "I could, yes, but the grief that brought it on would still be there and it would find some other way to manifest itself. Perhaps a worse one."

I looked away from him. He was right, I was the cause of Peter's suffering. Without my presence in his head, he would have no reason to drink or to destroy himself in any other way. He would be able to get his job back and get on with his life without having to drag sadness behind him. He could be happy.

Happy.

Something scratched at my mind. Something Aleister had mentioned.

Something...

My eyes widened as the memory came rushing back.

"On the night I came to live here, you told me that Peter would go on to get married and have children, that he'd lead a happy life without me. Is this what you meant? Did you know I would have to make this choice?"

Aleister's eyes glittered as if he were bubbling over with internal laughter but he said nothing.

"Did you know, even then, this was what it would come to?"

He still said nothing.

I didn't realize what I was doing until the knife by my plate was in my hand, its point plunging into the table with one violent stab. Anger swirled inside me, mixing with the exhaustion of nights filled with nightmares along with the worry for Peter that had reached its peak today, until I felt I would lift right out of my seat under its turbulent force.

"I deserve the truth!" I yelled. The hand still holding on to the knife shook along with the rest of me.

He went on watching me, his expression remaining the same.

"I've had enough of all of this!"

Aleister lifted an eyebrow. "All of what, Nora?"

"Of not knowing anything! You've forced me to live in this strange house, where I am always frightened, you don't tell me who you are, how you can do the things you do, or even what I'm helping you get back, and now you won't tell me if you knew all of this with Peter was going to happen. You could have told me. You could have *warned* me. These are our lives you're toying with! What gives you the right?"

I pushed away from the table with a shriek of wood on marble and stood up. He wasn't going to help me, and I wasn't going to sit here and allow myself to become his dinner entertainment. I turned from him and walked toward the dining room's door.

"What is so strange about this house?" he suddenly asked.

The question was surprising enough to stop me. All of the things I had mentioned, all of the rage that I had given voice to, and he asked me something so stupid. "You can't be serious," I said and turned to face him.

"I don't see anything very peculiar about it," he said. He glanced around the room in genuine bewilderment. A wrinkle of confusion marred his smooth forehead.

This was ridiculous.

"You don't realize that it's at least three times larger than it should be?" I said, motioning at all of the space that surrounded us. "That it's shaped completely different from its exterior? And there are no bloody curtains! Not on a single window! You're telling me that doesn't strike you as strange?"

"Ah." His forehead cleared and he nodded. "Curtains. I knew I'd forgotten something."

He was mad. I was living with a mad person.

I rubbed my eyes with my hands. The urge to cry or scream in frustration or plunge the knife still embedded upright on the table into Aleister's chest battled within me. Nothing made sense in my life anymore. It hadn't since the damned night I'd met him.

"And you say you are always frightened here. Why is that, Nora? What scares you?"

I walked back to the table to see his face, to catch his expression and make sure he wasn't mocking me because no one could be that obtuse. But there was nothing to read, nothing on his features at all.

I held his gaze. "I was almost suffocated with my own corset strings the first morning I was here. That bloody scares me, for one."

If I had expected him to flinch at the mention of a woman's undergarments, I would have been disappointed. I did manage, however, to extract a small frown.

"But that's impossible," he said. "Suffocated by whom?"

"By the damn shadows or whatever the hell sneaks around this place, or are you going to tell me I'm imagining them? That there is no reason why I should be sleeping on the sofa with a butter knife in my hands?"

I waited for him to deny their presence, to tell me I'd lost my mind along with everything else, that perhaps it would be better for me to retire to my chambers. Instead, he offered a laugh that was so dry it could have caught fire.

"The shadows mean you no harm," he said. "They are playful things."

"Playful! Robbing me of breath and squeezing so hard I thought my ribs would splinter is not being playful."

He shrugged lightly. "I'm afraid they don't know their own strength. They've never served a woman before, so it might take them some time to learn the correct way of doing so." He looked at me. His eyes could have been made of glass for all they revealed of his thoughts. "I can assure you that there is no need for fear. You are under my protection when you are within these walls and nothing can harm you. You have my word."

I scoffed. "That means nothing to me."

He rolled his eyes. Somehow the gesture didn't look entirely natural on him. "Then use your head, Nora. Why would I go to all the trouble of helping your brother and making a bargain with you to then sit by and let you die on your first morning here? When I need your help? It's nonsensical."

I'd had that same thought myself, and perhaps it didn't make any sense, but it also didn't change what had happened or the fear I felt. I crossed my arms over my chest.

"Oh, for heaven's sake," Aleister said and waved his right hand.

At once, shadows began to seep in from the walls, oozing in without a sound.

I gasped and took a step closer to the table, ready to lunge for the knife despite knowing how little protection it would provide.

In an instant the room was full of them, dimming the light of the chandelier above our heads with their darkness.

I hadn't seen any of them completely until now, only catching glimpses from the corner of my eye as they retreated after leaving a tea tray or lighting a fire. Now I saw their shapes were vaguely human, but the proportions were wrong. Some had arms that reached all the way to the floor, while others had torsos that went on for much too long, as well as heads that would never have been supported by a normal neck. They were taller than a person, too, and so thin it hurt to look at.

I swallowed. If Aleister had thought that allowing me to see them would reduce my fear, he had just succeeded in the opposite.

"It appears our guest had a misunderstanding with a few of you," he said, gazing from one side of the room to the other. "That will not occur again. From this moment on, you will obey her every command, no matter how small, and you will do everything in your power to make her feel at home. Anything she demands, you will provide." He gave me a sidelong glance. "Unless, of course, it goes against my own wishes." He tapped his fingers on the table, watching the creatures who had not yet moved or uttered a sound. "I trust I have made myself quite clear and that there will be no repetition of what has frightened Nora. If it does happen again, there will be consequences. That is all," he said and waved them away.

As one entity, the shadows bowed their heads, or whatever passed for them, and left the room as silently as they had arrived.

I released the breath I hadn't noticed I held only when the last one disappeared and the room's brightness returned.

They were worse than I had imagined. Monstrous. Something right out of a nightmare. I could still feel their presence crawling across my skin.

I shivered. "What are they?"

"My servants. And, for you and me, harmless." Aleister lifted his wine glass again and took a sip. "Now, I hope that little demonstration has put you at ease that you are not only safe here but that you are mistress of the place. Second in command only to me."

I shrugged. "It *would* be comforting, but only if I knew who you were and how you have those abilities of yours."

"You will. I promise you, Nora, you will know all there is to know soon enough, but it is not time yet."

The arrogance of the man. "And that is something you get to decide, then?"

"Yes, I do," he said, and nodded to my chair. "Sit. You look like you're readying yourself to run."

I swallowed the dryness in my throat. "Maybe I am."

He lifted an eyebrow along with a corner of his lips. "Well, how about I promise to keep myself from snapping your neck at least until you finish your dinner? Would that help?"

He really was a bastard. "Very generous of you."

"Yes, I think so, as well." He shook his head and started cutting into the meat on his plate.

I hesitated. He frightened me, as did everything in this house, but would bolting out of the room make a difference? All I was managing to achieve right now was looking like a fool.

Besides, if I didn't make a decision soon my stomach would offer a very undignified grumble and I could, just possibly, die of shame.

I bit my lips. *Fine.*

Not allowing myself any more thoughts, I sat down and began to eat.

The food was as delicious as it looked, the meat's juices in perfect combination with the pale cream that coated the vegetables I couldn't name.

We continued our meal in a silence which, though hardly companionable, could have been much worse.

As I ate, the room's quiet gave me time to think on Aleister's solution for Peter's grief. It was a hateful option. It would rob me completely of my life, ripping me from the minds of everyone who had ever known me. Erasing me from existence as if I had never been.

It was a horrible solution, but it *was* a solution. The only one I had.

"Will it hurt? Making Peter forget about me?" I asked.

"No," Aleister said without hesitation. "And it takes only a moment."

"Do you need to be near him or see him or something?"

He shook his head. "We can do it right here, right now, if you wish."

I put my fork down, the flame of hunger suddenly snuffed out by the immediacy of this decision. "I don't have anything else to offer in return," I said.

"I'm not asking for anything." He sat back in his chair. "Call if a peace offering, of sorts."

"A peace offering?"

"Of sorts," he added with a small smile.

I hadn't the slightest clue what that might mean, but if I wanted to do this, I would do it no matter what his motives were.

"Can it be undone if I change my mind?"

"No. This is final, I'm afraid. Because it involves not only your brother but everyone else who's ever known you, it requires a great deal of my power and it is too complex to be reversed."

I lowered my hands to my lap. This decision was one I would have to live with for the rest of my life. But what was the alternative? Watching Peter, the Peter I loved, disappearing as surely as our mother had.

I'd brought this on the two of us. If I hadn't agreed to Aleister's terms, my brother would be dead, true, but he'd also be at peace.

If I'd just remembered the cufflinks.

Well, I could give him a version of peace now. This very second. It was pure selfishness that I hadn't granted him that yet.

"All right," I said. "Do it."

He watched me for a moment longer before nodding, perhaps waiting for me to change my mind, perhaps relishing the pain the choice brought me. I didn't know and I didn't care.

When he began, there was no bright light show, no elaborate hand movements, no strange words, nothing at all, just Aleister's eyes dimming in front of me. All the unnatural sharpness slipping from them in the space of a breath.

With a soft sigh, he closed them. His body stilled, even the rise and fall of his chest coming to a stop, until he could have been a figure chiseled out of granite. It was only a moment before he opened his eyes again, revealing the full force of his gaze, but it felt like an eternity.

"It is done," he said.

That was it, then. That was all it took, a single blink to wipe away an entire life. I dug my fingernails into my palms. I would not cry in front of him again. "Thank you," I murmured.

"There is no need for that. I did it just as much for myself as I did for you." Aleister's hands shook slightly as he pushed his chair back and stood. "I'll retire now and leave you to your thoughts, if you have no objections."

I shook my head, not trusting my voice's firmness.

"One more thing, Nora. Please take what I said about your safety to heart. After tonight, I hope you see that neither I nor any of mine mean you harm."

I bit the inside of my bottom lip as a tear slid down my cheek. *Just go. Please just leave me alone.*

Without another word and without waiting for a response, Aleister walked past me in absolute silence and left the room the instant before a sob racked my ribs open.

EIGHT

I STOOD HALFWAY BETWEEN the sitting room and the bedroom.

Both doors were open, the fires in both rooms were lit, and neither was welcoming. But it had to be one room or the other. The study only had a chair, and I refused to spend the whole night trying not to fall out of it.

My eyes, swollen from crying, burned as I glanced at the large bed, where I would not have to contort my limbs to manage a fully prone position, where softness waited for me instead of the rigid spine of a sofa. Just the thought of having to rest my head on a beaded and lacy decorative pillow the entire night made me groan.

A long-necked shadow slid out of the bedroom's entrance as I debated with myself. This one didn't scurry from my eyes, but allowed itself to be seen. Perhaps now that I officially knew about them, all of them, it didn't feel the need to hide. Or perhaps it just wanted to scare me.

Whatever the reason, it stood still, the blank space where its face should have been turned in my direction, as if awaiting instructions.

Instructions. There was a thought.

I cleared my throat. "Away from the door," I said.

It did as I ordered with no hesitation, sliding along the walls until it was as far from the bedroom as the corridor allowed.

Not bad. "Close the sitting room door."

It was done in a heartbeat.

"Come here," I said, pointing to a spot in front of me.

It was suddenly there, immobile, towering above me. I felt a jolt of fear at seeing it so close, but I forced myself not to react. I had to show them I was their mistress, and I could hardly do so if I spooked as easily as a carriage horse.

"Go back."

With no sign of annoyance, of anger, of anything but mindless obedience, the shadow returned to its spot across the hall.

I watched it and it watched me.

"These will be the rules, then," I said when it gave no sign of moving on its own. "None of you will touch me without my permission. There will be no helping me dress or undress, not so much as tying a ribbon in my hair. I don't want any of you in the room while I slee—" No, that was wrong. "I don't want any of you in the room with me at all, at any time, unless I call for you. I don't want fires lit in any of the rooms unless I say so. If I need anything I will ask, but otherwise I want to be left alone. Is that understood?"

The shadow bowed its head as it and its brethren had done for Aleister.

"Let the other ones like you know my wishes."

It bowed its head again.

Well, that was something, at least. I wasn't entirely sure they could be trusted, but I supposed I would find that out soon enough. If I woke with a blade against my neck, that would mean that no, indeed, they could not.

Gathering every bit of courage I had, and as prepared to be shoved, scratched, or choked as I could be, I turned and walked into the bedroom. My hand trembled when I reached out to close and lock the door behind me.

It was stifling inside, worse than it had been on the first and only night I'd slept there. As if the fire had been burning unabated since I'd arrived. The heat was like a hand pressed against my face, making it a chore to draw breath. One minute under its heavy weight would be impossible, never mind an entire night.

I couldn't put it out now, not when it blazed with such fury, so I would have to wait for it to die on its own.

All well and good, but I needed to let in some fresh air or I would dissolve in a pool of my own sweat.

I crossed to one of the uncovered windows. My reflection greeted me with dark eyes that looked like they would roll out of my head from lack of sleep. My naturally pale face was even paler than usual and the soft roundness that had made me appear younger than I was for as long as I could remember had begun to be replaced by the angles of my cheekbones. For the first time since we'd left childhood behind and our features had taken on the qualities of our genders, I saw the resemblance between Peter's face and mine.

I unhooked the latch and opened the window. It was silent and offered no resistance this time.

Sharp, cold air swept over me and I exhaled with relief. Despite the smell of refuse from the nearby Thames and the noise of people and horses that it brought with it, there wasn't anything that could have soothed me better than common London air. I breathed in deeply, feeling the chill sweep the heat from my lungs and the crisp wind brush the remnants of tears from my face.

The night vibrated with movement. Just outside this house, people were living their ordinary lives, dealing with everyday problems as best they could. And out there, among them, a young man had woken from a nightmare, the name Nora Smith suddenly losing all meaning for him and with it, all sting. That had to be enough for me. I had to be satisfied knowing he was finally free.

Free.

With a surprising pang of guilt, my thoughts landed on the missing girls. They were less free than Peter and I had ever been, for all of our complaining. Even now, I had more freedom and an infinitely better life than they would be able to dream of if that ship left with them onboard.

But I would do my best to help. I would do everything in my power to save them. I was *already* doing it.

I stared out at the clear sky above the house. "I hope that will be enough."

The cloudless expanse held its silence.

I walked into the main hall, my eyes on the thick book in front of me. *Paradise Lost*. It was like trying to read sentences through a fog, Milton's slippery stanzas twisting and gliding out of view before finally revealing their meaning. I still wasn't entirely sure this was reading material I enjoyed, but trying to decipher what Milton meant kept me distracted, offering some respite from the ache of knowing that Peter, my Peter, no longer knew who I was. Between reading and planning for tomorrow's luncheon with Geary, I'd managed to get through the day without shrieking in pain.

I turned the page as I crossed the hall toward the kitchen to fetch a glass of water, my bare feet sure on the marble floors while my thoughts followed fallen angels through the depths of hell.

That was when I heard it.

A sound that brought me to an instant stop, that locked my limbs, that made me forget all about the book in my hands.

My head snapped to the large door leading to Aleister's wing, where the noise seemed to be coming from. My chest tightened with suspended breath as I listened.

It was a sound unlike anything I'd ever heard, so distorted I didn't realize at first it was a voice speaking.

Aleister's voice.

It barely resembled his usual tone, and it didn't resemble a human voice at all. No normal throat could make those screeching hisses and knife-blade sounds that blended with serrated consonants at the highest of speeds, one slicing into the next with no pause.

This wasn't a human language, I was sure of that.

I took a step forward, nearer the door.

The pain, when it began an instant later, made me recoil. But it was too late. It had already enveloped me.

All my mind registered was that, somehow, I was on fire. It was like someone had poured liquid flames into my veins and every second and every heartbeat fanned them deeper and deeper into me. My throat, my scalp, my hands and feet, my legs, my lungs, my stomach, my heart, everything started to boil.

I opened my mouth to cry out in a mixture of surprise and fear, but another wave of fire raced through me and burned my voice to nothing.

What was happening to me? I scrambled for any reasonable explanation, but the pain shattered through every thought.

I looked down at my hands still clutching the book, expecting to see flesh melting off to reveal steaming bones, but they looked just as they always did. Shaking but intact.

Aleister spoke again and the pain intensified. I could feel my blood bubbling like water in a kettle. It doubled me over.

It was him, I realized. It was his voice that was causing this pain!

My fingers dug into the book, pages curling into my palm as I lost control of all movement. And the only sound, unending, was his voice, the monstrousness of it.

I had to get away. Right now.

But I couldn't feel my legs beneath the burning. Were they even still there? As I looked down at my feet, my eyes blurred with tears that could not quench the heat that had infected every part of me. There was nothing visibly wrong, not with my legs or my feet, but they wouldn't respond.

My body was closing itself off to avoid the pain.

Stop it! I screamed at myself. *You have to do something!*

But flames licked at my insides, the agony of it making me gag on my own saliva.

Walk! Goddamn it, move your legs!

Gathering all of my strength, I forced myself to focus on my bare feet. I willed them to move, shoving aside the internal flames that threatened to consume me, narrowing my field of vision right down to my toes until everything faded, including Aleister's voice.

The paralyzing pain lost its grip on me for just a moment, but that was all I needed.

I took off down the corridor at the highest speed I could muster.

With every step away from Aleister, from his voice, the burning began to fade. Control of my muscles and my mind returned as I careened through the doorway to my wing of the house, down the corridor, and right into the bedroom.

I shut the door and locked it before running into the bathroom and doing the same. I yanked the bathtub and sink faucets open as far as they would go, the noise of rushing water becoming one more barrier between those nightmarish sounds and me. Launching into a made-up tune that echoed against the bathroom walls and vibrated on my palate, I waited for the pain to begin again without any idea of what I would do if it did. Run out of the house barefoot and in my sleeping gown, I supposed, and continue running until I couldn't anymore.

But the burning didn't return.

There wasn't a single remnant of its fierceness in my body, either. No singed hair or blackened skin that I could see. My insides weren't seeping out of my mouth or nose in goopy, melting ropes. I felt no pain at all. Not even discomfort.

I stopped humming.

Whatever I'd just experienced seemed to be over.

I exhaled a shaky breath of relief.

But that only lasted a moment before anger descended on me. "That's enough," I whispered.

I'd had enough of not knowing anything about who Aleister was or where his powers came from. This was the second time I'd feared for my life in this house, and that was two times too many. If he refused to tell me the truth, then I would have to find out for myself once and for all because this would no longer do. If I was successful tomorrow at the luncheon and got us invitations to Geary's ball, I wouldn't be able to do what I needed to with even remnants of the biting fear that coursed through me now.

Who was I living with?

The answers had to be in his rooms. There had to be at least clues as to how he did the things he did. The problem was how to get access to them. Aleister came and went so silently I never knew when he was in the house at all, and although he had invited me to explore his wing on the night I'd arrived, I doubted he'd be very amused if I walked into his bedroom without warning and began to open cabinets and drawers.

But I would have to find an opportunity, even if it meant keeping an eye on the front door for hours to see him leave. Getting into his rooms was the only hope I had of learning the truth.

It was vital, though, that I avoid suspicion of what I was planning to do until I did it or he would get rid of anything that might suggest the truth. Things had to go on as usual, as if tonight never happened.

No, I couldn't ignore any of this further. I'd been suspended in this murky limbo for too long. It was time to learn the truth of who Aleister was.

Whether he wanted me to or not.

NINE

"LADY BLAKE, ALLOW ME to introduce my sisters, Miss Evelyn Whitmore and Miss Maud Livingston."

Jonathan Geary smiled, his arm sweeping from one woman to the other in an exaggerated deference that would have made me roll my eyes in any other situation.

"Very pleased to meet you," I said.

Geary's sisters weren't what anyone would call attractive. Evelyn Whitmore, the eldest if appearances were to be trusted, had a nose that could have doubled as a coat hanger, while Maud Livingston wore spectacles so thick they looked more like magnifying glasses and had a mouth thin enough to border on invisible.

"I hope you don't mind that we've invited an acquaintance of my sisters', Miss Dorothea Giles, for luncheon," Geary said, nodding to a third woman I hadn't even noticed.

I batted my eyelashes. "Of course I don't mind. How do you do?" I said, turning to her, a middle-aged woman wearing a hat with an entire stuffed bird on it.

"Let us sit," Geary said, nodding to the table set out before us. "I've taken the liberty of ordering some refreshments."

As if plucked from thin air, a man in coattails appeared with a decanter on a silver tray. He waited until we had each taken our seats before filling our glasses with wine.

I didn't know what I had expected of *Rules*, but my imagination hadn't made it nearly as grand as it was. There were carvings everywhere, details and beauty to be discovered in every direction I looked, even above us, where a cupola done in tinted glass and adorned with golden flowers and curlicues allowed soft natural light to seep in.

I had passed by the restaurant's doors with Peter numerous times, but I'd never in my wildest thoughts imagined I'd step inside.

I realized my hands were trembling. After the luxury of Aleister's house, it was silly that this place would make me nervous, but it did. All I could see in front of me were glasses to spill, plates to break, utensils to drop, tablecloths to stain.

This is not the time to turn coward, Nora, I told myself. *You live with someone who can steal a person right from death's grip, and you're scared of looking foolish in a restaurant?*

As the other women took sips from their glasses, I removed my cream gloves one finger at a time and placed them on my lap. The wedding ring Aleister had given me to wear this morning caught the light from one of the small chandeliers above us and winked like an eye.

He had handed it to me with all of the irony and coiled laughter I'd expected and I had tried not to flinch too much as each syllable he spoke reminded me of that horrible language that had almost boiled my insides.

It hadn't been an easy morning, waking after hours of nightmares to remember once again that Peter no longer knew me and that I had almost died the night before. But it had strengthened my resolve.

I had to find the truth. And I would.

I picked up the crystal glass with care and tried not to wrinkle my nose at the wine as I brought it to my lips and pretended to take a sip. The smell alone was nauseating.

"Our brother told us you are not familiar with the city," Evelyn said.

"I'm afraid it's true. I've lived my entire life in Essex County. It sounds rather dull, doesn't it?" I forced myself to giggle in my most girlish manner.

"Essex," Dorothea said, as if tasting the word. "That's north of London, right?"

And I'd been worried about my accent! Dorothea sounded as if she had come right from Whitechapel this morning.

"No, it's to the southeast of here," Geary said.

"You have a coast, then?" Maud asked.

The extra puff on the "h" gave her away at once. It revealed how unused she was to enunciating it.

These women were pretending just as much as I was; they just happened to be worse at it. Compared to them, even Geary could have passed for nobility. Hadn't he realized that if I were a lady, the addition of his sisters and their friend would have harmed his position with me, not helped it? Then again, he might not have had anyone else he could bring and still hope to achieve what he wanted.

I cleared my throat. "Oh, yes, we have a lovely coast. One of our estates was by the water." I allowed my hands to flutter to my chest. "Is. I meant *is* by the water."

"Of course. It must be a beautiful place," Geary hurried to say.

"It is."

I busied myself adjusting the cloth napkin on my lap, granting the man more than enough time to signal to his companions. Which he did, giving all three a pointed look that I caught with a quick flick of my eyes. On his cue, the women turned to each other and began a sudden, nonsensical chatter, each choosing a different subject and trying to out-speak the other. Subtle, they were not. But at least I now knew they were in on the scheme, too.

After another look from Geary that was comical in its exaggerated fierceness, their voices smoothed out into a conversation on the latest fashions.

"I am so very glad you could join us today, Lady Blake," Geary said, turning to look at me. "I hope you have found the city more satisfactory than you did when we met."

"It is lovely, but I do miss my own home."

He leaned in a bit, lowering his voice to a level of intimacy that made my skin crawl. "Yes, I remember you said you had to leave it in a hurry."

Getting right to it, then. Maybe I wouldn't have to waste an entire afternoon with this man.

"Yes," I said, making sure he saw the way I clenched my hands in my lap, the way I avoided his eyes. All things he wouldn't be able to resist.

"I wanted to extend my help to you and Lord Blake. If you are in need of any assistance at all, I am fully at your service." He took up his wine glass. "I have many connections in the city. In all manner of areas."

And all under his thumb, I was sure. Though how they had gotten there was difficult to understand, unless they were all gullible idiots.

"That is most kind of you, Mr. Geary." I bit my lips and fiddled with the napkin again, allowing the silence to grow between us.

His sisters and their friend were still going on about the right shade of yellow for a silk dress, since apparently just a touch of extra blue or red in the color could ruin the entire season. They were emphatically not looking our way, but I could almost see their ears pricking up, listening for our voices even while they talked.

"I hope I haven't offended you with my offer, madam," Geary finally said.

"No, of course not. On the contrary, I am very grateful for all the kindness you've shown me." I leaned a bit toward him, lowering my voice, as well. "It's just...well, it's rather difficult for me to speak about it, because I don't really understand everything that's happened. It's a business matter, you see, and my husband doesn't want to bother me with it."

"Quite right, too, madam."

I smiled and nodded. "He's very considerate. He did tell me, though, that he's had a spot of bad luck with an investment and somehow it's become a bit of a fuss."

"Most unfortunate."

"It is, rather. Nothing very serious for us, of course, but—" I stopped, biting my lip and clasping my hands tighter on my lap.

"Madam?"

I leaned even closer. "This must stay strictly between us, you understand."

"Of course."

"Well, from what I have gathered, some of our friends followed my husband's recommendation and invested, as well, and now they are blaming him for the outcome. They're saying he knew it was bound to fail but he encouraged them anyway. Which is very silly. Why would he do that? Besides, no one knows how these things will turn out!"

He lowered his eyes, but not before I saw the gleam of excitement in them. "That's exactly right, madam. I'm sure your husband is blameless."

"He is, but he is very troubled by all of this. He is even thinking of selling our home in Essex!"

Geary nodded. "As a matter of fact, madam, I know quite a bit about the kind of investment problems you've mentioned."

"You do?"

"Yes. I'm considered an expert in these kinds of...uncomfortable situations. I've helped a number of acquaintances through similar moments."

But of course he had.

"It is usually a misunderstanding and it can be easily resolved."

I blinked repeatedly. "Really?"

"Yes, madam."

"Would you be able to help us, then? Settle everything with our acquaintances so that things can return to normal?"

"Without a doubt."

I clapped my hands and gave him a beaming smile. "Oh, how wonderful! You are a godsend, Mr. Geary!" An easily manipulated one, too.

The three women sitting in front of us didn't even turn in our direction but continued on with their chat, which made their listening in all the more obvious.

"I'd be happy to help, Lady Blake."

"I'm just so thrilled!" I touched his arm. "Of course, you will have to speak with my husband about the particulars, since I don't know more than what I have told you."

"Of course."

If it was going to happen, it'd be now. I held my breath and batted my eyes.

"In fact," he started after a moment, "I'm having a ball at my estate next Wednesday night. I know it's last minute, but I'd be honored if you and Lord Blake attended. Your husband and I could begin to speak of all of this then. Start thinking of how best to resolve the situation."

Oh, this was much too easy. And all of it done before we even selected the first course. "A ball?" I said, adding a flutter of excitement to my voice. "We haven't gone to one in ages, what with all of this nonsense."

He smiled too widely for it to look natural. "We can remedy that, as well."

I met his smile and topped it. "I know I speak for both of us when I say we'd be delighted to attend, Mr. Geary."

"Wonderful. I'm looking forward to making Lord Blake's acquaintance. With a bit of luck, we'll have you back in your home in Essex in no time at all, madam."

As he finished speaking, a man appeared at our side carrying cloth-bound menus. I stretched my hand out for one.

"I have full confidence in your abilities, Mr. Geary," I said. "I have no doubt at all you'll be able to help us."

After giving him another smile, I glanced down at the page in front of me and tried to focus on the words embossed on it.

I'd done it. We had invitations to the ball.

Now I could focus all of my attention on what I knew would not be nearly as easy to accomplish: learning who Aleister really was.

TEN

A KNOCK ON MY bedroom door pulled me out of the nightmare that had left my nightgown plastered against my legs, bringing me gasping into the waking world.

"Nora?" Aleister called.

Although his voice sounded as it always did, I still couldn't hear it without thinking of how distorted it'd been just a few nights ago, how much pain it had inflicted. It sent a shiver coursing through me every time I remembered.

"Coming," I said, my tongue still thick with sleep. I pushed the covers aside and sat up.

I forgot all about one of the leaning wooden figures carved into the bed as I stood. It hit me squarely in the forehead, its extended hand missing my right eye by a hair's width.

"Bloody angels or whatever the hell they are," I muttered, grabbing my dressing gown from the end of the bed and slipping it on before staggering to the door.

Despite the early hour, Aleister practically vibrated with energy in front of me. The corridor's gloom, barely touched by the pale rising sun, couldn't hide the brilliance of his eyes.

Seeing him sent a jolt of fear up my spine, which worked just as well as a splash of icy water to bring me fully awake.

"I know it's early, Nora," he said, "but I've been called away on urgent business."

"Oh? Is it to do with Geary?"

"No, another matter. I've been putting it off for as long as possible but it's unavoidable now. I will be gone for all of today and tonight, but I'll be back tomorrow morning. No later than noon, I should think."

Though a sudden flare of excitement lit up inside me at his words, I was careful to keep my face as impartial to the news as possible. I nodded and looked down at my hands. "All right."

This was it. This was the chance I'd been looking for. I would have more than enough time to go through the entire house if I wanted to.

"Is something wrong?" he asked softly.

I blinked. "No, I'm...I'm just not fully awake yet."

"Of course. And here I am, keeping you from your rest." A thin ribbon of scarcely disguised laughter was woven through each of his words.

If he'd been anyone else, any regular human, I would have landed a couple of blows to his groin to see if he still found me amusing, but that wasn't an option. Not unless I wanted to feel my brain sizzle like fat in a pan with just a few of his words.

Aleister cleared his throat and took a step away from the door. "Is there anything you need from me before I leave?"

I shook my head.

"Or anything you would like me to bring you back? More reading material, perhaps? Or a new dress?"

"No, thank you."

"Quite sure?"

"I'm sure."

He shrugged lightly. "Very well. I'll see you tomorrow, then, Nora."

I watched him walk down the corridor and leave my wing of the house.

This was my chance.

I made myself wait an hour. A full hour to make sure Aleister hadn't forgotten anything and come back to find me elbow deep in his personal possessions. One eye on the clock on the night table, I dressed and waited. Then waited some more.

At ten minutes past seven, I hurried across the entrance hall and stopped in front of the door to Aleister's wing.

The house was silent around me when I grabbed the doorknob and turned it. Nothing stopped me, not a single one of the shadowy creatures or their suddenly returned master. Not even a lock because the door opened without protest.

The corridor had become endless. It looked nothing like it had just a week and a half ago. It stretched in front of me, its far wall a distant horizon.

Spread along the wainscoted walls that flanked the dark marble floor were door after door after door, all of them crafted out of the same matching wood and all of them closed. There had to be at least fifty rooms.

Soft tinkling drew my eyes above me, where huge, many-armed and fully lit chandeliers moved gently with the current of air I'd created by opening the door. They scattered brilliant light against all of the walls and the floors, dispelling shadows with their glittering crystals.

For all of my urgency until now, I found myself reluctant to do more than hover in the doorway. There could be anything in those rooms. A thousand dangers.

But, also, all the answers I needed.

"Right, well, you'll learn nothing just standing here like an idiot," I told myself. I was wasting time. If I didn't do this now, I might never be able to do it at all.

Swallowing back a twinge of fear, I crossed the wing's threshold and turned to the study's door.

Everything looked just the same as the one and only time I'd been in here, down to the blazing fire. I scanned through the books in his bookcases, which had been built right into the wall, looking for anything of importance. There was a bit of everything: novels, poetry collections, atlases, books on religions, and even some written in languages that crossed my eyes just from trying to read their titles. All of them mixed together. I could have spent the entire day looking through the shelves and still not have known everything they contained.

Turning, I spotted a desk with four large drawers sitting beneath one of the windows. That looked more promising. I walked over to it, already pulling two hair pins out of my hastily built bun, ready to make Peter, the Peter who still knew me, proud. All it would take were the few quick twists he'd taught me, and the drawers would click open. No more than a minute's worth of work.

But they weren't locked.

There was also nothing inside them. Not so much as a piece of paper.

"Blast," I said.

With a sigh of frustration, I slammed the drawers shut and walked out of the study. On to the next door.

This one revealed Aleister's bedroom, which was almost entirely empty. There wasn't anything in it but a lit fireplace and a bed. It was smaller than mine, without a canopy, and adorned with large carvings of wings instead of with vaguely human figures. The feathers, done in wood, caught and frozen in flight, spread through the headboard and all along the frame, giving the bed fluid motion. As if it were about to take off. The memory of that feather I'd seen in his coat pocket, the way he had hidden it from me, made me frown. There was an answer there, I could almost see its glint, but I couldn't quite make it out. Not yet.

Except for these carvings, the room was severe in its simplicity. The blue and gray walls were bare of paintings or ornaments of any sort, and there was no night table, armchair, or even an armoire in which to store clothes. It was devoid of personality. It could have been anyone's bedroom.

I gathered my heavy skirts and knelt beside the bed, peering under it in case that was where he had stashed a trunk full of letters or documents. But there wasn't even dust.

Damn.

Standing again, I glanced up the length of the blue bedspread.

Perhaps there was something under the pillows, something so important the only way it was safe was if its owner slept with it. Peter used to sleep with the money we earned under his thin pillow, an uncomfortable arrangement considering we were paid mostly in piles of coins. I doubted Aleister needed to do that with his money, but there could be something else. Just a piece of paper with his real name somewhere on it would be a start.

It couldn't hurt to try.

My hands hovered over one of the pillows for a moment, an unexpected image of his almost unnaturally handsome face as it might look asleep flashing across my mind. I blinked it away but not before I felt a flush of warmth spreading up my neck and into my face.

Concentrate, Nora! You've hunted for rats in men's chambers before, so there's no need to be a ninny about it.

With more force than was probably necessary, I yanked the pillow up to uncover bare, crisp sheets. Nothing remotely interesting.

Time to move on.

As with the other two rooms, the next one's doorknob turned easily in my hands, revealing people.

I gasped and took a step back before I realized what I was looking at. Me. My image repeated over and over across the full-length mirrors that covered all of the walls in the room. I frowned and at least seven versions of me did the same.

This was odd. What did he need with all of these mirrors? He couldn't be that fastidious with his appearance when he hardly ever bothered to wear gloves or a hat.

I stepped inside. Patches of darkness closed around my feet, which the tear-shaped crystal light dangling from the ceiling could not dispel.

So far, this was the only room in the house that did not have any windows.

I neared the mirrors and looked around. My copies echoed every move in a precise dance. It made me uneasy, for some reason, like a shrill sound repeated one too many times.

Tapping the glass in front of me, I listened for the hollow sound that would give away a hidden room or a secret door. There had to be something, some hint as to who I was living with.

That was when I caught a shift out of the corner of my eye. A change in one of my duplicates.

I turned as quickly as I could but that only created a wave of movement through the room that hid what I'd seen. Gripping my skirt, I made myself to stay still despite the urge to look all around me, focusing only on the reflection right in front of my eyes. I held my breath and waited for motion.

There!

One of my reflections' heads twisted to the left, like an invisible someone had snapped her neck with one sharp jerk. Her body slackened, hanging upright for a moment, before returning to her original position. I watched in horror as one by one all of the other images did the same, the movement like a ripple that spread and spread.

It reached the last mirror, the last image of me, and stopped. Every single reflection stood still and stared straight ahead, just like I was doing.

My heart thumped violently in my chest as I stepped away from my doubles. The hairs on the back of my neck prickled with energy.

With such speed I winced, the reflections scurried closer to their edge of the mirrors, their heads snapping to look at me retreat. One more step and they would slip right out of the glass.

I didn't stay to find out if they actually could leave their crystal homes.

Lunging back quickly, I ran out into the corridor and slammed the door shut on all of those faces. I put all of my weight against the wood, listening for footsteps or crunching glass that would let me know I was about to be attacked by versions of me that belonged in a mad ward.

I waited a good long while until nothing tried to punch its way through or attempted to turn the knob, and then slowly removed my hands from the wood.

Nothing but quiet.

"Small blessings," I said.

I gazed down the long corridor, at all of those waiting rooms, at all of the horrors that could be ready to pounce on me the moment I opened each door. Because there was little chance now that they would reveal only elegant sitting rooms and dressing rooms. No, this wasn't going to be a dull day.

Taking a steadying breath, I prepared myself to tackle the next nightmare.

And I was right.

Every door I opened led to a sight more awful than the previous one. Floors that gave way to sheer drops; ceilings that cracked and buckled as I watched, threatening to bring plaster and who knew what else raining down on my head; a room swaying with enough water to drown in but that somehow did not splash out into the corridor; walls teeming with spiders that rushed at me the moment I opened the door; a room that was completely upside down, with furniture dangling from the ceiling; sliding walls that grew spikes as they neared each other; and on and on and on.

Each a new shock, each a new opportunity to turn around, run back to my wing and hide until Aleister returned.

But I didn't run. I had to find something that made all of this worthwhile because so far, I knew nothing about the man I lived with that I hadn't known already.

So I continued, cracking doors open enough to peer inside and slamming them shut after a few wide-eyed seconds. Over and over until I ran out of rooms.

"The last one," I said and walked toward the one door I hadn't yet opened, relief and disappointment staining my voice in equal measures.

Except, I realized when I drew closer, it wasn't a door but a shadowed arch leading into another corridor.

"This house is never-ending," I said, slumping against one of the walls to catch my breath. I wasn't sure what I would do if I saw another hall full of rooms when I walked through that dim entrance. How much more fright could I take before my mind unthreaded itself like a ragged hem and I just collapsed into a pile of maniacal laughter?

"Let's find out, I guess," I said with a sigh and pushed away from the wall.

A thin line of sweat dripped down my back when I moved and I found that my hands were moist. It was warmer at this end of the hallway than it had been at the opposite one, a dry heat that scratched at my throat and made me wish one of the many rooms around me had a decanter of water.

I stepped through the archway, its dimness giving way to the sight of a tight corridor created by more marble floors and bare walls. I started down its length and followed its path when it curved to the left, opening up into a larger passage that ended in front of a gate.

A large iron gate that blocked the way to the spiral staircase beyond it.

I stopped walking.

It didn't take a genius to tell from the house's exterior that it was made up of two stories, but I hadn't thought Aleister owned both. When he'd told me about the rooms on the night I'd arrived, he hadn't even mentioned the second floor. I'd imagined that someone else had access to it from a back entrance or some other arrangement, or that no one lived up there at all, because I hadn't heard anyone walking above our heads. Not that I could trust the way the interior of the house was set up when it was at least six times larger than it should have been, but still, I would have heard *something* if people lived upstairs.

There was also a large, thick chain with a metal lock around the double doors that made up the gate, so perhaps Aleister didn't own this section. Perhaps these were safety measures to keep strangers out of his side of the property.

Only one way to find out.

"I need one of you," I called out.

At once, a shadow appeared, the one I had named Long-Neck, for all of the obvious reasons.

I pointed to the gate and beyond it. "Is that part of your master's house?"

The shadow followed my arm with its sightless gaze but did nothing.

Did everything have to be so difficult? "I order you to answer me."

Its head turned back to me and stayed there, all motion suspended for an instant before it nodded, once.

So he had kept me from knowing about the second floor. That had to be significant.

"Give me the key for the lock, then," I said, extending my hand.

It could have been a statue made of solid ink for all its movement.

"I'm waiting," I said.

The shadow took a step back and gave a sharp shake of its head.

That was all the confirmation I needed. The truth of who Aleister was had to be hidden beyond that gate and up those stairs. Why else would he use a lock now when he hadn't bothered with the other doors? Why else would he have forbidden his servants to allow me access?

"Get out of here, then," I said. "I don't need you anymore." I made myself turn around, though every inch of my body yelled for me to do the opposite, to keep the shadow I could still sense at my back in full view.

I focused, instead, on the gate.

It loomed before me, appearing to grow taller as I drew nearer. It was crafted out of thick black iron, with sets of spikes at regular intervals along the top. Despite this, it looked easy enough to climb over. Almost too easy. The horizontal bars that began at the bottom of the frame and rose like steps all along its length made it child's play. A minute or two of climbing and I'd be on the other side.

Still, it seemed like too much work to undertake with the layers and layers of elaborate skirts I wore. I'd end up tripping over a lacy hem and impaling myself on one of the spikes. And it was even hotter in this side of the house, much too hot to exert myself if I could avoid it. Which I could. There was a much quicker option.

I again pulled out the two hair pins from my bun and got closer to the chain and thick padlock that sat heavy against where the gate's double doors met. I had never seen such a large one.

"Never mind," I muttered. "It's still just a padlock. Like many I've opened before."

Peter and I had done a good amount of lock picking, especially when I was younger and hadn't yet discovered my skills with rats. We'd kept ourselves fed with it, opening kitchen doors and stealing whatever was at hand. When we joined with Sharpe, Peter eased off on it, saying we no longer needed to take things now that we had a somewhat steady income and a roof over our heads, but I'd kept my skills sharp through the years. I'd stolen a series of padlocks and even a rusty set of handcuffs to practice on and not a week had gone by before all of this insanity occurred that I hadn't sat on the floor of our room seeing how quickly I could open them all.

A pang of grief made me close my eyes. I'd never again hear Peter tell me to drop the hair pins and pick up a book or a periodical instead, his gruff tone never fully concealing his smile at my speed.

I shook my head. Now was not the time to grieve over one more thing I'd lost.

I bent over the padlock and peered into the keyhole. Nothing strange there. It looked just like all the other ones I'd ever opened.

The hair pins in my hand were the ones I usually wore at the top of my bun, long and strong, without any ornament other than a small mother-of-pearl oval at each end. I'd snatched them from a woman's dressing table a few years ago during a job, and not purely out of vanity, either. They were the perfect length and shape for lock picking. The only adjustment I'd had to make was to turn the end of one of them with a few hits of a hammer.

I inserted the straight one as low into the padlock as it would go and turned it. Just the right amount of pressure came down on it. So far, everything was in order.

It took some effort not to scream when the shadow was suddenly there, right beside me, its silhouette a spot of darkness in the corner of my left eye.

"I told you to get out of here," I said, without removing the pin from the keyhole. I wasn't sure what I'd do if it decided to attack me but I was losing my patience with the spook routine.

"If you are going to hurt me, do it, otherwise stop distracting me."

I grabbed the other pin, and inserted it into the padlock, curved tip facing up. My hands shook slightly from knowing that creature was close to me, I couldn't help that, but I was used to working with a bit of nerves.

The shadow hovered at my side for an instant more, thinking god knew what, if it thought at all. And then it retreated. It was surely just behind me, but at least I didn't have to see it.

I brought all of my concentration back to the lock. This was the fun part.

I began to tap up lightly with the curved pin, feeling for the number of tumblers.

Really? Only four?

"That's disappointing, Aleister. I expected more of a challenge."

Always maintaining pressure on the bottom hair pin, I started to lift each tumbler with the curved one until I heard sharp clicks. One by one, they got out of the way, the bottom pin slowly sliding in.

Child's play.

The padlock opened with a dull thud.

I removed it and unwound the chain from around the gate doors, which swung open without a sound.

If I'd expected fanfare of any sort, unearthly screams alerting my intrusion or dogs foaming at the mouth ready to rip me limb from limb, I would have been even more disappointed than I was about the four tumblers. Because all I was greeted with was more silence. More and more nothingness.

Wiping sweat from my forehead, I walked to the spiral staircase which was made out of the same kind of iron as the gate. It was simple, just a basic, solid structure that rose up into a patch of darkness I couldn't see into.

"Maybe that's where the foaming dogs are waiting," I said, turning with a smile toward Peter...who was not at my side.

He would have been laughing, rolling his eyes at me. He would have been debating whether climbing those stairs was a safe enough thing for me to do and would have gone on debating until realizing I was already halfway to the top.

But he wasn't here. He wasn't smiling or rolling his eyes or debating with himself.

For better or worse, there was no one to stop me. Not even the creature I still sensed behind me.

I stepped onto the staircase, feeling the cast-iron structure shift slightly under my weight, and looked up again. I should have been able to see the second story from here but all I saw was blackness. That wouldn't stop me.

It started a few steps later.

The shrieking of metal on metal.

"What now?"

The cast iron started to shake under my hands and feet, the entire structure trembling. Was it falling apart?

The stairs gave a sudden jolt and I had to grab on to the banister again or risk falling. I was still near the floor, I could easily hurry back down, none the worse for wear. That would be what Peter would have shouted for me to do. It was the safest choice. The obvious choice.

I hesitated, my right foot dangling between steps.

But if I turned around now then I'd never know what was up there, what Aleister had worked hard to conceal from me. I couldn't do that. I *wouldn't* do that.

The metal frame seemed to spasm.

No, not seemed, I realized with widening eyes, it had *actually* contracted. The iron banister was suddenly closer to my side, the curve of the next section of the stairs almost touching my head.

It was shrinking!

No sooner had I thought it, the frame gave another jolt and twisted closer.

Time to move.

I lunged forward. The frame bucked again and I had to duck under the curve of the banister above me to pass on to the next section of the stairs without hitting my head.

"They had to be spiral!" I yelled as I slipped out of the way of a spasming metal coil, my voice echoing back to me like a slap. "Bloody spiral stairs!"

The noise was teeth-grindingly loud as every inch of the frame twisted in on itself, tighter and tighter. Iron rubbed against me, my arms and legs banging on the curved, cold edges as I ran past them at full speed. Up and up and up.

Another jolt shook the steps from under me too quickly to prepare for and I fell. I tasted blood and realized I had bitten down on my tongue.

Before I could rise, or even move, the stairs shook again and one of the steps twisted sideways, closing around my foot. For a moment I was sure I'd heard the crunch of bones, but there was no flare of pain. Nothing seemed to be broken.

Which didn't matter. Because I was stuck.

Unable to do anything as the metal drew closer, tightening like a fist around me, ready to crush and suffocate. If I couldn't move out of the way, I'd die right here.

After all that had happened... How pointless.

I shook my head. "Yeah, well, we'll see about that. It's over only when it's over."

Gathering all the strength I had, I pulled. I tugged until my fingers turned white from the pressure, but there was no chance of setting myself free like this. The shoe I wore was just wide enough to prevent it. The only option I had left was to try to yank my slightly narrower foot out from inside it.

I started to pull on the knots. I had tied them well this morning, too well.

My fingers slipped.

Concentrate! Panic will solve nothing.

With a trembling breath, I forced myself to narrow my attention, to wipe away every distraction, even the insistent thumping of my heart, until the only parts of my body I felt were my fingers. The rest evaporated.

In a moment, I had the knots undone.

The stairs creaked and shook as they got ready to shift again.

I leapt up and gripped the banister with both hands as I began to pull again. I would not die like this.

But it wasn't budging. If I could just have turned it sideways a little—

The metal trembled around me.

With a scream of frustration, I redoubled my efforts until it felt as if I were ripping my foot from the rest of my leg. I didn't care. If that was what it took to make it out of here with my life, I would gnaw my leg free like an animal in a trap.

And then I felt something give. My foot popped out of the shoe and I almost went careening off the side of the stairs. There was no time to celebrate my freedom, however. Everything was twisting again, tightening, one section of the stairs curling into the other. Now not even someone like me, small enough to crawl through the tightest walls, could fit through the gaps without risking getting trapped and crushed.

I looked down at the marble floors I'd left behind what felt like ages ago. The fall wouldn't kill me if I jumped, but I'd surely break something. That would force me to tell Aleister the truth of what had happened, or at least parts of it, and I would still know nothing worthwhile.

No. I'd come too far to be stopped. All I needed was a bit of courage, just a few more minutes of it. I could do this.

Besides, I had an idea. Maybe not the wisest one, but it was the only one I had that could still get me to the next floor.

I jumped over the edge, hands gripping the banister tightly.

The force of the swing brought me back toward the stairs and I slammed against the metal. The pain echoed through all of my bones, robbing me of breath.

"Damn!" I said. I had no time for this.

There was just empty air beneath my dangling form now. I held on as tightly as I could, but I knew my hands would not be able to hold me for very long. Not with the constant movement. I had to find a better grip.

With a grunt, I placed my feet on any groove I could find. The edge of a contorted step, the curve of a banister, the curlicue of an ornament. Anything that provided the slightest bit of purchase.

I started to climb up the side of the stairs like a ladder, going from one makeshift foothold to another. The corset bit into my ribs and I had to kick the skirts out of the way with each step to avoid slipping, shifting my hands quickly as the metal twisted tighter together and tried to trap my fingers within its cold folds.

A ribbon of light landed on my hands. I'd been so focused on climbing I hadn't realized I was finally nearing the top.

I was almost there!

As if reacting to my excitement, the next contraction was the worst one yet, sections of the stairs splintering as parts that were never meant to join together did so now. I continued to climb up, but all the edges were beginning to disappear, to meld into one another the tighter the staircase grew. Now only parts of my fingers could grasp the metal and only the tips of my toes found a perch.

I sped up, exchanging some caution for swiftness.

The light continued to spread around me. The entrance to the second floor was right above me.

"Yes!" I hissed, and quickly scurried up the few inches I had left to climb to reach the top.

What I now realized was sunlight poured down on me from the large windows that were coming into view. A bare room greeted me, just marble and light.

But there was another problem I hadn't thought about. Because the stairs had curled into themselves, the step and part of the banister that would have connected them to the second floor was gone, also wrapped in the roiling structure beneath my hands.

Which meant there was a gap between me and my goal. Empty space.

"It's not that big of a gap," I said. "Not more than an arm's length."

And there was no other option.

I brought both of my legs up as high as I could, ignoring my protesting ribs, and braced my feet against the staircase.

This time, I sensed the shifting in the metal before it happened.

Pressing all of my strength down into my legs, I did my best to turn into a human spring and shoved off the staircase.

For a moment, I hovered in the empty air. Weightless.

And then my elbows and torso slammed against the marble floor, ripping a gasp of pain and relief from my throat. Half of my body still dangled over the edge, but not enough to pull me down.

I'd made it to the second story.

"About bloody time, too," I muttered as I started to lift myself up.

Without wasting a moment, I crawled away from the edge before collapsing right onto my stomach. I lay there, flat against the floor, just panting.

Everything ached. My ribs bruised by the corset, my hands and bare foot scratched and bleeding from the metal edges, and muscles I had never noticed I had twinging from all the climbing and running and pulling.

But I was alive and I was on the second story. The rest, be damned.

"'You're perfectly safe in the house, Nora. Nothing can hurt you,'" I said, one of my cheeks against the ground. "That bastard. If he thinks this is safety, I dread to think what he considers danger."

With a prolonged groan, I sat up. Everything seemed to creak back into place without excruciating levels of pain. Good enough. Now I just had to stand.

I was about to attempt it when another shriek of metal stained the air.

I frowned. Would the stairs not stop even now that they had no one to squeeze to death? Seemed like a waste of energy or magical power or whatever else made that trap from hell spring to life.

Slowly, and ready to bolt away if there was the slightest danger of being grabbed by the rabid pile of metal, I shifted to the edge again and peered down.

"Oh, that's just grand," I said.

Instead of the column of blackness I'd expected, the staircase looked just as it had before I set foot on it, as solid as London Bridge. Like I hadn't almost lost my life to it half a dozen times. Which meant I would have to go through the same song and dance on the way down unless I found another option. Wonderful. Something to look forward to.

My missing shoe, twisted and cracked into almost unrecognizable shape, lay on the floor next to the stairs, where it had been spat out by the metal.

"You bloody thing. You liked that shoe? Well, I've got another one for you!" I took hold of the laces of my remaining one and undid the knots. "Here, enjoy!"

I slipped it off and flung it down, hitting one of the stair's steps and part of a banister.

"Hope you choke on it."

Turning, I stomped off down the large bare space to an arch on the opposite side that led into another room. It was time to see what all of that trouble had earned me.

There wasn't much, I soon realized.

Two rooms empty of furniture, of paintings on the walls, of everything. They were submerged in sunlight, though, which flooded in through the curtain-less windows that faced into the street. None of them were the small square ones visible from the pavement outside, of course, another of those inconsistencies I was learning to shrug off or risk going mad.

There was a door at the end of the second room. A replica of all the other ones in the house. Not very impressive at all. Nothing about it spoke of the kind of awful secrets someone had to have to require the protection of a gigantic gate and a murderous staircase.

I walked toward it, shaking my head. "There have better be piles of gold behind that door," I said. "If it's another bare room, I might just set fire to Aleister's bed."

I paused before touching the doorknob. Who knew what I might unleash by trying to open it.

Still, this had to be done. I wouldn't be stopped now, no matter what happened.

I took hold of the knob and turned it.

Neither fire nor stones nor anything else rained down on me in punishment. No sharp stakes jabbed up from the floor to skewer me.

I exhaled in relief.

The door was locked, though. A promising sign that there was, after all, a worthwhile secret to be discovered.

I was about to get started picking the lock open when something pulled my hand from the knob with enough strength to turn me around. Long-Neck was beside me again.

"Get your hands off," I hissed and yanked my arm away. "I told you, all of you, not to touch me. Not ever."

The shadow turned its head to the door and shook it with violence.

"Oh, now you want to warn me, is that it? Well, where the hell were you a few minutes ago when I was about to be crushed to death? I could have used your help then, but no. You and all of your kind only show up when you're not needed or even wanted." I pointed across the room. "Go stand back there. Or better yet, go all the way downstairs. I don't want to see you."

It seemed to be staring at me, to be listening to my words, but it didn't move.

"I am your mistress; Aleister said so himself. You have to do as I order."

If a shadow, a mere silhouette, could display reluctance, this one did so now.

I narrowed my eyes and made myself as tall and imposing as someone of my stature, barefoot, bruised, with ripped skirts, and still somewhat afraid of the creature in front of me could hope to be. "Go downstairs."

It finally started to move, slowly shifting back toward the arch that led to the stairs without turning around, without taking its gaze off me. Like it was expecting me to change my mind and call it back.

Little chance of that.

I waited until the shadow had disappeared completely before pulling the two pins out of my hair.

"Let's see if he chose a tougher lock this time," I said, kneeling in front of the door.

I inserted the pins. "Ah, six tumblers. Better." Not that it added much difficulty, just a few more seconds to the time it would take to get it opened.

Tapping each tumbler into place, I waited to hear the dry click of an opened lock.

"There," I said with a smile a moment later. "Nothing to it."

I slid the hairpins back into my bun with practiced ease and turned the doorknob.

Darkness greeted me. Absolute blackness, like I had opened a door to pure night. The flood of sunlight that surrounded me didn't make the slightest dent in the room, not lightening the gloom in the smallest degree. It was like the rays couldn't slip past the doorway.

I rolled my eyes. This was Aleister being theatrical again, providing another obstacle to the truth. Well, *this* wouldn't work on me, either.

I reached out with my left hand to tap for a light switch. No matter how strange its contents, every room in the house had a chandelier connected to electric light and there was no reason to think this one was an exception.

My fingers touched bare wall.

The switch could be a bit further down, or on the opposite side of the door, but that would mean having to walk in.

The idea of entering the room blind was not exactly pleasant. There could be anything waiting for me.

Yes, sure, but I was quick. Always had been. I could run down the wall, find the light, flick it on, and run back out into the corridor in seconds. It would be ridiculous to turn around now after everything I'd done to get here just because I was afraid of tripping over a lounge chair. A possibly enchanted lounge chair out for my blood, but a piece of furniture nonetheless.

I placed a hand on the door for solid reassurance and took a step into the room. I opened my eyes wide, as Peter had taught me to do at night, allowing them to gather whatever light there may have been even in the blackest of rooms.

There was no light to gather, though. All that they saw was darkness, almost solid in its thickness.

Taking a deep breath, I let go of the door and darted to the left, my hands flat on the wall, feeling for anything that could be a light switch. I reached as high as I could and as low as I thought probable, but found nothing.

I gasped when the door slammed shut, my eyes widening even more at what was simultaneously occurring beneath my hands.

It was the wall. It had disappeared from under my fingertips, the rough, reassuring surface of the plaster turning into air.

I swallowed back a jolt of surprise that already carried the cold edge of fear.

This was just another trick. The wall had to have moved somehow, retreated or shifted. I only had to find it and the door again, that was all. It didn't call for a surrender to panic.

Blinking, I turned my head in the hopes of seeing something now that my eyes had had time to get adjusted, but it was useless. How could any place be this dark? I'd assumed I knew what complete blackness was from my hunts through walls or through sewers at night, but it had never been like this. There had always been some light. This had to be what blindness felt like.

"It's just a few seconds," I whispered. "I'll be fine."

As long as nothing is hunting me.

Stretching out my arms, I started slowly walking forward. My fingertips tingled with the anticipation of touching something but each step brought me to more emptiness. The more I walked, the less possible it was to feel only air. The wall couldn't have moved this much without upsetting the way the entire second story was built. I should have been in the middle of the corridor by now.

Maybe the wall hadn't moved. Maybe I had without realizing it. Perhaps the door closing triggered some mechanism or magic or whatnot that shifted me about, like had happened on my second morning in the house. Without the light from the door as an anchor, I might not have noticed it happen.

Choosing another direction at random, I turned left. I kept one arm in front of me and the other stretched out to my right, and started walking again. Step after step, hoping for the feel of a wall.

The sound of something scurrying a few feet in front of me brought me to an immediate stop. It was a rough, dry clatter, like animal feet.

"Is it one of you?" I called out before I realized the stupidity of the question. It wasn't one of the shadows. They were as silent as Aleister when they moved. Which meant there was something else in the room with me, something which might well be able to see me while I was wholly blind. Even if it meant me no harm, it wasn't the most calming of thoughts.

The sound had grown closer now.

"Stay away," I said. The last syllable shook and cracked as a shape brushed against my skirts. Fear was like a splash of cold water down my back.

I had to keep moving, even if I didn't know which direction was the way out. Standing still would not help me at all.

I launched into a faster pace, my arms extended, searching for what had now become a necessity.

Sudden laughter, very close to me, rippled over my skin. It was a shrill sound and there wasn't anything human to it, but it was laughter. An imitation of it, like a captive bird's repetition of its name.

I didn't allow it to stop me, not even to slow me down.

"Get away," I said. My voice scraped against my dry throat and seemed to peter off as soon as it left my mouth, swallowed up by the darkness.

That sparked more of the same laugher, this time from behind me.

I turned on my heels and yelled, moving my arms wildly, trying to scare off whatever was making that horrid sound. Whatever had decided to stalk me.

The noise only increased and drew closer.

Without warning, without so much as a growl or a hiss, something so cold it burned sliced into one my outstretched arms. I yelped in pain and leapt back from where the swipe had come from. The shaking hand I brought up to the wound touched wet, warm blood.

The scurrying came from two different directions now.

"Get away from me!" I screamed. The rising panic was impossible to keep out of my voice. If there were two creatures, there could be a dozen or a hundred, for all I knew. And if I couldn't see them when they could obviously see me—

The unmistakable pain of teeth sinking into one of my feet flung all thoughts away. The stinging rose up my leg, extracting a cry of agony from me just as another set of teeth bit through my skirt and into my calf.

I kicked out with violence, shaking off the creatures, but the pain was unbearable. It made my head throb, the inside of my eyelids burning red with its power, my breath hitching into a tight fist.

Hot tears slid down my cheeks as I stumbled back. A chittering, gurgling sound was building all around me.

I had to get out of here. Right now.

I started running, hurtling through the darkness at full speed. Sharp hissing joined the laughter behind me, and a vibration of movement shook the floor beneath my bare feet.

Panic gripped me. They were giving chase.

I forced my legs to move faster, to fly me through this endless room.

"Help!" I screamed. "Help!" I had no idea where the exit was and I wouldn't find it on my own. Not in time to save myself. But the shadows had to be able to hear me, they had to! I was still in the house. All they needed to do was open the damned door and I could make it out.

The sound of my feet was swallowed up by the rushing and scraping of sharp limbs. The creatures were getting nearer and I had no more reserves of speed to draw from. I could almost feel their hot breath as they hissed. The slippery surface of their teeth as they chittered and growled.

Air brushed my skirts as a claw swiped at me, not close enough yet to connect with skin. But it would be. In moments it would be.

"Help! Hel—"

A body, heavy and hot, landed on my back and sunk its icy teeth into my shoulder. I screamed and tried to yank it off without slowing down, but it wouldn't release me, its grip deepening. An instant later, another creature slammed into my side, knocking me off balance.

I couldn't right myself, not in the absolute blackness, and I fell on my back. My head hit the floor with a thud and ringing filled my ears.

I knew I had to get up, but every thought had an echo to it and I couldn't focus on the limbs I needed to move to stand. My head felt full of foam, my body like it belonged to someone else.

They were suddenly on top of me, five, six, seven horrors I couldn't see. I reached out to shove the nearest one away, but its jaws latched onto my hand, sending bolts of pain shooting up my arm.

The haze cleared, my mind sharpened again.

I didn't have time to do anything before more teeth bit down on my thighs, on my arms, on my feet and hands. I screamed and kicked out, managing to throw off some of the creatures, which were just replaced by more and more of them.

"No!" I shrieked, flailing my arms and only managing to get them further trapped beneath the multiplying weight of teeth and hot bodies. Calling on everything I had, I lunged forward, trying to sit up and shake them off so that I could get to my feet again.

Jaws bit down on my stomach, cutting through the layers of cloth, through the corset stays, slicing my breath off in a surge of pain. So many teeth it was impossible to know the number of creatures that had a hold of me. I fell on my back again as waves of red filled my head.

Laughter and hissing surrounded me. Bile rose to my throat.

"Help! Someone help me!" My voice had lost its power, though not the bright fear that stained it. The truth raced through me: I was going to die here.

"No!"

I kicked out again with legs that were covered in scurrying bodies, that burned under the agony of teeth and claws.

There were too many of them.

I gasped as I was yanked up by my arms and lifted off the floor completely. My feet dangled in the air, the grip of whatever had a hold of me tightening as I tried to lunge from it, to kick and twist away from its touch. It wasn't one of the creatures, it was something else. Something much stronger.

A rectangle of light unexpectedly appeared in front of me, cutting through the darkness, and I was being shoved through it.

Into the sunny hall I had left behind what felt like centuries ago.

"You foolish girl," Aleister said.

My legs gave way under me at the sound of his voice, at being able to see again, at not having any creatures tearing at my skin, and he had to tighten his grip again to keep me from falling. My entire body shook, my teeth chattering with the sudden relief that mingled with pain and fear.

"They would have killed you. If I hadn't gotten you out, you would have died, Nora," Aleister said. There wasn't a trace of kindness or worry in his voice, only a degree of coldness I had never heard in it before. That I had never heard in anyone's voice before.

I looked up, blinking in the light.

His eyes blazed with anger. It coiled through them, turning them even sharper than they usually were. Blades that could, and would, easily cut me.

"Let go of me," I said. My voice was a husk of itself.

Aleister released me from his grip at once and I stumbled back, away from him.

Every step, every movement, was torture. Blood flowed from the countless wounds on my arms and legs, dripping to the marble floors below me. I looked down at my dress, ripped, its original cream and blue design unrecognizable under the stains. I touched my stomach, where the most blood had pooled, and flinched.

And he was the one who was angry? My hands contracted into fists. "You lied to me," I said.

"In what way?"

I looked up at Aleister again. "You told me I was safe in the house."

"And so you are."

Rage bubbled under my skin, increasing my trembling. My knees quivered. My whole body was screaming for rest.

"Sit down, Nora. Before you fall over."

I shook my head fiercely. "You just said I would have died in there! You said those words! You must have a very poor understanding of safety."

Aleister held my gaze without blinking. "That room is not part of the house."

"What?"

"Do you need me to say it a bit slower, Nora?" His voice bit out at me, as cruel as those creatures' teeth had been. "That room is not part of the house."

He had to be joking. "You mean to tell me that that bloody door right there, that door I touched and opened, that *you* touched and opened, and which is clearly in your home, is somehow not connected to the rest of this building?"

He lifted an eyebrow. "Exactly. I'm glad I've made myself understood."

If my hands hadn't ached so much I would have hit him, or at least tried to. "All right, let's say I take you at your word and choose to believe that. Where was I a minute ago, then, if not in the house?"

"That is none of your concern."

For an instant I thought I had misheard. Because no one in their right mind could have said that and meant it. Then the amazement twisted into further rage.

"None of my concern!" I spread my arms, giving him a full view of my state. "Every drop of *my* blood on your floor makes it my concern!"

"And whose fault is it that you got hurt? You should not have been in that room in the first place."

"What did you think would happen? You tell me nothing about yourself, about who you are and how you do the things you do, and then you give me permission to roam the house. Any dullard on the street would have been able to predict what came next!"

Aleister grew very still at my words, his features wiped clean of the slightest trace of life.

At once, something began to change in the room. I felt it on the edge of my skin, crackling energy that lifted the fine hairs on my neck and forearms. A slight hum of power that pressed against my ears. A sudden need to run enveloped me, so strong I dug my fingernails into my palms' open wounds to distract myself.

I would not be cowed into silence. He could threaten me all he liked, using all of his bloody powers if he wanted. "I deserve the truth. If you won't give it to me, I'll keep searching for it myself until I find it, even if it means going in that room again."

The energy built by the second, pulsing against me and making me shiver with its feverish strength. And still Aleister said nothing, made no indication that he hadn't turned to marble in front of me.

Exhaustion dropped on my shoulders like a heavy coat. Everything I had done today, every moment of fear, every bruise and scrape, every bite, had been for nothing, then. He could stand there all day, refusing to answer my questions, boiling in his own fury.

I tried again. "What difference would it make? The truth wouldn't change anything about our bargain. I can't run off, not when you hold Peter's life in your hands."

My head throbbed under the increasing pressure in the room and my thoughts were becoming difficult to arrange. I wrapped my arms around myself and tried to hold back a shudder.

"Enough, Nora. You're tired."

Snow would have been warmer than his voice.

"I'm fine," I said, but I knew I wasn't. Aleister's palpable anger and the pain from my injuries had blended together and they were asking a lot from my body.

Too much.

My legs buckled, unable to hold me up any longer. I fell to my knees.

Aleister made no move to help. "You have lost quite a bit of blood. We can continue this later, when you've rested."

"Like you give a toss." I shook my head to clear it but didn't bother trying to stand. If I attempted it now, I was sure I'd lose consciousness.

"Of course I care," Aleister said.

"You care about what I can do for you. Because that's all I am, an investment, and that's fine. I'm used to it. That's what I was for Sharpe all of those years." I closed my eyes and shivered. "You don't have to give a damn about me. All I want is the truth."

The heaviness in the room kept increasing. The air felt charged, like a storm was about to begin. Even the curls on my head prickled with the energy he was creating.

"You are in no position to demand anything," he said.

"Goddamn it," I said, my voice just a murmur. I forced my eyes open again and looked at him. "I know that. I know I have no power over you. I know that you can turn me inside out with a wave of your hand if you feel like it. I'm..." I clenched my jaw. "I'm *asking*. Because I'm afraid. Of you, of that awful language you speak"—I motioned around me—"of what you're doing right now. And I don't want to be. I want to understand."

His eyes narrowed slightly.

I would've preferred to eat my tongue than to say it, than to beg, but it was the only thing I had left to try. "Please."

He held my gaze in silence for a long moment.

Then he nodded once.

The pressure around me eased as quickly as it had started, ebbing away and back to its source. Aleister's face once again had life in it. His eyes, no longer glittering like beautiful but cold jewels, were marbled with flashing thoughts. He walked toward me.

I scurried back, but he lifted a hand. "It's all right, Nora."

With a sigh, he lowered himself to his knees in front of me. I searched for any sign that he meant me harm, but the rage I had felt up to a few seconds ago had evaporated. He looked, more than anything, tired.

"If you want to know, I have to show you. I can't just tell you," he said.

"How?"

"Oh, that's simple enough. I'll transfer some images, some of my memories, into your head. I just need your permission to do so."

I swallowed. The thought of allowing Aleister inside my mind wasn't in the least bit pleasant, but this is what I'd asked for.

"Fine," I said. "You have permission."

He smiled faintly. "You're going to regret this."

"I understand," I said.

"No. You don't."

His arms sprung from his sides quicker than I expected and in an instant, his hands were pressed against my temples.

The room around me disappeared. It didn't fade, but vanished all at once into a darkness as thick as the one I'd almost died in. For a moment, I thought I was back in that room, that I'd never left and had just conjured up a fantasy of a rescue, but then the darkness changed. Colors seeped in, grays and whites, greens and golds, inking themselves into slow shapes. Into feathers. A multitude of them, large and gleaming, transforming into entire wings. Two pairs of them, facing each other.

The wings on the left, the gray and white, lunged fiercely at the green and gold ones without warning, the sound of the flapping feathers echoed by a clash of metal against metal. Sprays of red streaked across both pairs at first, but soon enough it was only the left wings that were drenched in it, the color darkening almost to black.

The wings disappeared and I was falling from a great height.

Fear ravaged my (*his*) mind as I—no, as *Aleister*—tried to think of a solution, his back burning, muscles twisting in an effort to halt a descent that had no end.

Darkness once more and heat, so much heat. A hiss began, and a glitter of scales cut through the emptiness, ripples of colors that moved like water. A snake. Coils and more coils appeared, wrapping themselves around something I couldn't yet see.

A laugh broke out of my chest. It wasn't my voice, though, and I didn't know what there was to laugh about, but I couldn't stop the sound. It wasn't in my control. I blinked and a woman's body seeped in through the darkness, naked except for the serpent's coils that wrapped around her left leg. They slid up her thigh, the creature hissing softly. It was a familiar image, like something I knew or ought to have known, but before my mind could grasp its meaning, the picture vanished.

It was replaced by a spot of red, like a drop of blood, that pierced through the black canvas and began to grow.

An apple, blooming in front of me. It shone wetly, drops of dew on its surface glinting in the light coming from somewhere above me. Only a jagged bite marred its perfect shape.

Pale images flashed in and out of my view, layered over the piece of fruit. Black hooves stamping against dusty ground. A pair of goat horns lunging forward. A tail whipping out sharply.

And I suddenly knew.

I gasped, my eyes flooded with light as Aleister removed his hands from around my head. But no amount of brightness could erase what I had just seen, what I now knew about who the being in front of me was.

"Nora—"

"No," I whispered and scurried backwards again. "No, it can't be."

He sat back on his heels and looked at me. "You understand, then?"

"It's just a story! It's not real. None of it is."

He cocked his head, waiting.

Nausea twisted my stomach. "There's no Devil!" I screamed.

He smiled thinly. "I'm afraid there is," he said. "And you have him right in front of you."

ELEVEN

I LEAPT TO MY feet, all the weakness and exhaustion I'd felt moments before erased by the new horror I was facing. "Stay away from me," I hissed, taking a handful of steps away from Aleister, or Satan, or whatever his name was. He only watched me, making no effort to rise.

"I know this is a shock, but—"

I didn't wait for him to finish. I bolted, running down the center of the room, through the archway and across the next one, heading for the spiral staircase. Without a second thought, I started down its length, ready to leap off and risk broken limbs at the slightest shift in the metal. But the staircase was just like any other now, solid, lifeless, and I made it to the floor in seconds. I ran past the still open gate and down the corridor that housed a multitude of nightmares without pause.

Tears sprung from my eyes as I raced out of Aleister's wing and through the main hall to the house's front door. Fear bit at my heels.

He wouldn't let me escape. I knew it. He'd lock the door, block my every attempt at leaving until I had no other option but to cower in front of him. In front of the creature Peter and I had heard about as children on the few Sundays we had snuck into one church or another in search of a refuge from the cold. The Devil. The actual *Devil*.

But the doorknob turned under my hands and opened into a bright London afternoon. There were no screams from behind me or hooved feet chasing after me, only the pulsing silence easing out of the house and the contrasting chatter of nearby people.

I ran. Down one street and another and another, my mind full of the things I'd seen.

How could I have been so stupid? So blind? The clues had been there, from the moment he had appeared in the alleyway all of those weeks ago, and still I'd missed the truth. Even while reading that blasted book Aleister had given me, I'd missed that I'd made a bargain with the Devil himself.

"Goddamn it!" I screamed and ran on, ignoring curious stares and the way the rough pavement scraped against my bare feet with every pounding step.

I made it to Trafalgar Square before the uselessness of fleeing finally struck me and brought me to an immediate stop.

Panting, I glanced around, looking for Aleister's tall silhouette.

Wherever I ran to, wherever I hid, he'd find me. There was no question about that. Even if for some reason he didn't come after me, he still held Peter's life in his hands. I couldn't break our bargain and he knew it. Sooner or later I had to return.

I shuddered at the mere thought.

"How much?" a man asked, stopping abruptly in front of me.

"What?"

His gaze traveled down my body. "How much are you askin' for your services?"

I followed his eyes, seeing the rips in my dress, my corset half-visible through the ragged cotton bodice, my ankles bare for the entire world to see. It was no wonder he had assumed what he had.

I shook my head. "Sod off."

"I'm sure we can come to an arrangement, girl," he said. He stepped closer. His clothes reeked of alcohol and food.

"I told you to sod off, unless you want a kick in the bollocks."

But he smiled and came closer. "Spirited. I like that. Makes everythin' more enjoyable."

I turned away from him, ready to walk in the opposite direction. If I had little patience for this type of scum on most days, today I had none at all.

The man's moist hand closed over my wrist. "We ain't done talkin'," he said.

"On the contrary. I think she has made her position perfectly clear." Aleister, suddenly beside the man, placed a hand on his arm. "Release her."

"This ain't your business," the man said, turning to face Aleister, whose lips twitched into a half-smile.

It only took an instant of staring into his bright eyes before all the color drained from the man's face, his jaw slackening with surprise or fear or both. He let me go at once and took off at a near gallop past Nelson's Column and into the street. A carriage managed to avoid running him down only by a quick maneuver on the driver's part.

I shivered in the sun. If I'd ever felt as frightened as I did now, I couldn't recall it. Not even the panic I'd experienced in that monstrous dark room compared.

"Let's sit down," Aleister said after the silence and stillness between us had grown loud enough to deafen.

I shook my head, but couldn't bring myself to look up at him.

"You can barely remain on your feet, Nora. You're trembling like a newly born calf." He motioned with his hand toward the steps that led up to the National Gallery. "Come. Just for a bit."

All I wanted to do was run away, but he was right. I was still standing only because a strong breeze hadn't brushed against me yet. I needed to rest, if only for a few minutes. Then I'd be able to gather myself together again.

I followed him to the steps and sat down just out of his reach. A woman perched a substantial distance away raised a bag of what appeared to be bird seed in our direction, to which Aleister shook his head.

There were people all around us, a few on the steps, a clump laughing loudly by one of the fountains, and chattering groups above us heading into the museum. In any other circumstances, this might have been comforting, but what they could possibly do against the Devil, if anything, I didn't know. If he wanted to harm me, he would, even with all of these people nearby. I was sure of it.

A flock of pigeons took to the sky with a sharp flurry of wings and I flinched.

Aleister sighed and turned toward me. "You can see now why I was reluctant to tell you the truth. I've revealed my real identity to only a handful of humans throughout my long life, and the reactions were all very similar to yours. You do hold the distinction, however, of not having fainted. Which, I suppose..."

His voice faded away and I looked up despite myself. His eyes were on my hands, which I was clasping together so tightly they had turned almost white. Not even that, though, could stop their shaking.

"Nora," he started after a moment, his voice a murmur, "I have no intention of harming you. I hope you know that by now."

I kept my silence.

"I know this is all a shock, but nothing has changed from what it was a week ago except that now you know who I am. You are still safe in my presence and in my home."

Safe. He kept insisting on that, yet the last thing I could say about my situation, then and especially now, was that I was safe. I opened my mouth to say as much, but it was hard to form the words. Everything I would have thrown at him before today, every harsh word, every scoff, turned to ash on my tongue.

"Go on. You've never censored yourself before. Say whatever you need to say without fear."

Taking a deep breath, I shook my head. "I'm *not* safe. Even if I somehow ignored who you are, I was in serious danger today. At least twice. And it's not just been today, either."

I glanced up again to find him watching me carefully. He had leaned in slightly and I realized my words were only a bit louder than a whisper. I made myself speak up. "How can you say I'm safe when that staircase of yours would have crushed every bone in my body if I'd been just a little bit slower than I am? When I would have been eaten alive in that room?"

Aleister nodded. "What happened today was unfortunate and I should have foreseen it. The blame is entirely mine. The truth is that you were not supposed to even make it to the second story. That was what all of those rooms were for, to deter you. That was what the *stairs* were for. Not to hurt you, but to frighten you and keep you from reaching the top. If you'd taken a single step in retreat once they'd started shifting, you would have seen them return to normal, allowing you to descend safely. But you continued climbing, putting your life in mortal danger without any other incentive than to satisfy your curiosity." A small crease grew on his forehead. "I pride myself on knowing humanity well and still that wasn't something I expected."

"I needed to know," I said, daring another brief look at him. "Once I heard you speak that awful language a few nights ago, I suddenly couldn't do it anymore. I couldn't continue to ignore that I was living with someone who could boil me from the inside out with a few words if he felt like it."

He shifted on the step and I cringed away, ready to spring up and run. He lifted a hand gently to stop me. The gesture, so human, done with a pale, thin hand that could have belonged to any gentleman in the city, made my mind reel. How could this man, who spoke, looked, and behaved like a member of the highest levels of civilized society, be the vilest, evilest being in the world?

"I didn't know you'd heard me until you mentioned it back at the house. If I'd realized you were listening I would have stopped at once. It is not a language meant for human ears."

The words leapt out of my mouth before I even finished thinking them. "Is it what demons speak?"

Aleister's eyebrows shot up in surprise. "No, Nora. It's my native tongue. The language of angels."

I blinked. "Oh."

"There is no demonic language. Not in my dominion, at least."

A shriek of laughter turned his head and my eyes to the center of the square, where a young woman stood, arms outstretched. Pigeons flocked to her, reaching for the small mounds of seeds she held in her open palms.

Silence descended on the two of us as we watched the mad flurry of wings. The woman's laughter was bright and free, the laughter of someone whose life still had some semblance of logic in it.

I glanced at the people around us. Did any of them have the slightest idea that the Devil existed? That he could be right here, sharing the afternoon with them?

No, none of them could even imagine it. How could they? I'd been living with him and it hadn't so much as crossed my mind.

My gaze flicked to Aleister, who was watching everything that was happening with the rapt attention of someone looking in from outside a window. His eyes followed every single person, every flick of a wing, every seed that dropped to the ground only to be snatched up by a beak. He seemed to vibrate with contained energy. But I sensed no malice, none of the anger I'd felt back at the house. It was easy to believe he was who he said when he did the impossible, but like this, perched on a stone step on a sunny afternoon watching pigeons...

"It's hard to accept," I whispered.

Aleister turned, catching the words even though I had barely heard myself speak them. "I'm sure it is. Even more so in this era of reason and science. But after everything you've seen me do, it can't be that much of a leap to accept the truth. I would imagine it'd be more surprising if I were just a regular human who'd somehow acquired these abilities."

I shook my head. "But if you're the Devil—"

"Which I am."

"Right. But then, does that mean that God exists? Because I've never believed in him."

I waited for a growl or a hiss, or at the very least an angry recoil at the mention of his legendary enemy, but Aleister just shrugged.

"Neither have I," he said. "That is why I ended up in exile."

I frowned. "That's not what I meant."

Aleister nodded. "I know what you meant." His sharp eyes met mine, and I had to look away. "Yes, God exists, as do heaven and hell. I can guarantee, however, that none of them are as you've imagined."

That was just the thing, though. I'd never imagined any of it because I was convinced they were just stories. Everything Peter and I had heard at church those Sundays, everything he had read to me from the bible I'd stolen for him one Christmas, all of it had been fantasies for us. But now, from one moment to the next, it had all become real.

The questions that fear had kept at bay until now managed to finally break through. They poured into my head, one rushing in after another and another, until it felt like my skull would crack open with their demand for answers. I pressed my lips together to keep from blurting them out.

"Go on," Aleister said with a trace of a smile in his voice. "Ask. I'll answer what I can."

Eyes wide, I forced myself to look up. "Really?"

"I don't see why not, now that you already know the worst. If a bit of knowledge will stop you from flinching every time I speak, it would be foolish of me not to provide it."

Had I been flinching?

He motioned around us. "You have an opportunity many of these people would trade their souls for. So ask. What is the first thing you want to know?"

What came immediately to mind was a surprise for me. "Your real name."

From the slight raise of an eyebrow, it was a surprise for him, too. "My name?"

"Yes. Is it Satan? Or the other one, um—"

"Lucifer?"

I nodded, ignoring as best I could a stab of hot pain in my stomach.

"Neither, actually. My real name is impossible for humans to pronounce or to hear without feeling the effects you experienced. It's the same for all the other angels. But people had to call us something, so they chose what they could pronounce. Michael and Gabriel and Raphael and all the rest. In my case, they settled on Lucifer and followed it with Satan when I became God's adversary." He shrugged. "They are no more my names than Aleister Blake is. Which I chose only because I rather liked it."

"That is still what I should call you, then?"

"Of course. I wouldn't expect you to go around civilized society addressing me as Lucifer. I imagine it would draw some stares." His smile was a blade's edge. "What else would you like to know?"

There was so much, so many different things to ask, that it was difficult to choose. My thoughts were in knots.

But something he'd mentioned a few minutes ago had latched on to my mind. "You said people would trade their souls to have this opportunity."

He nodded.

"Have you ever asked for someone's soul in exchange for...for what they wanted?"

"Yes, I have, though not nearly as many times as people imagine. The majority of hell's population got there without any help from me."

I bit my bottom lip to hide the next painful spasm in my torso. "Is that what I did? Did I give you mine when we made the bargain for Peter's life?"

"Ah," he said, clasping his hands together. "No, you can rest easy on that front. For me to own someone's soul, it must be given voluntarily and in full knowledge of what he or she is doing. This includes knowing who you're giving it to, which you didn't. All you promised me that night was your life. Your soul is your own."

I knew I should have felt some sort of relief, but it was difficult to feel grateful that I still owned what I hadn't believed existed until this afternoon.

"And hell is your kingdom."

"That's right."

"But that means you're powerful. Second only to God, right? What could you possibly need my help to get back that you can't get yourself?"

It would be something awful, of course it would be, and I wouldn't be able to stop him.

Aleister met my eyes and it took every bit of strength I had left not to recoil from the power behind his gaze. He held his silence for a moment.

"As I've told you, Nora, my abilities have their substantia limitations. Angels can be powerful beings, but I was stripped of a lot of those powers when I rebelled so that there'd be no danger I'd try to usurp heaven again. I can manipulate objects and create illusions without much trouble, but when it comes to humans, my abilities are weak. Free will, and all of that. I can do little when they're involved and what I *can* do takes twice the amount of effort it should."

"You saved Peter, though."

He nodded. "Yes, but it took me days to recover from that expenditure of power." He sighed. "And, to answer the rest of your question, what I'm trying to reclaim are my wings. Nothing more threatening than that. I've been searching for them for millennia and I finally found them. Or rather, I know that *Pandemonium's* crew found them in their travels. Pulled them right out of the ocean's depths. That's why I need to know when the ship will be in London. I can't lose them again."

His jaw clenched and he looked away.

His wings, then. That was what all of this was for. "Will we still be able to save the girls?"

Aleister turned back to me again. "If that is what you want."

"It is."

"Then we will do so."

The manner he said it made it sound so simple, as if preventing the horrors those girls would face if the ship left with them onboard meant very little. But then, knowing who he was, perhaps that shouldn't have surprised me. Would human lives be worth anything to him?

I frowned as that thought brought up another question. "What do you do? What is your purpose? Do you really punish people who've done evil things?"

"You mean do I prod them with pitchforks and hold them over flames?" He smiled. "No. All I do, really, is ensure that the souls that have earned their place in hell arrive there when it is their time and that no mistakes are made. Mistakes like today's."

A shiver racked through me, the cuts on my arms and legs burning with pain.

"The room I was in..." My voice wavered. "That room was hell?"

"That's merely the entrance. The foyer, if you will. I must have access to my dominion at all times, which is why wherever I am, that room will also be. In some guise or another. I've always gone to great lengths to ensure that no one is able to enter it without my permission, so I am still somewhat puzzled as to how you managed to do so today."

His words brought back the terror I'd felt in that darkness, the pain, the conviction that I was going to die in there.

I started trembling again and once I did, I couldn't stop. Not this time. I had to clench my jaw to keep my teeth from chattering.

Aleister cocked his head and watched me for a few seconds before speaking again, his voice softer than it had been until now. "Nora, I realize you are still frightened, but you are also extensively wounded." He motioned to my still stinging torso and my aching hands and feet. "You have lost blood and you're battling pain as well as shock, which is one of the reasons you can't stop shaking. Let me help you. I can make all of that disappear in a moment, but I am not allowed to do so without your permission."

Shaking my head, I wrapped my arms around myself. The day had gotten much cooler all at once, even in the sun.

"And why not?"

He really had to ask? "Because you're the Devil," I said in as expressionless a voice as I could muster.

"That makes no difference. I am offering genuine assistance. Your injuries are mostly my fault, and I would like to set things right. A bit of an apology for not telling you the truth sooner, if you will. Surely you won't deny me that opportunity."

Another shiver raced through me. I felt like my bones had lost their consistency and were now made of pudding or something equally wobbly. I knew my body well enough to realize I was getting to the end of its strength. It had been a long, long day.

As little as I wanted the help Aleister was offering, I might not have another option if I wanted to avoid the risk of fainting when I stood and tried to walk more than a step or two.

"I don't have anything to give you in return," I said, the words clipped by my clenched jaw.

He looked away from me, at a pigeon that landed on the floor beneath us. The bird went on bobbing its head and pecking at the bare ground, without any sign that it recognized the man watching him for who he was.

"There is something, actually."

My stomach clenched. "What?"

"Since we're here, I would like for you to come with me right up these steps, into the National Gallery. I'd like to show you something."

I blinked repeatedly.

"I think it's a more than fair exchange, don't you? I heal your wounds and you grant me fifteen or twenty minutes in a public place where you will be completely safe from any wickedness I might be planning."

"And that's all?"

"That's all."

The Devil wanted to take me into an art gallery. If it were happening to anyone else, I might have found it funny, or mad, or both. I looked down at my dress, all stains and rips. "I don't think I'd be welcome inside like this."

"I can take care of that, too."

Despite the mounting pain, I hesitated.

That was when a ripple of darkness swept across my eyes. Everything disappeared for the length of a heartbeat and returned covered in a dull haze. I could barely feel my fingers and toes. Unconsciousness was not far off. Could I risk that now that I knew the truth, when I could wake up anywhere, in the middle of any horror? Even if I managed not to faint, I still had no strength left to run or defend myself, and that just wouldn't do.

"All right," I said, with a sigh. "You have my permission, I suppose."

"Excellent." Aleister nodded once and turned fully toward me.

"Wait, you're going to do it right here? In front of all these people?"

His lip curled into a smile. "One thing I've learned in my long life is that humans are not nearly as perceptive as they think they are. The most extraordinary things happen right in front of them and they're oblivious. They won't notice this, I can assure you."

He caught my eyes in his strikingly beautiful ones. A shifting movement swept through them, leaving them empty, as lifeless as the glassy eyes of a dead animal.

My skin began to tingle.

The sensation spread from wound to wound, followed by a slight pulling that reminded me of closing a drawstring bag. The shooting pain and throbbing I'd felt from the very first bite dulled into mild discomfort before fading altogether.

As I watched, the blood disappeared from my clothes, as did the rips. The skirts grew like living things to their original lengths once more and shoes identical to the ones I'd lost to that maniacal staircase covered my feet again. With just a flick of his power, Aleister had erased the damage of the past few hours. As if none of it had ever happened.

It all lasted the span of a moment and, as he had predicted, not a single person looked our way.

"That's much better," Aleister said once life had returned to his eyes and face. He stood and extended a thin hand that now, after the use of his powers, trembled slightly. "Come on. This will be interesting, I promise."

He had lost his bloody mind if he thought I would take his hand just like that, as if he were a regular man and not the source of all evil in the world. It would take more than an afternoon of talking in the sun to earn my trust, if he ever managed to earn it at all.

Ignoring him, I stood on my own and breathed in quiet relief at the steadiness of my legs, at the lack of pain in my torso, at the energy in my limbs. I felt like I could run for hours. I hoped I wouldn't have to, but if I did, Aleister had given me everything I needed to at least have a chance at evading him.

He watched me in silence, the palest smile on his lips.

I was about to start up the steps so that we could get this expedition over with when I saw the large black rat. It sat beside the fountain on the far right of the square, half in shadows. Immobile and watching us.

"Is that one of your servants?"

"My servant?" He turned in the direction I was staring.

"There, that rat. It's chased me around the city since I met you."

"I'd forgotten all about him! Yes, I employed him weeks ago to make sure you are safe when you're out of the house."

"You're spying on me?"

He rolled his eyes. "He's hardly a spy, Nora. It's not like he can tell me where you've been or what you've been doing. He is just there to fetch me if you run into any problems and require assistance, that is all. There's nothing sinister about it."

"Nothing sinister about having my every step outside watched?"

"When you know the dangers of this world as well as I do, it is difficult to allow someone in your care to roam without a safeguard of some sort. You have been in my care since we made our bargain, and you will continue to be in my care for as long as that bargain holds, which means I will also continue to protect you." He waved a hand in the animal's direction, and it immediately ran off. "I settled for the rat because it's something you and all other Londoners see every day."

"I don't need your protection," I said.

"Really? I thought you rather did earlier today."

"Yes, and it took you bloody long enough to help!"

He didn't make an effort to hide his amusement.

I grit my teeth and lowered my voice. Making him angry again probably wasn't the wisest choice. "But what bothers me is not only that it's following me," I said. "It's that that rat was in the pit the night Peter was injured."

"They all look similar," Aleister said.

I shook my head. "That one is the exact one that was in the Lantern. I know about rats. I can tell them apart as well as people."

He frowned. "Well, then I suppose it's just a peculiar coincidence."

"A coincidence? That's all it is, then?"

Aleister scoffed. "Of course. How would I have found the exact animal you saw that night when I wasn't there? And even if I had been, would I have taken the time to find a specific rat so that it could follow you when any of them would do? To what purpose?"

I looked up at him but his face was once again impossible to read. He could easily be lying, but I didn't know what he could gain by it. I already knew the worst of his secrets; this was just a detail. And I was sure he hadn't been in the Lantern's cellar. I would have remembered him. His eyes alone would have made him difficult to miss even in the crowd that night. He couldn't have seen the rat that tried to escape.

"A coincidence, then," I said, my voice still edged with doubt.

"Unless you can think of another explanation that makes sense." He motioned to the steps. "Shall we?"

Like I had a choice.

I followed him up the steps and into the National Gallery.

I'd only been inside once, a few birthdays ago, when Peter had thought to make a day of it. It was free and it was warm, all things to consider in the fall when money was always limited, but it hadn't been the most exciting of adventures. The paintings were nice enough, but after a while, they began to blend into one another, one landscape or one portrait turning into all of its predecessors. There were just so many Duchesses of Whatnot I could stare at before my mind wandered.

Aleister held the door for me and nodded to the man who welcomed us into the gallery.

"It's this way," Aleister said.

He led us through a number of corridors without hesitation, acknowledging nods and tipped hats from other visitors in a perfect imitation of humanity while I scrambled to keep up.

We finally came to a stop in front of a set of four painted panels, long and narrow. At the center of each stood a figure done in intricate detail. Aleister pointed to one of the paintings, in which an angel in battle armor brandishing a sword and a set of scales stood over a green, horned creature.

"Saint Michael," he said. "Done by a man called Carlo Crivelli. A beautiful representation of an angel, one meant to inspire awe and perhaps even a bit of fear. And that, at his feet, is supposed to be me."

I frowned and leaned forward to look closer at the prone figure at the angel's feet. It was a frightful being, all claws and flailing limbs, making the contrast with Saint Michael's rippling strength all the more apparent.

Aleister sighed. "Quite a difference, isn't it? Somehow, I have transformed into a gargoyle-like being who retains nothing even vaguely angelic. Now"—he glanced at me—"would you say that is an accurate representation of my appearance?"

"How would I know?"

"Because I am standing right in front of you."

"You could change form. Maybe *that's* how you really look and this is a disguise."

"Alas, altering my appearance is not a power I possess. Nor does any celestial being. What I look like now is what I've always looked like. Except, of course, for my lost wings. But all right; let us imagine that you're correct and that the form you see in the painting is my true one." He motioned for me to follow him again.

We swept by more corridors until we arrived at a room empty of people. Aleister led me to a large, dark painting. It showed a multitude of figures, with six suspended in mid-air and three others on the ground. The plaque read *Christ Appearing to Saint Anthony Abbot by Annibale Carracci.*

From the golden halo it was easy enough to tell which figure was Christ. The Devil, too, was simple to pinpoint. In this version, he was a large man with a bare torso, thick claws, and horns, and he was about to grab hold of who I assumed was Saint Anthony.

"This is better, I suppose," Aleister said. "At least I'm no longer green and I am somewhat human. But it also looks nothing like the previous painting. So, which one is showing the truth? Is my real form closer to a goblin or a human that still possesses horns and claws? Or perhaps one with a goat's head and hooved feet, or one with a forked tongue, or one that breathes fire? And I could go on. In every gallery or museum in practically every city in this world there is at least one image that is meant to represent me and none of them look the same. Even if I could change form, I can't be all of those disparate ones. I can't think why I would want to be, either. If they can't all be right, then what's to say which one is and which one isn't?"

"But in the memories you showed me—"

"I showed you the classic images that everyone associates with the Devil so that you would understand, but they are not necessarily the truth. And that's my point, Nora. Just because something is told often enough doesn't make it reality." He shrugged. "If there are inconsistencies with something as trivial as my appearance, it follows that there might also be inconsistencies about the things people say I've done throughout the millennia."

The reasoning behind his words was sound, but it was hard to accept that the entire world could be mistaken.

"There are all manner of versions of my life out there," Aleister continued, "from the fall from heaven to that made-up nonsense with the snake and Adam and Eve. I've not bothered to correct them but that doesn't mean they state what really happened."

"One moment," I said when I saw where he was heading with this. "Are you trying to tell me that you are some kind of misunderstood hero or something like that? Are you asking me to believe that?"

He shook his head. "I'm not asking you to take anything on faith. All I want is that you make your judgments about me from your own experience and not from the things people tell by rote. Who knows what you may discover. You may even come to enjoy my company." He gave me a sleek sideways glance and started down the length of the room slowly, his eyes straying from one work of art to another.

I remained where I was and watched him.

He was wrong. He had already asked me to take a lot on faith, especially now that I knew who he was. I had to *believe* he wouldn't hurt me just because he said so, that he wouldn't force me to do something I didn't want to do. I had to trust him when everything pointed for me to do the opposite.

But what other choice was there? This was it. I had to honor the bargain I'd made.

With a deep breath, I followed after Aleister.

"There is something I'd like to ask you, Nora," he said when I'd almost reached his side, leaning in to look at a painting of a man on horseback attacking a dragon. "If you'll allow me."

"I suppose."

"You see, I'm curious to know how you managed to enter that room without drawing my attention to the intrusion. The gate leading to the stairs should have alerted me to your presence the moment you started climbing over it and the room's door has countless enchantments on it to keep anyone from forcing their way in. So how is it that I only learned about what you'd done when one of the servants came to fetch me?"

I frowned. "It was one of the shadows? They told you?"

He nodded. "I hope that proves once and for all that they have nothing against you. On the contrary."

Not sure I would go that far. They more likely feared their master's wrath if he returned home to find me dead.

A group of six people walked into the room in a fog of conversation and perfume, the women in the arms of their partners. They didn't so much as glance our way.

I walked closer to Aleister and lowered my voice. "I didn't climb over the gate, and I didn't force the door open. I used this." Lifting a hand to what was left of my bun, I reached for the hairpins.

There was only one.

"Damn," I said.

Aleister's eyes didn't leave the painting in front of him. "What is it?"

"I just lost one of my pins, that's all." The other one must have fallen when those creatures threw me to the floor. One more piece of my past life gone. It was surprising how much the loss bothered me even now, when it should have been something minor in the wake of all that had occurred today.

He looked at the remaining one in my hands. "You can purchase ten more beautiful than these, if you like. A hundred."

"No, these...I liked these." I clutched it tighter.

"Well, if they mean that much to you, I'll try to find the other one. Things tend to move around in my dominion, however, so I am not making any promises."

I started to thank him, but he waved my gratitude away as usual.

"That still doesn't tell me how you managed to enter the room," he said, walking forward to the next painting.

"Oh." I thought it'd be obvious. "I just picked the lock."

He turned to me, his expression as blank as if I'd spoken gibberish.

"You picked hell's door open," he finally said.

I shrugged. "It was easy, too. You should think of getting a more complicated lock."

He blinked once and then burst into laughter.

It was so unexpected a reaction that I took a step back before I realized he didn't pose a danger to me.

Holding my breath, I watched as Aleister's face lit up with genuine mirth. It was so different from his usual sarcastic chuckles and sharp smiles. Now, his features softened and he appeared younger than ever, until it was impossible to believe he could be the same being the paintings he had shown me had tried to represent. He looked nothing but human.

His sparkling, silver laugh bounced off the artwork, and surrounded me and the other people in the room. It tugged on my own lips until I felt them curl up into a smile without my full consent. I started to feel weightless, as if I didn't have a worry in the world. Was this what drunkenness felt like? Somewhere within me, I knew it wasn't a normal sensation, that it was probably some strange reaction to hours of fear and exhaustion.

But at that moment I didn't care.

All I could do, wide-eyed, was watch the Devil laugh.

TWELVE

"MISS, CAN I HELP YOU?"

I flinched in surprise and looked up at my brother.

Peter's eyes were on me for the first time in weeks, but there was no recognition there.

I'd done my best not to search him out after Aleister wiped his memory of me, trusting in the promise that my brother would be well once more and waiting until the burn of what I'd done was reduced to an ache before heading to the Lantern to see how he was. But today, after everything I'd learned, I'd needed to see him.

I realized it was a mistake in an instant. Years could go by and I'd still feel the scorching pain of loss deep within me. Always fresh. There was no comfort to be found here.

"No, I'm just waiting for someone," I said, grabbing hold of the first thing I could think of.

Peter frowned slightly, taking in my silk and velvet walking dress. "Would you like me to wait with you, miss?" He motioned to the Lantern and its surroundings. "There can be some rough characters in this part of the city."

I couldn't help smiling softly. I'd lived my life among those rough characters. I *was* one of those rough characters, ready to snatch anything that wasn't nailed down and even then, trying. And anyway, I'd spent weeks trailing after him wearing these same fine clothes and others like them without losing so much as a button. Still, he had given me an opportunity I couldn't allow to pass.

"That would be very kind, thank you. It should only be a few minutes."

"Of course, miss." Peter smiled.

He looked better than he had in weeks. The shadow that had fallen over his features at my disappearance had been swept away by the natural brightness I'd known all of my life. He looked like himself, once more.

It was difficult to keep my eyes from straying to his face as we waited for my imaginary someone together, to keep my lips from smiling as widely as they were able, to keep my arms from reaching out to embrace him. It was difficult to just stand there searching for something mundane to say when there was so much I wanted to finally tell him and still couldn't.

I settled for the simplest thing I could think of. "I hope I'm not keeping you from anything. Were you on your way to work?"

"Yes, miss, but it's no bother. My employer can wait a few minutes."

I exhaled in relief. He had his job, then. He'd gotten that back, at least. "What is your employment?"

"I'm a rat-catcher, miss." Peter smiled. "Though maybe that's not entirely true. I'm more of a bag-holder. My sister does the catching while I do the carrying."

His words were like blows.

He had a sister. Who was not me. Someone who was living a version of the life I had been exiled from, sharing all of the memories and experiences that were, by right, mine.

I had expected, I had prepared, to be forgotten, but not to be replaced. There was no readying myself for that.

I forced myself to smile and continue the conversation. "What is your sister's name?"

"Sarah. We're not really blood related, but I raised her since she was a tiny thing, so she's my sister in every way that counts. She's one of the best rat-catchers in the city." Pride wafted off of him while my insides twisted into themselves.

This was harder than I could have possibly imagined. I should have been leaping with joy that he was himself again and that there was not the slightest whiff of alcohol on him, but it was impossible. It hurt too much.

"Do you have siblings, miss?" Peter asked.

I swallowed and focused on the pavement in front of me.

Peter shuffled his feet beside me. "I'm sorry it that was too forward, miss. I meant nothing by it."

"No, it's all right." I looked back up at him, at the face that I had known since the moment I was born. "Yes, I have a brother. He's who I'm meeting here. His name is Peter."

His eyes widened. "That's my name as well, miss!"

"Is it? What a coincidence. Well, Peter, I'm Nora." I extended my gloved hand to him.

He hesitated for a moment, his eyes darting around us as if he expected coppers to crawl out of the very floor to stop him. But he finally took my hand in his and pressed it gently. I wanted to grab on and never release him.

"Pleasure to meet you, Miss Nora."

I nodded and looked away, using the excuse of searching for my sibling as a way to wait out the overwhelming urge to cry. How much I had lost!

My mind returned to those minutes in the alleyway once again. Aleister must have had a good laugh at my expense that night. He'd gotten exactly the help he needed without having to tell me anything while I lost my entire life. He had fulfilled his part in seconds, while I paid and paid, and would continue to pay for the rest of my days.

An idea bloomed slowly in my mind as I stared out at the street I knew so well. I could do something for myself right now. Something that would make *me* happy, even if just for a little while. After this morning, I thought I rather deserved it.

"Actually, Peter," I said, "it's been a definite blessing to meet like this because I think I could use your assistance."

"Oh?" Peter said.

"Yes, there seem to be rats in my home. I've heard scratching coming from inside the walls at night. I can't think of what else it could be."

He nodded. "It's most likely rats. They're everywhere at this time of year."

"I was wondering, then, it if would it be possible to hire you to remove them." I smiled. "I don't know any other rat-catchers, and it seems almost like fate that we have come across one another today. I'm not one to argue with destiny!"

Peter smiled. "Of course, miss. My sister and I would be happy to help."

I clenched my teeth together but nodded. "That's wonderful. How does tomorrow sound? Or is that too soon?"

"Not at all, miss. We'll be ready." His cheeks reddened. "Beg pardon, but could I have your address? We usually speak with gentlemen about these removals and all of their details."

"Oh, of course, how silly of me!" I told him the address, knowing all too well I would only have to say it once for him to memorize it. "Well, I don't want to keep you any longer, Peter, and create problems with your employer. I think I'll just head home, since my rascal of a brother seems to have forgotten all about our meeting."

"Would you like me to get you a cab, miss?"

A cab in this area would have been quite the trick but he looked ready to run across the entirety of London to fetch me one. Even when everything changed, some things never did.

"No, that's all right. I told my driver to go have a bite for breakfast and to wait for me in the park a couple of streets away from here. I'll just go meet him."

"I could walk you there, if you'd like, miss."

"I couldn't possibly impose on you anymore, Peter. You have been much too considerate. I'll leave you to your day, now, as I'm sure you have a busy one in front of you, and hope to see you tomorrow."

"You will, miss."

With a nod, I forced myself to turn away, to not linger and make things more difficult. I would see him tomorrow, in any case.

Whether Aleister liked it or not, I would spend the day with my brother in the Devil's own home.

There were curtains in my room.

Simple, wine-red curtains in a material so heavy they kept out even the early afternoon sun. They'd been purchased, delivered, and hung in the space of a couple of hours, which would have been astounding if it had happened anywhere else but in this house. Once Aleister was involved, all bets were off.

"Are they to your liking?"

I leapt at the voice. "Bloody hell!" I said, turning around.

Aleister stood by the bedroom doorway, his tall figure taking up much of the entrance. "It wasn't my intention to startle you," he said.

I pressed a hand to my thumping heart. "Well, you did a marvelous job anyway."

"I only wanted to make sure the curtains met with your approval." He waved a hand in their direction. "I chose the burgundy on a whim, but they could be done in a different color or a different fabric, if you'd prefer."

I shook my head. What did that matter, after everything that had happened today? "No, they're fine. Perfectly lovely."

"Good." He cocked his head. "I trust everything was well with your brother?"

The change of topic was so abrupt I wasn't prepared for the renewed flare of pain that came at the mention of Peter. I looked away. "Did the rat let you know I saw him?"

"No, I've been keeping watch over him myself. Nothing too intrusive, of course."

That was unexpected. I met his gaze, which was like a weight on my skin. "Why?"

"He is important to you."

The simplicity of his answer, as if it were the most obvious thing in the world, made me frown.

"I've been ensuring he receives a generous amount of coins each day and that your old employer has plenty of work to send his way. If there is anything else you would like me to do for him, you need only ask."

My mouth opened in what I imagined was an unsightly manner. "That's...Thank you," I said, and was surprised to find that, at least right now, I actually meant it.

He held my gaze for a heartbeat before waving the words away as he had done every time I'd shown him gratitude of any sort, genuine or not.

"I won't disturb you any longer," he said, the edge of mockery back in his voice. "I think you've seen more than enough of me today."

"I would have to agree."

He smiled lightly. "I have duties that I really do have to attend to now, so do I have to worry about you making your way upstairs again or can I trust you?"

I blinked.

The Devil wanted to know if he could trust *me?* That had to be one of the most ridiculous things I'd heard in my entire life.

Aleister lifted an eyebrow. "Well?"

"Yes, you can trust me."

"I have your word?"

I rubbed a hand against my forehead and sighed. "Yes, for what it's worth, you have my word. I, like all of humanity, want nothing to do with hell."

"You'd be amazed, Nora," he said, softly. "You really would."

I looked up at him but he had already disappeared, slipping out of view in an instant and in the most absolute of silences.

THIRTEEN

MY SITTING ROOM'S DOOR opened early the next morning.

I kept my eyes on *Paradise Lost* and waited, preparing myself as much as I could for an argument with the Devil.

"Your brother is at the door," Aleister said. His voice betrayed no emotion at all.

I put the book down and turned to him.

"It's peculiar, isn't it?" he asked, leaning against the door's frame. "That he has just appeared at our house. It's almost like magic."

He fixed his eyes on me, waiting for an explanation.

I searched his face, but I still couldn't identify if he was angry or irritated, not from the curling of his lips, which was the only trace of any expression at all. I supposed that if he was angry, I would have felt it.

"I couldn't resist when I saw him yesterday," I said. "You never forbade me from inviting anyone into the house, so I didn't think you'd mind."

"And I don't, Nora. I do know quite a bit about loss and the things it can lead us to do. My only concern is that this will be more painful than rewarding." He pushed away from the door. "He's brought a young blonde girl with him who he claims is his sister."

"Sarah. He told me about her."

"Well, your voice tells me all I need to know of how you feel about her."

I nodded, crossing my arms. "Yes, I'm not thrilled she's here. But I can stand one day of seeing Peter and Sarah together if it means I can just talk to him a bit."

"You're certain?"

I didn't allow myself to hesitate. "Yes."

"Very well." He motioned to his left. "They're in the foyer."

My eyes widened. "You've let them in already?"

"Of course I have. I'm not a brute who just leaves people waiting in doorways."

Peter was in the house, and I was just standing here like a ninny.

With a quick swipe of my hand, I smoothed my skirts and hurried towards the door. Aleister moved to the side to let me pass and I kept a sharp eye on him as I did so. If I saw any signs of anger, I was ready to drag Peter out of the house.

"They brought bags and sticks, so I am assuming it's not a social call."

"I told them we had rats."

Aleister chuckled. "But of course."

We walked to the door leading out of my wing of the house. If Aleister didn't say anything about the imaginary rodents, I might have at least two hours with my brother before he and Sarah gave up searching. I almost vibrated with excitement at that thought.

"I have to warn you," Aleister said, grabbing the doorknob. "I had to make certain quick adjustments to the house so that it appeared more ordinary. The servants are gone for now, as well."

He opened the door.

It was a good thing he warned me.

The foyer looked like it could have belonged in any other wealthy home in London. I'd been in dozens just like it, down to the red and gold carpet that covered most of the floor. The marble columns were gone, and the walls were now covered in the kind of floral wallpaper I'd always thought belonged more as lining for the inside of a lady's jewelry box than on actual walls.

After the beauty and spaciousness of the original, this was a stuffy, ugly and utterly normal room.

And one which I forgot all about when I saw that Peter was just a few feet away, standing in front of the door.

The impulse to launch myself at him was as strong as ever. Strong enough that I had to curl my toes inside my shoes to avoid giving in to it.

Would I ever be able to look at my brother and not feel like I had just been robbed of everything that mattered?

I clenched my teeth and blinked away the pressure behind my eyes. I couldn't cry in front of Peter, I couldn't let him know anything was wrong.

I focused, instead, on the girl beside him. My replacement.

She looked a year or two younger than I was and thinner, with a narrow, boyish figure that looked much better in the trousers she wore than I ever had. Her face was covered in scratches, some healed, others still wet with blood, and there was dirt on every visible inch of her, even in the golden curls that framed her face.

I hated her on sight.

I knew it wasn't fair of me; I knew all too well that at this moment she was the only thing keeping Peter from drinking himself into his grave, but I couldn't help it. She had the love that had been mine for all of these years and I hated her for it.

Still, I had to try to be civil. For Peter.

"How very nice to see you both," I said, hoping it didn't sound as insincere as it felt to say.

"Mis—" Peter stopped himself with a quick look at Aleister. "*Lady* Nora, it is a pleasure to see you. And, sir, it is an honor for me and my sister to make your acquaintance." He bowed his head.

Aleister nodded. "Lady Blake has told me quite a bit about you."

A spot of color rose to my brother's cheeks. He had always been much humbler than I was, much more prone to feeling inferior to people with wealth and status. It was one of the reasons he had stopped stealing from homes and from pockets as soon as we'd had other means of staying alive.

"Sir," he said, and bowed again in acknowledgment.

It struck me that this was the first time since that terrible night that all three of us were together. The circumstances couldn't have been more different.

Sarah shifted in place. "There are rats in the house, then, sir?" she asked abruptly, turning away from me. Peculiar.

Anyone who didn't know him as well as I did would have missed the way Peter winced at her tone.

From the sudden tension I sensed coming off Aleister, I was sure he was going to tell them I had lied. That they should head home. Just to assert his power over me once more.

I prepared myself for his words.

What he actually said made me turn to look at him.

"Of course. Why else would my wife have called you here?"

His voice had a thin column of coldness at its center, his eyes locked on Sarah. Why was he helping me?

"Yes," I said, ignoring my surprise at his response. "We've heard them quite a bit these past few days. Scratching inside the walls of this very room."

Peter looked around. "Then we'd best get to work and find them. Where did you hear the most sounds from, if you can remember?"

I chose the back wall at random. "All manner of noises from there. It sounded like there were a good number of rats, I'm afraid."

My brother nodded and motioned to Sarah, who pursed her lips for a second but lowered her gaze and followed him to the wall I'd pointed out.

"Is it all right if we move the furniture?" he asked.

"Of course," I said before risking a glance at Aleister. He was watching them in complete stillness, but he didn't seem to mean them, or me, any harm.

They lifted a small table from the far corner, Peter showing his usual care with the trinkets resting on it that Aleister had conjured up. I half-expected Sarah to try to palm one of the smaller pieces, as I would have done, but she made no attempt at all. A wasted opportunity, in my eyes.

They began inspecting the wall, looking for holes, for bite marks or rat droppings, tapping it and listening for movement. I could predict everything they did before they did it. There was nothing for them to find, though, and with each second and inch of wall that passed, I began to see Sarah's face tighten.

"We need to look at the rest of the walls. At the whole room, if that's all right," Peter said.

I smiled. "Whatever you have to do."

Sarah sighed loudly enough for me to hear. She obviously didn't want to be in this house, though I couldn't imagine why. She was a rat-catcher and she was being asked to catch some rats. Where exactly was the problem?

I clenched my jaw to keep from saying something that would prompt her to convince Peter to leave. I had to remember I was on the other side now, I was no longer the one who could do no wrong in his eyes. If I attacked his false sister in any way, he would turn against me.

The pain of that thought bit into me and I had to look away from them.

Perhaps this whole thing was too hurtful for me. Perhaps Aleister was right, as much as I hated to think so. Maybe the Devil did understand loss better than I imagined.

I felt the weight of his gaze on me and I turned.

He was watching me, the smallest of frowns on his face. There was a peculiar muted look to his eyes, though, that I hadn't seen before. What I would have said was sympathy, if I had been speaking of anyone else.

A sudden sharp whisper brought my eyes and my thoughts back to Peter and Sarah, who were huddled together in one corner of the room, speaking in hushed tones.

I cleared my throat. "Is something the matter?"

Sarah stepped away from Peter, ignoring the sharp tug on her sleeve that was meant to hold her back. "Madam, I don't think we can help you."

My eyes bored into her. "Oh? Why is that?"

"Well, madam, we haven't found an entrance into the walls, not so much as a bite in the wallpaper." She sighed. "We haven't even heard a sound in all the time we've been here. Both of us have been doing this long enough to know what those signs mean."

"Which is?"

She looked down at her hands. "That if there are rats in the house, it's just one or two of them."

I almost laughed. If I had ever heard such a load of rubbish, I couldn't remember it. The entrance into the walls could be in any room, even in the roof. They would have to walk through the entire house, inspect every single crevice, before she could say something like that. And she expected to hear a lot of noise from animals who slept during the day? Nonsense. She was either incompetent or a bad liar.

From the way Peter's gaze avoided mine and instead dropped to the floor, the latter seemed like the more accurate of the two options.

"Madam," Sarah continued, "our employer told us that if we didn't see evidence of a lot of rats, we were to go on to the next house on our schedule. It has an infestation in its walls and will earn us quite a bit."

"Sarah—" Peter started.

She cut him off without even looking his way. "I'm sorry, but we can't afford to miss that opportunity. We'll tell one of the other rat-catchers to help you, those who are less busy."

The strength of her dislike settled on me for the first time. It was more than a casual irritation, which was strange, since I hadn't done anything obvious enough to have earned it in the few minutes since we'd met. On the contrary, I was being as friendly as I knew how to be. But she seemed to sense there was something about me which didn't quite *fit*.

I shouldn't have blamed her, I should have grudgingly admired her perception, but that was impossible. I couldn't feel anything but mounting anger.

Swallowing back the bitter words I wanted to say, I smiled. "We'll pay you for your time, of course. For each hour you are here."

"With respect, madam, we can't show up at our employer's without a single rat, even if we do get paid."

Absolute bollocks. Sharpe would have been just fine with it.

I searched for something, anything which might keep them there, but if money wasn't enough of an incentive, I didn't know what would be.

I looked at Peter, who seemed to want to sink right into the floorboards, and then at Aleister, who had remained strangely silent throughout this entire exchange.

He was watching Sarah, his entire body so still it didn't look like he was even breathing.

The intensity of his gaze should have drawn the girl's attention, as it would have drawn mine if it had been directed at me, but she was unaware of it.

Perhaps she wasn't quite that perceptive, after all.

A slow smile began to spread across Aleister's lips.

At the same time, the walls erupted with noise; the scrambling of claws, the chattering of teeth, the movement of dozens of creatures within the brick and plaster. It was as if the walls themselves had come alive.

Sarah's head jerked up, turning left and right in search of the cause of the noise. Peter, too, glanced around him, wide-eyed, his mouth falling open.

"Speak of the Devil," Aleister said lightly, still not taking his eyes off the girl. "Sounds like there are quite a few rats in those walls, doesn't it?"

I only just stoppered my own gasp.

Sarah had wanted an infestation and here it was. From the sound of it, Aleister had called on the entirety of London's rodent population to surround the foyer.

But why had he bothered? I couldn't imagine a single reason. At least not one that fit neatly into my idea of who he really was.

We listened, immobile, as the noise built and built with each second that passed. It was an impressive amount of sound.

Just when its volume was becoming a painful pressure in my ears, it reached its peak and broke, the whole thing receding into a more manageable series of hissings and scratchings.

Peter was the first to shake off his surprise a moment later, exhaling forcefully. "Well, that settles that, then."

Shifting the tool bags from his shoulder, he lowered them to the floor. "I think anyone would say, without a doubt, there are rats in this house. And plenty of them." He chuckled. "Now the problem is whether Sarah and I can manage them all on our own."

The girl didn't appear to have heard him. She looked away from the walls and turned to Aleister, blinking in obvious confusion. She winced as soon as her eyes met his, which only made his smile widen.

"It certainly seems so," Aleister said. "You will likely be here for most of the day, but I am sure your employer will be more than happy to see you return with bags brimming over with rats."

"Oh, no question about it, sir. Sharpe will be pleased," my brother said.

With a final curl of his lips, Aleister turned his head, finally releasing Sarah from his stare.

Peter was too busy tugging open one of the sacks they'd brought with them to notice the way his false sister had paled, the way she couldn't stop watching Aleister.

It had taken her longer than I'd expected, but she now sensed he was not who he said he was. She had shifted her stance slightly, as if she were getting ready to race out of the house at the smallest provocation. I realized something in that instant which chilled me: she would leave Peter behind if it came to it. I saw that in the fear on her face. It was fear that left room for no one else, not even her supposed brother. If her life was threatened, she would plunge through our door back into London without so much as a glance back.

If I hadn't hated her before, the knowledge that she would flee and leave Peter to fend for himself would have been everything I needed to make me want to set her on fire.

"Come on, Sarah, we've got to get started," my brother called as he pulled out a sledgehammer I would have recognized anywhere. It was the same one we'd had for a decade.

"Sarah," Peter said again when she still hadn't moved. There was an edge of irritation in his voice.

The girl yanked her gaze away from Aleister and hurried to my brother's side.

"We will need to make a hole in the wall so that she can crawl inside," Peter said, standing up. "I'll do my best to keep it as small as possible."

I cleared the anger at the girl from my throat. "Whatever you need to do, of course."

My brother walked to the wall I'd pointed to when they'd first asked about the noises and brought the sledgehammer up in a gesture I had seen hundreds of times. With a swing of his arm, it connected against the plaster.

"Why did you do that?" I asked Aleister as soon as I was able to hide the words beneath the noise of destruction. "Why help me?"

He didn't hesitate. "Because it would make you happy and I will not deny you happiness if it is in my power to grant it."

His words settled against my skin along with a thin layer of surprise. He had done this to make me happy? But what did that matter to him? I was bound to him by our bargain and by my own growing desire to help the missing girls. Happiness did not come into it, not in the least, yet he'd helped me anyway.

He had erased me from Peter's memory, had begun watching over my brother to ensure his safety, and had now done *this*, all without asking for anything in return.

Just to please me.

The thought brought with it a peculiar stillness to my mind. The feeling of a knot loosening or a fist unclenching.

I cleared my throat. "Will they actually find rats in there?"

"Oh, yes. Enough to keep them here for hours." He gave me a sideways glance. "Be sure to pay them substantially, however, because those rats will disappear three or four blocks from here. The two of them will arrive at their employer's with empty bags, which, we can only hope, will give that exasperatingly stupid girl a fit."

I bit back a smile. At least I wasn't the only one who disliked her.

"I'll leave you to it, then," Aleister said. "I'm sure you will not miss my presence in the least now that you have your brother here to entertain you."

His voice had regained its biting tone, placing me back on somewhat surer footing.

I nodded.

"We'll speak later about the ball, yes? I know you are more than capable of running circles around Geary, but there are some things to discuss. No more than a few details."

"Well, you know what they say about those," I said, my words held out as a simple offering of peace. A way to call a truce.

He paused for an instant and then laughed, that same genuine, sun-streaked sound I'd heard in the National Gallery. "Very good, Nora." He held my gaze for a moment and then turned away.

I watched him walk out of the room in his silent, graceful manner.

Would he move with that same sureness through hell? Would he smoothly make his way through the horrors which had almost killed me while I sat here and chatted with Peter as if this were just a normal home with normal occupants?

What awful things would those eyes, which had once gazed on heaven, see?

With a sharp exhale, I turned and focused on the most important thing in the room, in the entire house.

My brother.

"PANDEMONIUM!"

Peter's scream shook the ground on which I stood. My teeth chattered together as the pavement beneath me split open, giving way to a pit swarming with darkness. A shifting black maw, its writhing life reaching up. Reaching for me.

My feet moved on their own, taking me toward the edge. The crowd that pressed against me started to laugh, shrieking hysterics that grew and grew with every step forward, with every step closer to the waiting blackness.

"Stop!" I screamed. "Peter, help me!"

But Peter couldn't hear me over his own screams, over the pulsing, biting repetition of that one word.

I felt the edge of the pit under my feet. One more step and I would fall into it.

"Help!" I flung my arms back and tried to grasp someone, anyone, who could keep me from tumbling into death, but my hands slipped, unable to hold on.

"Help! Someone help me!"

Two hands suddenly touched my shoulders, cool against my hot skin.

"Nora."

That voice. I knew it. I tried to turn to see who it was but I couldn't. My body refused to cooperate.

"NORA."

I woke with a gasp.

The first thing I saw were eyes, brilliant in the moonlight spilling into the room. The power coiled inside them cut into me.

Even half-asleep, my entire being recognized them.

"Nora," Aleister said, leaning slightly over me. "Are you all right?"

"Oh, god," I said, my voice cracking under the force of the nightmare that still clung to me. That pit and Peter. Those screams. The need to cry was suddenly so strong, my stomach contracted with it. "God."

I sat up and Aleister moved away, carefully dodging one of the wooden carving's protruding limbs before sitting down at the edge of the bed.

I couldn't seem to catch my breath.

"You're safe, Nora. It was a dream," he said.

Placing my entire focus on the reality of the room, my room, I took slow, deep breaths. This was real, not that nightmare. *This.*

Seconds ticked by like years and slowly, slowly, the pressure on my chest eased. The blazing fear faded. I wasn't going to die right now.

I looked up at Aleister, who was watching me.

"What happened?" I asked, my voice still tight.

"You were screaming." He frowned. "I apologize for entering your room without permission, but I didn't know how else to help you."

I nodded and a bead of sweat rolled down my forehead with the movement. I realized I was drenched, my nightgown clinging to me like a second layer of skin. Shifting on the bed, I swallowed back the remnants of the screams that still wanted to find their way out of me.

"That was the worst one yet," I said.

Aleister shook his head. "I don't understand why you are still having them. I've been careful with my thoughts since you told me about the dreams. They should have stopped."

"I don't know." I shuddered. "I thought I was used to them, but this one..."

Even now, with my heart beginning to slow down to its normal rhythm, I could still sense the nightmare waiting in the darkness. Ready to envelop me again when I fell asleep.

"You're hurt," Aleister said.

I followed his eyes to my left hand, still in a tight fist, from where a ribbon of blood glittered darkly in the moonlight.

"Oh," I said and opened it.

My palm was soaked with blood, as were the cufflinks resting inside.

Gently, Aleister reached out and plucked them from my hand. He studied them, unaware of, or unconcerned with, the drops of blood staining his elegant fingers.

"Were they your brother's?"

"No. I stole them on the last day of my other life," I said. "I've just gotten into the habit of sleeping with them, I suppose." I looked down at my palm, which bore several puncture marks. Blood trickled out with each of my heartbeats.

"May I?" Aleister asked.

I glanced up and he motioned to my hand.

I nodded.

He placed the cufflinks on the night table before turning his attention to my wounds. In an instant, that strange, empty look overtook him, and the injuries puckered shut, the blood seeping back into my skin.

"Thank you," I murmured when he blinked back into himself.

For the first time, he didn't wave the words away or curl his lips into a sharp smile. Instead, he nodded. "You're welcome."

The sincerity of his response took me by surprise. Where were the sharp edges I was slowly becoming used to?

With a frown, I shifted on the bed in an attempt to untangle my legs from the mess of sheets I'd created in my sleep, and my movements uncovered the book I'd been reading earlier.

Paradise Lost.

Aleister reached for it. "Are you enjoying this?" he asked.

"I am, actually."

"It's been centuries since I've bothered with it, though I was fond of it when it was first published," he said.

He traced the well-worn cover with a finger and then opened the book at random, bringing it up slightly to read the words in the moonlight. I'd become so used to not having curtains that I'd forgotten to draw them shut.

I watched him flip through the pages, stopping here or there to read whatever caught his eye.

As he was now, haloed by light, it was easy to believe he had once been an angel. It was there in the cold lines of his face, in the absolute stillness that reminded me of a figure in a painting. In the brilliance of his eyes.

Then he smiled at something he read and he was suddenly no longer angelic but human, a handsome young man with a tumble of dark curls framing his face. Someone who radiated intelligence. Who thrummed with energy.

Aleister's gaze flicked from the page in front of him up to me as if he had felt the weight of my stare. Because I knew I had been staring.

I looked away. A flush rushed to my face and I could only hope that the moonlight would not reveal it.

Clearing my throat, I said the first thing that I could think of to break the silence. Something I realized I actually meant only as I finished uttering the words.

"He's a lot like you."

He blinked. "Who?"

"Milton's Satan."

He closed the book, placing the entire focus of his attention on me. "How so?"

"He's..." I searched for the right words, fully aware of the intensity behind those bright eyes. "I suppose he's almost human. Not at all like the other angels. They seem to follow orders without question, and there's no real, um, substance to them. They're interchangeable. They don't display anything that even resembles humanity, either, which most of the time makes them much more frightening than Satan."

Aleister's eyebrows rose.

"Yes, he's frightening, too, but he also shows doubt, anger, even happiness at moments. He can be sarcastic, he feels despair. He has very human passions." I stopped. Did I believe that Aleister possessed that range of emotions, or were well-sculpted verses muddling up the reality of who he was?

A long beat of silence stretched between us, my words hanging over our heads.

"That paints me in a rather more favorable light than I am accustomed to," Aleister finally said. I could almost feel his soft voice against my skin.

I swallowed. "Well, it's hard not to feel at least some sympathy for Milton's version of Satan."

"Sympathy for the Devil." He smiled. "Now there's a notion."

I looked down at my hands. For some reason, I'd become aware of my heart's thumping.

"You know, I actually met Milton once."

I almost exhaled with relief at the more casual tone in his voice. "You did?"

"Yes. This was a few years before he started *Paradise Lost*, before he went blind. I didn't tell him who I was, of course, but I remember we had a very pleasant conversation on religion over dinner."

"Maybe that's where the resemblance comes from," I said. "Maybe he based his fictional Devil on the real one without even knowing it."

He chuckled. "Perhaps. Stranger things have occurred."

"And the events he wrote about in the book? Are they accurate?"

"Not quite."

It didn't look like he would elaborate on that answer. I would have liked to know, but there was something else I wanted to ask. I hadn't been able to gather enough courage to ask it yet, and I wouldn't have had the courage to do it now, either, except for the way he looked.

Maybe it was the late hour or maybe it was the light that surrounded him, but there was something about Aleister right now that made me feel as if I could say or ask anything and it'd be fine.

I took a breath and hoped I wasn't wrong.

"Do you ever regret what you did?" I asked.

I expected, if anything, a quick answer, an offhand comment or biting sarcasm, even anger, but he was silent for what felt like an endless moment. He lowered his eyes and frowned, his head tilted slightly.

A minute passed, then two.

Just when I thought he wasn't going to answer, he looked up again.

"No one has ever asked me that. Not a single human or creature roaming heaven or hell, not in the millennia I have been who I am." He exhaled sharply. "I know it's hard to understand why I did what I did. Who in full possession of his faculties gives up heaven? But I...I couldn't live in chains any longer, Nora. Blindly following orders, bowing down to a power I didn't find infallible anymore. I was a prisoner who was expected to be glad of my imprisonment."

There was an edge of defiance in his voice. And I realized I could understand it. At least I had made a bargain with Aleister offering my life, my freedom, for something invaluable to me, but he had been created just to serve. With no options.

It amazed me that I hadn't thought of it quite like that before now.

He shifted and his face fell into shadow. "I miss my home, of course, and bearing the weight of all of the lies that have been told about me throughout the centuries never gets easier, but I couldn't return to that servitude. What would be worth that?"

I frowned. Perhaps when we first met I would have believed those words, that fierce refusal to show his care or his need for anything, but I wasn't sure I did now. I wasn't here, in his house, just on a whim of his.

"Not even your wings?" I said after a moment, my voice a murmur.

He made a small sound in the back of his throat. Even with his face hidden I could sense his hesitation. The way he must surely be averting his eyes from me.

"My wings," he finally began. "Yes. Perhaps I would accept chains again for them." His hands tightened into fists on his lap. "Do you know, Nora, they were ripped from me the moment I rebelled."

I winced.

"The best part of me, torn away."

A spot of pain bled into his words and it was still fresh, as if what he spoke of had not happened before humanity even came into existence. As if it still jolted him awake at night.

I should have known what to say. With my own experience in losing everything that made me who I was, the words should have come naturally to my lips, but I'd never been any good at comforting anybody. Not even myself. That had always been Peter's strength.

"Were they the gray ones I saw in your memory?" I asked, not at all sure that asking him about them was the right thing to do but unable to think of anything else.

"Yes. All shades of silver and white."

"Were they large?"

"Oh, yes." Aleister moved again, allowing the moonlight to fall over his features once more. "Extended, they would have been the length of this entire room. I suppose that's why I feel most comfortable in large spaces, why I begin to feel trapped in smaller ones. I still haven't gotten adjusted to not having them, even after all this time." He forced out a chuckle. "Ridiculous, I know."

I shook my head. One thing it was not was ridiculous. "Was the feather you had in your coat that day at the café part of them?"

His eyes darted to my face, the intensity behind them almost burning into me. Before I could say anything, he reached into his dressing gown and brought out the feather.

It glinted silver in the moonlight.

"It was the only one I was able to save." He held it out to me.

My eyebrows shot up. "No, I don't want to hurt it."

Aleister smiled. "You won't. It's stronger than it looks."

Wiping my hands against the bedsheets, I carefully reached for it.

It was heavier than any feather I'd ever held, but it was also silkier. Warmer. It was dizzying to think that it had helped propelled Aleister through heaven and had now roamed the depths of hell along with its master for thousands of years. This soft thing.

I could feel his despair at losing the wings, his frantic effort to save at least one feather, anything at all to remind him that they'd once been his.

Oh, how I understood that despair!

With the tip of one finger, I traced the quill down to its point and looked up, ready to tell him how beautiful it was, but the words faded from my lips.

Aleister was watching me, his head cocked slightly. An almost imperceptible frown appeared on his forehead as he searched my features...for what?

The hairs on the back of my neck rose.

Beside me, the half-empty glass of water resting on the night table gave a strange crystalline quiver.

The sudden realization that I was in bed, in only my nightgown, jolted my heart into a gallop. I sat up straighter, bringing the sheets up to my chest, and handed the feather back.

Aleister took it and looked away. Unnatural emptiness smoothed out his face.

I opened my mouth without any idea of what would come out of it, but he spoke first.

"I think it's about time I let you rest, Nora. I always forget just how much of it humans need." He stood but paused before heading for the door. "I hope you have no further nightmares tonight."

I swallowed and nodded.

"Would you like me to draw the curtains?"

"No, it's all right. The light doesn't bother me all that much anymore."

Aleister gave me a sideways glance that was meant to have all the sharpness and amusement that his looks usually did, but which right now seemed forced. "It appears as if I'm becoming a bad influence on you."

"It's a possibility," I said, trying to make my voice as light as I could.

I expected him to smile or to lift an eyebrow, I hoped for it, but he only nodded and slipped silently out of the room.

My heart pounding in my chest, I blinked in the moon-streaked night.

What had just happened?

FOURTEEN

AS SOON AS I tried to button up its velvet bodice, I realized there was no chance I could fit into the new evening gown using my regular corset. None at all.

"Damn it," I said, pulling on the strings again. But it was useless. I needed to shave a good three inches more from my waist than my maid's undergarment was built to do. "These blasted fashions."

I sighed and undid the laces before slipping the corset off and tossing it across the room. As nervous as the idea made me, there was no other option but to use the silk-lined one Aleister had purchased along with the dress.

He had appeared with the exquisitely-wrapped parcel three days before, handing it over with the offer to have something else made for me if I didn't like it. It had only taken an instant after pushing aside the tissue paper and seeing the deep, wine-colored velvet that seemed to shimmer with each movement of fabric to know there wasn't a lovelier gown in the entire world. With luxurious velvet, contrasting cuffs done in crisp cream lace, and a plunging lace neckline in the center of which a single chiseled stone rested like a large drop of fresh blood, it was something a princess in a story would wear.

Since Aleister had managed so well with all of my other clothes, and because I'd been too afraid of ripping it or damaging it in some way, I hadn't tried the gown on to make sure it fit before hanging it up in the wardrobe until Geary's ball.

Something for which I now cursed myself. If I'd known the waist was so small, I would have planned ahead for it.

I turned to the new corset lying on the bed. Of beige satin and silk, and with thin but powerful stays, it was much heavier than any other ones I'd ever had, and much more beautiful. It bore the same stamp as the gown, so Aleister had to have had it made especially for me, as well.

With surprise, I realized my cheeks warmed at that thought.

I shook my head at myself and held the corset up to my torso. Right, well, this had to be done now unless we wanted to be more than fashionably late to the ball.

"I need one of you," I called out.

In an instant, like it had been waiting for the opportunity, one of the shadows slid in through the closed bedroom door. It was Long-Neck, at least, which brought me a small measure of reassurance that I wasn't about to do something very stupid.

"I want you to listen carefully."

It waited, immobile, for my words.

"I need help cinching up this corset and—wait," I said, lifting a hand to stop Long-Neck when it started moving toward me. "Wait. I need to be sure there will be none of what happened on the first morning I was here. I don't know whether it was done on purpose or not, but I almost died. Do you understand?"

Long-Neck nodded.

"All right." I turned around and held the corset in place. "You have to pull on the strings until I tell you to stop, and then you *have* to stop. Immediately."

My heart thumped loudly as I felt Long-Neck lift the laces, the memory of that awful morning racing through my head despite all attempts at reminding myself that the shadows hadn't harmed me in any way after that. That they had actually saved my life.

The corset tightened. I closed my eyes. *Please let me not have made a mistake.*

I allowed the garment to get as tight as I could possibly stand it without risking a swooning episode in the middle of the ball and then lifted my hand. "That's enough."

The second that passed between my order and the shadow's response could have been a lifetime.

The pressure stopped increasing, but Long-Neck did not let go of the strings.

A moment later I realized why. I'd made it promise it would do exactly as I told it, and I hadn't said what to do next.

I exhaled. "Now tie a double knot and tuck the tail of the laces into the corset."

With the whisper of silk against silk, the shadow did as I said before releasing its hold of me. I allowed myself to breathe in with relief. Or breathe in as much as I could manage while wearing the damned contraption.

Swallowing back nerves, I picked up the gown's bodice from the bed and slipped it on. The fabric closed easily around my waist now and I had the buttons done up in a moment.

I turned to grab one of the underskirts next and gasped when I saw Long-Neck had drawn closer. It was near enough to reach out and throttle me if it wanted to do so.

I was about to order it out of the room, preparing myself to call for Aleister if it continued to move, when something about its posture stopped me. There was no aggression in it. It was hard to say how when it had no features I could read, but it all at once gave me the impression that it wanted to speak.

"What?" I asked.

It shifted its feet.

Was that hesitation? "Go ahead, what is it?"

Long-Neck lifted an arm much too quickly and I flinched. No matter how long I spent in this house, I didn't think I'd ever get used to these creatures' speed.

The shadow pointed the silhouette of its index finger at my head.

I frowned. "I don't understand."

It motioned again, this time bringing its hand close enough to touch one of my dark curls with its finger.

"My hair?"

Long-Neck nodded.

Blinking, I turned to look in the mirror. There was nothing wrong with it. I'd washed it this morning, though I had forgotten to comb it afterward and it was starting to look a bit like the rat's nests Peter and I had always searched for, but—

I sighed. Right. "You mean I need to do something with it for the ball?"

Another nod.

This was nothing if not bizarre. I hadn't considered that the shadows could have thoughts that didn't in some way relate to either frightening me or following the orders they were given, and here one was, commenting on my appearance.

I shrugged. "I'll put it up in a bun."

Long-Neck shook its head.

"Well, it's the only thing I know how to do. It's either that or it stays just like it is."

The shadow moved its arm sharply again until its index finger was pointing at its own chest.

"You...you want to do it?"

It nodded.

I blinked. One of the Devil's servants, a creature probably straight from the pits of hell, perhaps even one of the group that had almost killed me that first morning, wanted to do my hair for a ball.

For the first time in a good number of days, the madness of my situation rushed over me and a bubble of laughter that had an edge of hysteria to it rose up my throat.

Long-Neck pointed to itself again.

Damned insistent thing. "Well, I suppose you can make an attempt," I said after a moment of hesitation. "As long as you don't try to strangle me with a ribbon or stab me with a hair pin. Oh, and that's all I have to work with, too, so you'll have to make do."

It nodded and raced past me into the bathroom.

With a groan, I started after it. I had to have lost my bloody mind.

Aleister paused midway through sliding on his white evening gloves as I came to stand in front of him. He cocked his head, a frown creasing his forehead.

His eyes traced over me for a long moment, taking in the gown and the mass of curls that Long-Neck had by some miracle managed to shape and arrange so that they tumbled gracefully down my back.

I raised an eyebrow at his unusual silence.

"You look beautiful," he finally said. "Truly beautiful."

There was a muted tone to his voice that sent a flutter through my stomach.

"Thank you. You look very nice yourself."

As soon as I said the words, I realized just how true they were. In his dress coat the color of a raven's wing, the contrasting crisp white shirt and matching necktie, and the dark curling hair that framed his pale face, he didn't just look "very nice." He looked handsomer than any man I'd ever seen before.

The thought made my face warm.

"Thank you," he said, with a small incline of his head.

"A thank you from the Devil," I said. "That's a first."

He thought for a moment before speaking again. "Compliments tend to be rare when you're me. When you have spent millennia alone. I have learned to appreciate each one."

His words gave me pause. I would have never imagined that he, by his very nature, was someone who might need reassurance of something as basic as the way he looked. But being alone for so long had to leave scars, no matter who you were.

All at once I wished I could take my glib comment back.

"I'm sorry. I hadn't thought of that," I said.

Aleister watched me carefully, his eyes glittering under the light of one of the foyer's chandeliers. "You don't have to apologize to me, Nora. Not ever."

I met his gaze.

Just like on the night he'd woken me from that nightmare, a pulsing, strange energy grew in the air between us all at once. A tension that heightened the silence and stillness. Like the moment before lightning struck. It licked at my skin, making my breath catch in my throat and the hairs on the back of my neck tingle. I couldn't help shivering.

Aleister's lips parted to say something just as the chandelier's light flickered above us.

As if abruptly being woken from a dream himself, Aleister breathed in deeply and looked away from me. The words he'd been about to say dissolved.

"Aleister?" I said. "Is everything all right?"

"Perfectly." His usual curling, shallow smile was on his lips in an instant, the sharpness returning to his eyes. "How civilized we both are tonight, Nora. Who would have imagined it when we met?"

I made myself smile, too, though my skin was still prickling and my stomach was still knotted by a sensation I couldn't place. One I couldn't quite recognize.

"We should get going," he said, turning to take his coat and top hat from the table by the front door.

"Yes."

The remnants of the energy between us was almost gone. I wanted to know what it was, but I wasn't sure how to ask.

Long-Neck appeared beside me a moment later with my own light coat, which it draped over my shoulders.

"Thank you."

The shadow inclined its head.

"That's unexpected," Aleister said when I joined him by the door, his voice back to its usual, amused tone. "That level of cordiality. Up to a few weeks ago, you didn't even want my servants in the same room with you."

"Opinions can change, can't they?"

He nodded. "I suppose so."

He held the door open for me and we stepped into the night, where a carriage already waited for us. This was no regular hansom cab, but one of the larger growlers that could easily sit four people. The driver, who stood beside the carriage door, was in full livery.

"You hired all of this?"

He gave me a sideways glance. "Well, I considered making you walk to the ball, but it seemed too harsh, even for me."

"Amusing," I said. It was a relief, though, to hear that the edge of laughter was back in his voice.

Aleister extended a hand to help me up into the carriage.

"You'll have to be patient," I said. "Maneuvering all of these layers of fabric as well as a bustle and train is new for me."

"I have all of eternity."

I snorted. "It won't take quite that long."

Gathering as much of the velvet skirt and silk underskirt as I could in my free hand so that I wouldn't get my shoes caught in their folds, I climbed the first step. Aleister waited until I had regained my balance before bending and grasping the end of the elaborate crimson train.

I ducked into the carriage, the corset's stays digging into me enough that I knew I'd have bruises in the morning. With a swoosh of fabric, I shifted my weight, lifting the bustle slightly, and sat. Aleister tucked the gown's train partly under my seat before climbing into the carriage himself and sitting down opposite me.

Once we felt the shift in weight at the front of the vehicle that indicated the man had climbed on, Aleister thumped his hand on the roof to let him know we were ready to depart.

I'd never ridden in a growler before, but I knew why they had gotten that name. It took me only a second to see that it was more than well deserved. The noise this one made against the cobbled strerts was astounding as we sped away from the house. My teeth rattled with it.

"You remember what to do tonight?" Aleister asked once we were well on our way.

Shifting in my seat to try to find a way to breathe more easily and to keep the stays from stabbing anything vital, I nodded.

"I have to introduce you to Geary and then hurry out of the ballroom while he's distracted." I looked up at him. "How sure are you that the information we want is in his study?"

"Moderately sure. The thoughts that I've been able to gather from him about *Pandemonium* seem connected to a particular desk in his home, one with a hideous set of cherubim carved onto its sides." He grimaced. "I assume that means a study. I hope that proximity to Geary in his own house will help me narrow down where that study is actually located."

I tugged on one of my gloves to smooth the fabric out. How could society women wear them constantly?

"Fine," I said. "The evidence is in a desk. What if it's locked?"

"Since you picked open the door to hell, I assume you can handle a drawer, Nora."

"That would be true if I had hairpins with me, but I didn't know I would need them."

He frowned as if he'd just remembered I didn't have magical abilities that would open locks at my whim and actually needed tools. "Of course. Well, we can return to the house to pick up one of the replacement pairs I bought you. We'll be a little late, but we can't risk losing this chance."

Aleister was about to thump on the carriage ceiling again but I lifted a hand to stop him.

Holding his gaze, I reached up to my elaborate hairdo. From the ripples and folds of curls, I pulled out the set of ruby encrusted hairpins he had given me when it became obvious hell would not return mine. I'd tucked these in after Long-Neck had finished the look so they were not essential to holding the entire thing together. I could remove them as I pleased.

Raising an eyebrow, I held them up so Aleister could see. "Just teasing you. Of course I've come prepared."

He was very still for an instant before breaking into one of his rare, real smiles. "You've actually managed to fool me. That has to be the first time in a long time. Well done."

"I just wanted to see if I could." I smiled and lifted the pins to my hair again. "I can't promise these will be intact after I use them, though."

He dismissed the words with a hand. "I can buy you a hundred more of them."

Now that we'd addressed the few concerns I'd had about the evening, we allowed ourselves to fall into a comfortable silence. It was the kind that I'd experienced before only with Peter. Everyone else in my previous life had been full of noise and activity, people who demanded constant conversation about anything that crossed their minds to stave off the silence they seemed to fear, but not my brother. And not Aleister. When we were together, we shared the kind of quiet that didn't ask anything from either one of us.

The growler rumbled on, street after street, until we were out of the main part of the city. I stared out the window and watched the landscape of buildings begin to give way to trees swaying lightly in the darkness. I looked out of the opposite side of the carriage and found the same view. We were surrounded by greenery.

This was entirely new for me.

Neither Peter nor I had ever left London. Our entire lives, we'd lived among cobblestones, coal dust, and the noise of a city that was as restless as its people. Riding out of it now brought a surprising jolt of excitement, the realization that there was, indeed, a world outside of my small territory. That the places I'd read about were more than just names on a page, and that there was no reason why I shouldn't be able to visit them some day.

Stranger things had happened in just the last few weeks.

I was so distracted by the view and by my own thoughts that it took me a second to realize we were already approaching a large, well-lit estate.

"Is that it? Is that where Geary lives?" It was hard to keep the surprise out of my voice.

Aleister nodded. "He's done rather well, I would say."

I couldn't argue with that. The closer we got to the house, the grander it appeared. It was a large, rectangular structure done in an austere gray stone that stood solidly in the center of a manicured lawn. The simplicity of the house made it appear larger and statelier, and it seemed to glow against the night sky with the amount of electric light that poured out of each window. I didn't have the slightest idea how many rooms a house like that could contain, but it looked like every chandelier and every lamp in each one had been lit.

There were a substantial number of carriages lined up at the entrance as we neared, a flurry of colorful movement surrounding them as women descended in gowns of all hues, followed by men in variations of what Aleister wore.

"Do you think he's blackmailed all of these people?" I asked, my eyes following this or that couple as they walked into the house with all the grace years of similar evenings had taught them.

"Not all, surely, at least not yet, but enough of them. He wouldn't be able to afford such a place, otherwise."

"And they still come to his ball?"

"Of course. They don't want to give Geary any reason to be irritated with them. Not when he holds full control of their lives."

I shook my head and stared out at the chattering, smiling people dressed in their finest. "I don't understand it. Why not just have their secrets out and be done with it?"

Aleister chuckled. "It is difficult for us to comprehend, isn't it? But then, we don't rely solely on our names and reputation to go about our lives. These people have nothing else. Their wealth is tied to their being able to keep their place in society intact and if that means paying obscene amounts of money to a man who can barely read and allowing him into their social circles, then they will do so. Anything but live with a stain to their name."

He was right. I didn't understand it. I might have if the secrets would send them to jail once revealed, but not everyone making their way into the house could be a criminal. It wasn't possible. Which meant that for most of these people, whatever Geary held over their heads was something thoroughly commonplace. What precarious lives they must live, then, if just a whiff of everyday gossip could destroy them.

We drew to a stop a fair distance away from the entrance, behind five other carriages.

"Do you want to wait to get nearer the door, or would you rather get out right here?" Aleister asked. "It could be a few minutes still."

"Let's go down."

With a nod, he tapped the carriage ceiling. At once, the driver jumped down from his post and opened the door.

Aleister looked at me, tilting his head slightly to motion me out. Right. Ladies exited first.

I made sure my feet weren't tangled up in fabric before I made a single move. The last thing that would be helpful to us right now was for me to fall and smack my head on the pavement. I leaned forward, ignoring the pain from the corset, and placed my hand in the driver's gloved one. Taking my time, I lowered a foot to the step leading out of the carriage, lifted my skirts right to the edge of decency, and stepped out. Nothing tugged or pulled me backward, nothing made me tip forward. I breathed with relief.

Behind me, Aleister adjusted the gown's train so that it would slip out without snagging on anything, and I climbed down to the path that led up to the house. In a moment, Aleister had followed me out and had dismissed the driver with a wave of his hand.

"Nicely done," he said. "I've seen actual society women with less skill."

I smoothed out the velvet. "I just can't understand how they do this, night after night. The effort it takes just to walk, just to breathe, is ridiculous."

He chuckled. "They lead dull lives, Nora. They have nothing better to do than to fuss with their gowns." He motioned towards the house. "Are you ready?"

"I am."

"Excellent. Come then, lovely Lady Blake, let us go to the ball."

My face warmed at his words, which somewhat bothered me. I'd never been the kind of girl to dissolve into giggles at a compliment, so why was it so different with Aleister? Every time he said something pleasant to me or praised me in some way, I blushed or had another idiotic reaction. It made little sense.

Aleister smiled and offered me his arm, as the husband he was pretending to be would do for his wife. I made myself accept it in a casual manner, like it was an everyday occurrence for me to walk on the Devil's arm, and allowed him to start leading us toward the glowing house.

Because I'd never touched Aleister before except on the morning when he'd pulled me out of that awful room, my body in too much pain to take in much of anything, I wasn't prepared for what I felt the moment I placed my hand on him.

Even through the layers of clothing he wore and my own satin gloves, it was impossible to ignore the strength, the power, that twisted inside him. It writhed like an animal in a cage too small for it, as if the only thing keeping it contained within his body was Aleister's sheer will. Which, for all I knew, was the truth.

The memory of his voice when he'd spoken about his wings returned to me. It was easy now to imagine him slicing through the sky with them, this leashed energy breaking loose to propel him onward. And it was just as easy to comprehend the pain of their loss. I thought I'd understood, but it was only now, feeling the coiling power within him which no longer had its natural outlet and which he could no longer fully wield, that I sensed the real measure of just how trapped he'd been from the moment they were ripped from him. How much he'd lost of himself.

It sent a ripple of sadness through me.

Aleister slowed down and turned to look at me. "Is everything all right?"

I found I couldn't meet his eyes. "Yes, why?"

"You shivered."

I hadn't even noticed it. "Everything's fine. I'm just anxious to get this done, I suppose."

The weight of his eyes remained on me for a second more before he turned away and we resumed walking. With each step, I made myself concentrate on what needed to be done tonight, nothing else. It would not do for me to be distracted.

When we reached the entrance, it was not as crowded as it had been just a few minutes before. A blessing, that. There was only a man in uniform waiting, someone who didn't look us fully in the face but who bowed deeply from the waist as we passed him.

The foyer brimmed with people. The space, which was nowhere near the size of Aleister's, held at least ten couples at the moment, some of whom I'd seen descending from their carriages. A few heads turned in our direction as we handed our coats to another man in full livery, gazes flicking up and down the length of my gown before moving on to Aleister. I clenched my jaw. Didn't these fashionable people know that staring was considered a rudeness? Even *I* knew that.

It took me an instant to realize that the couples weren't just standing at random, but seemed to be in a makeshift queue of some kind in front of the double doors that led to the room beyond the foyer.

"What are they doing?" I asked.

Aleister followed my eyes. "Ah, well, there's a man by the doors who officially announces each person into the room. Sometimes the hostess is there to greet her guests, as well, though it doesn't seem like that's the case tonight." He shrugged. "They do this at most large balls, and it is exactly as tedious as it sounds."

"What for?"

"It is meant to help the guests mingle. With the added benefit, of course, of allowing the host and hostess a chance to boast about the kind of people that attend their soirees."

That sounded just like something Geary and his sisters would revel in.

More chatter and the swoosh of skirts sweeping across stone floors came from behind us as further guests entered the house.

"I think we'd better make our way to those doors or we'll still be standing here two hours from now," Aleister said.

He led us closer to the group of people, which was slowly growing thinner as each couple was announced into the next room.

I wouldn't have said I was nervous, exactly, though my heart was beating faster than it had been until now. It was just that I'd never even been near a ball before.

One by one, the man in uniform who stood by the doors introduced the people in front of us, booming names and titles into the next room.

And then we were the next couple.

I swallowed as we walked forward.

"Viscount Aleister Blake and Lady Nora Blake," Aleister said, his voice as casual as I'd ever heard it.

The man bowed his head and repeated the words loudly enough that they cut right through all of the noise. More heads turned our way, something which would have irritated me much more if my mind hadn't been immediately wiped clean by the astounding ugliness of the room we'd just walked into.

I hadn't seen anything like it in my entire life. The clash of colors alone would have nauseated a sailor. The room was festooned with bright yellow and purple ribbons hanging over the long tables which were set along both sides of the room and which were draped with red tablecloths that were much too shiny to look elegant. Not to be outdone, the ceiling above us had gaggles of fat painted angels holding golden harps and resting on white cotton clouds, the whole thing framed by a carved border that was meant to be gold, but which looked more like it had been painted a sickly yellow. If it was supposed to add anything to the room but gaudiness, it was a failure.

And then there were the plants. Small, spindly trees which had been stuck into white and blue pots and tucked into every free corner in the room. They weren't real, that was easy to see from any distance, probably made of silk by someone who either had never seen trees before or who had no skill in the art of recreating them. Fruits that were meant to be apples hung heavy from the thin branches, giving the trees a stooping look. How anyone could have thought filling a room with them would be a good idea was beyond me.

"Are you seeing this as well?" Aleister murmured.

"Unfortunately, yes."

"Good. I thought I might be having an apoplexy."

I snorted. "Can that even happen?"

"If anything could do it, it's this room."

The people around us seemed to be having the same sort of trouble with the décor, if their slightly widened eyes and pursed lips could be trusted. The women who had fans were busy using them, as if the assault of bad taste had been physical, while the men gazed about themselves like they couldn't quite recall where they were or what they were supposed to be doing.

We walked a few steps away from the entrance and slipped into the crowd just as the man behind us announced another set of names.

Now that I could set aside the shock of the room's ugliness, I was all at once struck by the lack of space. There wasn't nearly as much of it as I'd imagined when I'd thought of a ball in a grand estate.

The room already felt crowded enough to make me worry about my gown's train and it was only eight thirty. In just half an hour more, if people kept entering, walking could become a challenge. How could I stealthily find my way to Geary's study when I'd have to squeeze through half of London society to get there? It was impossible.

"This is not it, right? We won't have to spend the entire night here?" I asked.

Aleister shook his head. "There should be another room beyond this one where the dancing will take place. At least I very much hope so, or some of these women will start giving serious consideration to gouging their eyes out."

"That's a relief, then." I smiled, adjusting my hand on his arm.

I noticed I felt more at ease now about being so close to Aleister. It was as if my body had attuned itself to the onslaught of energy that radiated off him, allowing the power to envelop me without trying to fight it. It was a surprisingly pleasant sensation.

"Would you like a refreshment?" he asked, motioning to the many decanters of water, wine, and lemonade that rested on the tables set along both sides of the room.

"No, I'm all right." I glanced around at the clumps of people surrounding us. "Do you see Geary?"

"I can sense he's in the house, but no, he's not in the room yet."

I wished he'd hurry up so we could get started. The sooner I got the papers we needed, the sooner I could claim a headache or some other malady and we could head back home. Away from the chatter and this nightmare of drooping silk trees.

"Lord Blake, Lady Blake," a man said with a bow of his head as he walked past us, a crystal full of wine in each hand.

Aleister nodded in acknowledgement and I hurried to do the same.

The exchange earned us more looks, this time from a group of older women. Even after they noticed I'd seen them, they continued to stare.

"They are higher ranking in society," Aleister murmured, turning us slightly away. "That is why they won't do much to acknowledge us unless they absolutely have to."

"What they are is rude."

"Many times, you'll find that those two characteristics go hand in hand."

His words brought to mind a question that the room's lack of elegance had stomped down. "Why did you choose the title of viscount?" I asked. "You could have been an earl or a duke. It seems oddly modest on your part."

He glanced at me, a curling smile on his lips. "I wanted a rank that was high enough to garner attention but not so high that people would be too intimidated to come up to us without a proper introduction. We want to blend in just a bit so that you can disappear when the time is right. If I'd made you a duchess, people would keep their eyes on you the entire night, which just would not do."

He had thought of everything, then. "I see. So that means we will have to mingle with the guests?"

"That is generally one of the things that happens at balls."

I groaned.

"Don't tell me you're afraid?" Aleister said, a ribbon of laughter through his voice.

"No, I'm not afraid. I'm just not very good at casual conversation, especially if there isn't a clear purpose for it." I exhaled. "It always feels so awkward, so forced."

"Oh, it's very straightforward, Nora. You just need to remember three things: smile often, keep the conversation simple, and tell them exactly what they want to hear. That's all it takes to become irresistibly charming."

He turned to nod at another couple walking past us, leaving me with his words echoing through my head.

If he knew so well how to win people over, why hadn't he tried it with me when we'd first met? He had actually done the very opposite of what he'd just recommended. None of our conversations had been simple, not a single one, and he'd never told me what I wanted to hear. He hadn't even managed more than a sarcastic smile at the beginning.

It was peculiar, as if he hadn't cared to make himself likeable.

"Lord Blake!" said a man with a full head of white hair who was suddenly in front of us. "What a pleasure to see you here. I don't know if you recall, but I believe we met in Venice last year. James Argyle, from Sussex."

Without the slightest hesitation, Aleister nodded and smiled. "Of course, Mr. Argyle. How fortunate to meet again, and under such pleasant circumstances. May I introduce my lovely wife, Lady Nora Blake?"

I forced out a smile. "How do you do?"

Argyle bowed his head. "Very well, madam, thank you. I'd introduce you to my own wife, but she's already selecting a prime spot on the ballroom floor. She'd dance the night through, if I allowed her."

Aleister nodded. "Perhaps we'll make her acquaintance later."

"She'd be honored. She's heard all of the stories from Venice."

"It was a wonderful experience, wasn't it?" Aleister said with a chuckle that to anyone but me would have seemed genuine.

"It certainly was," Argyle said. "We must repeat it."

"Yes, we must."

Argyle laughed. "Marvelous." He turned to me. "I shall hold your husband to that."

I nodded. "By all means. Perhaps Ms. Argyle and I can even join you on the next trip."

"Without a doubt, without a doubt. Have a pleasant evening, Lord Blake, Lady Blake."

"And you."

Aleister waited for the man to walk off before turning to me. "See? Nothing simpler. He wanted to insinuate himself into our acquaintance and all I did was allow him to do so. He'll now praise both of us to the high heavens because he thinks he outwitted us." He lowered his voice. "Here comes another group. Care to wager where they will claim to have met us?"

I held back a laugh and followed his eyes. Three women were walking toward us, each one wearing more rouge than the previous. I took a breath. If these ladies were remotely like Geary's sisters, this could be a tedious conversation.

"Lord Blake, Lady Blake," they said almost in unison.

Aleister and I both acknowledged their greeting.

"We hope you forgive our brazenness in coming to speak to you without being introduced," one of the women said. "But we've learned that you are new in the city and we wanted to welcome you."

The gossip had already spread, then. Good.

They prattled off their names, one after the other, all three of them so long I couldn't recall a single syllable once they were done.

Aleister's smile was resplendent. "How very kind of you all. I must say, London has been most welcoming since we arrived."

"We do our best," the woman in the middle said with a giggle.

"Have you been to the galleries?" the third one asked. "There are some rather marvelous works of art to be seen." She let out a little gasp as she looked past us. "Oh, this is exactly the person you should get to show you some of the lovelier sights. I'll introduce you!"

I allowed Aleister to take charge of the conversation, which he did with ease. No one would have ever imagined he lived his days almost in seclusion from the way he navigated three women and a man clucking at the same time about different subjects.

The chatter around the rest of the room was increasing, as well, as people continued to enter, making it more difficult to concentrate on what was happening in front of me. It was also getting warmer by the second, enough that I felt a trickle of sweat running down one of my legs.

Aleister seemed to be having no trouble with any of this, however. He continued to smile, nodding every so often at the idiotic comments on upcoming events in the city or on the latest fashions. Anyone looking at him would have thought he had never participated in a more fascinating conversation.

I waited for the group to leave us be, but they carried on, made bold by Aleister's attention. A few minutes later, two more people joined us, as if drawn in. They were followed by another group, and another, until we were thronged by men and women eager to offer invitations to balls or recommendations on where to dine in the city.

It was easy to see why.

Aleister was nothing if not captivating.

I watched, smiling at the group around us to make it appear like I was invested in the conversation, as he slowly became the center of attention, as heads turned, fans fluttered, and men began nodding at his words. He wasn't doing much more than asking questions a child living in the city would have known the answers to and agreeing with all the comments, but it didn't matter. I even heard him contradict himself in the space of five minutes without consequences. They weren't listening; they were just basking in his attention.

In less than half an hour, Aleister had become a different being from the one I lived with. This was the charming angel who'd had no problem convincing a third of heaven to revolt. Not the Aleister I knew, but *this* one. This glittering person who flattered without shame, smiled shallowly, and said the exact words these people so wanted to hear.

It was the first time I'd seen this side of him.

He had never done this to me. Had never tricked me like this. Not once. From the moment we'd met, he had been his difficult, sometimes infuriating self, with as many flaws and doubts as I had. Someone who was nowhere near the false perfection I now saw.

For some reason, he had decided that I was the person who could handle the truth of who he was. All aspects of it. The person with whom he didn't have to pretend.

My hand tightened around his arm slightly with the sudden need to make sure he was still there.

He turned to me in an instant. A small curl lifted the corner of his lips and his real self glinted out of his bright, sharp eyes. The relief I felt at seeing that ironic amusement was surprising.

"If you will all excuse us," he said, "I think my wife and I will make our way to one of the refreshment tables. I, for one, am parched after all of this lively talk."

It was like a light went off in the room. The smiles on the faces of the people surrounding us dimmed. If seemed that if it had been up to them, they would have stayed there talking until the ball was over.

Aleister nodded to the group at large without waiting for a reply from any of the individuals and I did the same. We eased through them and started walking down the length of the room.

"That was unbelievably dull," Aleister said when we made it a fair distance away. "I'd forgotten just how boring most humans are. How easy to manipulate."

"It was incredible," I said. "What did you do to them?"

"Nothing, not to them. I just heightened my own friendliness. Made myself as likeable as possible in case we need some allies in the future."

"Well, it was effective. They were practically worshipping you."

He chuckled.

"It's true! You could have told them to hand over their most precious belongings and they would have done so without blinking. Why didn't you try that on me when we met? It might have saved you a lot of trouble."

Aleister turned his head to look at me. "It wouldn't have worked."

"It worked now." But had it? I'd found him captivating, yes, but I had seen through the falseness quickly.

"I'm not so certain," he said, echoing my thoughts. He shrugged. "Even if I did manage to hold you enthralled for a moment or two tonight, it was only because you didn't put up any resistance. That would not have been the case then. If I recall correctly, you were furious with me. Perhaps even beyond furious. If I'd tried that on you in those first couple of weeks, you would have clawed the smile off my face."

I snorted. "So you did notice how angry I was."

"It was hard to miss."

I thought back on that time, on the constant fire that had settled in my stomach, fire fueled by fear and the loss of Peter. "Maybe you're right. Maybe it wouldn't have worked."

"In this case, I believe I am."

We maneuvered through the crowd until we were at the opposite end of the room. It was no easy feat, but it did earn us a bit more breathing space once we'd accomplished it. Like animals soothed by large numbers of their own kind, the majority of the guests congregated at the center.

We came to a stop close to the entrance to what looked to be the ballroom.

"What you have to understand," Aleister continued, "is that you are not like most humans." He smiled. "Actually, you are not like *any* human I've ever known. The things that work on the rest do not appear to work on you."

His words gave me pause. "Why do you say that?"

"Nora, you know exactly who I am, yet you are still on my arm right now as if it were the most normal thing in the world. I sense no fear of me in you anymore, no hate or disgust. You have kept your wits about you and have not disappeared into madness as the few to whom I've revealed my identity have done in the past. I can assure you, none of this has ever happened before. You are unique."

He watched me, his head cocked, like *I* was the mystery. Not the fallen angel who was a symbol of all evil on earth, but me, a seventeen-year-old human.

I opened my mouth to tell him that there was no secret here, that the reason I was able to live with him as I did was because of Peter and the threat to his life that my disobedience would bring, but the words died before they left my lips.

Because it wasn't the truth. Not the whole truth, at least.

Before I could consider what that meant, however, his head snapped to the right, toward a door half-hidden behind one of the monstrous apple trees, his entire stance tensing.

"What is it?" I asked, drawing closer to him.

His voice came as if from a long distance away. "Geary. I can sense him nearby."

I waited, not wanting to break his concentration. His arm grew rigid under my hand.

After a few seconds, Aleister inhaled and turned to look at me again. "He's in his study. It's through that door, along the second corridor on the right, but I can't narrow down the exact room."

I nodded. "All right. I'll have to check each one, then. As long as there are less of them than you have at home, it should be fine."

A flurry of movement tugged my eyes away from Aleister and toward a woman wearing a gown with so many folds, beads, and jewels on it, it was a wonder she could walk under its weight.

It was Maud Livingston.

"One of Geary's sisters is walking toward us," I murmured.

"Ah. It's about time, too."

"Lady Blake!" Maud said once she had pushed her way through a clump of guests. "I am so happy you've come! Robert, this is the lady I mentioned."

From behind her, where he had been completely hidden, stepped a man half Maud's size and twice her age. If he was a day under sixty, I would have been shocked.

"Mrs. Livingston," I said, matching her enthusiasm, "how wonderful to see you! Allow me to present my husband, Lord Aleister Blake. Darling, this is Maud Livingston, one of our gracious host's sisters."

"Of course," Aleister said. "A pleasure to meet you."

"Sir, it's an absolute delight," Maud said with a curtsy. "And this is my husband, Mr. Robert Livingston."

Both men exchanged a nod.

"It was most kind of your brother to invite us and welcome us into his home. And a lovely one it is, too," Aleister said.

"It is, isn't it?" Maud said. "He always gets a barrage of compliments."

"I'm sure he does. This room is especially striking. Lady Blake and I were just speaking about it, saying how we'd never seen anything quite like it."

I cleared my throat to hide a laugh. The sarcasm was blatant, but neither Maud nor her husband caught it.

On the contrary, Geary's sister was all smiles. "It is of my own design, in fact. My brother is not married, and doesn't have much of a feel of how a room should look, so I took it upon myself to help him. Every home should have a woman's touch."

"I heartily agree," Aleister said. "Men have no sense for these things. If it weren't for Lady Blake, we would still be living in a home without curtains. I forgot about them entirely."

I looked up at him and he met my eyes with the smallest of shrugs. My lips twitched as I remembered his face the night I'd demanded them from him. Demanded curtains from the Devil.

Maud burst into laughter. "No curtains! Oh, that's exactly what I always tell Mr. Livingston. Women just have a knowledge about these things that men lack. Isn't that ri—"

A trumpet call from behind us cut her words off. I flinched at the noise and even Aleister turned his head.

"The dancing!" Maud said, clapping her hands like a child. "The dancing is starting! Come, Mr. Livingston, so we can find a good spot on the floor. Lord and Lady Blake, you must join us. My brother hired a wonderful quartet for tonight that is known for their exquisite waltzes. It can't be missed! Mr. Livingston, don't dawdle!"

She gripped her husband's arm and pulled on it, half-dragging the poor man past us and toward the ballroom doors.

"And I thought living with you was a trial," I said.

Aleister chuckled. "Yes, it appears Mr. Livingston has a much tougher time of it." He turned to look at me. "So, what do you say?"

"About what?"

"About a dance."

I blinked, heat rising to my face. He couldn't be serious. "You want to dance?"

"I haven't done so in centuries and I have the perfect partner on my arm. I can't think of a reason not to if you're willing to join me."

"But...shouldn't we be on the lookout for Geary?"

"He's still in his study. There's more than enough time for a waltz." He smiled, a challenge written on his lips.

My heart thumped loudly in my chest. Not from nerves, but because all at once I realized I wanted to do it. I wanted to dance with Aleister. That thought alone was dizzying, full of implications that were too frightening to even begin to explore.

"Well, I don't know how to waltz," I said after a moment.

His smile brightened when he heard the reluctance in my voice had disappeared. "Oh, don't worry about that. If Maud and all the rest of these people can do it, you'll have no trouble at all." He shifted so that I would have room to turn around without stepping on my own train. "Just follow my lead."

"Because that has never ended badly."

His laughter enveloped me in its sparkle, making my skin tingle. "Touché," he said.

The ballroom was a much larger space, square, with gleaming floors and windows that stretched all the way to the ceiling. It wasn't a handsome room, with none of the stateliness of Aleister's home, but at least it had no silk monstrosities spread throughout its length.

At the far end, four men sat holding musical instruments that I somewhat recognized. I was rather certain two of them had violins and another had a cello. The other instrument was harder to name.

Aleister and I found a spot among the many other couples. Thankfully, it wasn't too close to the center of the room, so perhaps not all of the guests would see what I was sure would be my disastrous attempt at dancing.

Imitating the women around me, I bent to pick up the loop of fabric that would work like a handle to lift the gown's train up from the floor, and slipped it around my wrist.

"When the music starts," Aleister murmured, "your first move is to take a step back with your right foot, followed by a diagonal step with your left. Then feet together. That's three counts. The next three are done in the opposite way, with your left foot coming forward, a diagonal step with your right, and feet together. That is all there is to it."

"Oh, that's all, is it? How fortunate for me," I said, trying to hold on to at least some of his instructions but knowing they were already hopelessly tangled in my head.

The quartet took up their instruments, putting bows to strings to create a humming sound that overtook the room.

The couples around us shifted into position.

"Place your left hand on my right shoulder," Aleister continued.

I did as he said at the same time that he slipped his right arm around me, his hand coming to rest against my shoulder blade. Gently, he took my free hand in his left.

"You do realize I'm going to step on your feet, right? Probably more than once."

"I am fully prepared," he said, his lips curling. "You forget I have cloven feet."

I smiled. "So this is what they're for, then. Now I understand."

Aleister cocked his head and was about to say something, but the music began, robbing him of his words. There was no choice now but to dance.

I took the first step...and landed squarely on Aleister's left foot.

He smiled and pressed his lips together as I stepped on him again. And again.

"Right, left, together, left, right, together," he said, his voice brimming over with laughter.

"Goddamn it," I hissed, glancing down, as if looking at my feet would actually make a difference.

The couples around us had begun to spin without effort, conversation flowing along with the music. It looked so natural when they did it, while I seemed to have forgotten which was my left foot and which was my right.

I missed the next two steps and bumped my hip against a woman beside us. She hooted in surprise, blinking, her mouth open in horror. Her partner looked at us the way he would look at someone who'd insulted his mother.

The absurdity of the moment, of someone who used to catch rats with her bare hands trying to learn to waltz from the Devil in the middle of a crowded ballroom, was impossible to ignore any longer.

Laughter broke out of my throat, the sound so bright it cut through the music.

Aleister met my gaze, eyebrows lifted.

"I have no idea what I'm doing!" I said in between gasps.

"Really? I hadn't noticed."

His words brought on another wave of mirth and I made no attempt to rein it in, no longer giving a toss what the people next to us might think. I lifted my head high and just cackled.

As if my merriment were catching, Aleister too began to laugh. His voice was soft at first, just a chuckle, but it soon rose to become the perfect complement to mine as we danced through the room. Couples began to turn and look our way, each stare propelling us into more laughter, not less, until I had to lean into him to avoid tipping over. He tightened his grip on my hand and upper back, bringing me closer.

We lost all track of the steps, merely spinning now, clasping on to each other, enjoying the deliciousness of pure movement and music. I could hardly feel my feet on the floor as we turned faster and faster. It was as if we had risen high above the ballroom, as if it were just the two of us. The only ones left in the world.

The blood in my veins seemed to sparkle, bubbling with something I couldn't name. All I knew was that I didn't want this moment to end. Not ever.

I met Aleister's eyes, which shone so brightly they were almost painful to look at. I felt the warm pressure of his hand on my back, the closeness of our bodies, his laughter like fluttering fingertips trailing up and down my spine.

I shivered.

Without warning, he brought us to a sudden stop. His smile dimmed as he watched me, but his eyes blazed.

He drew me in closer.

The sound of glass shattering cut the music in two. Screams rose around us as one of the violins shrieked, bow slipping across strings in violent surprise when the ground began to shake. All of the lights went off at the same time, a collective gasp rising from the guests as darkness flooded the ballroom.

Aleister released me with a sharp exhale and took a step back. His chest rose and fell rapidly, matching my own, his luminous eyes competing with the moon's rays as the brightest source of light in the room.

My heart pounded with such force I could hear the blood rushing through my veins even over the constant sound of breaking glass.

The ground rumbled again, bringing more screams along with it.

Aleister closed his eyes and turned away from me.

An instant later, the lights flared back to life and the ground steadied. The sounds of human fear and excitement quickly replaced the noise of shattering glass, with nervous chatter and worried voices bubbling up to the ceiling along with the first barrage of shrill questions.

"What was that?"

"Could it have been an earthquake?"

"There are no earthquakes in Britain, are there?"

"But what else *could* it have been?"

And on and on.

I held my breath and looked at Aleister.

His gaze was now locked on the floor, his body rigid. I took a step toward him, following an illogical impulse to make sure he was all right, but he flinched back.

"Aleister—"

"I'll go see where Geary is," he said in a voice empty of all expression. He turned without waiting for my response and walked away.

I watched him weave through the crowd as if he were invisible, stepping across the puddles of glass shards scattered along the floor, and out of the ballroom.

Still panting, I pressed a hand to my racing heart.

It was the third time now something like this had happened. The lights going out, the rumbling, the shaking, and now the breaking of glass.

From his reaction, Aleister had done all of this without meaning to, as if he hadn't been able to control it. Just like the last two times, I'd felt the energy building in him, the power that grew until it enveloped me in its folds and wound the two of us together, and I'd done nothing to stop it. On the contrary, I'd welcomed it. His power, his closeness, his touch.

More than welcomed it.

My face burned at my thoughts.

"Pardon me, madam."

I looked up at a man in uniform carrying a broom. He bowed deeply. "Just starting to clear the glass, madam, if you'll just step to the side..." His voice faded and he frowned. "How strange."

Swallowing, I glanced down at the floor.

A perfect circle had formed where Aleister and I had stood. There were shards around the entire border, pressed against it as if a physical barrier had stopped them, but there wasn't a single piece inside the circle. Not a sliver.

The man looked up at me.

"How fortunate of me to be standing here, in exactly the right place," I said, forcing lightness into my voice.

"Very fortunate indeed, madam."

Before anyone else could see what the servant had seen and begin asking questions, I stepped out of the circle and walked away.

From the amount of shards on the floor, every wineglass in the room had to have shattered. Beads of blood marred many of the guests' white gloves as they removed pieces of delicate crystal from their palms, while some of the unluckiest ones had to submit to having their loved ones pick slivers out of their faces.

I made it across the floor and was about to step into the next room when Aleister appeared.

"Geary is on his way here," he said, his voice still on the edge of hollowness.

"Oh." I nodded. "All right."

As usual, there were too many things I wanted to ask him.

"There's quite a bit of...of damage in there," he said, motioning to the room he'd just come from. "All the wineglasses are in pieces. When it's time, be careful where you step."

There was nothing I recognized in his eyes. They could have been made out of crystal themselves for all the life they revealed.

"I will."

I wanted to say more but the words refused to form and then Geary appeared in the doorway, his eyes wide, jaw visibly tight, and there wasn't any more time. He barked out an order at a servant, who scurried out of the way.

"Lady Blake," he said the moment he caught sight of us. "I'm terribly sorry about all of this. You're not hurt, are you?"

"No, Mr. Geary, I'm quite all right, I assure you." I smiled and swallowed the dryness in my throat. "May I present my husband, Lord Aleister Blake?"

I didn't look up at Aleister but instead began searching for any excuse that might explain away the strangeness in his eyes and voice. Geary wasn't what I'd have called intelligent but even a child would be able to tell something was off about my supposed husband.

"A pleasure, sir," Geary said with a bow.

I held my breath.

"The pleasure is all mine. My wife has spoken at length of your graciousness and of the invaluable assistance you provided for her."

Relief washed over me when I heard the light hint of mockery was back in Aleister's voice. He'd managed to regain whatever steadiness or control he'd lost when we danced.

But why had he lost it?

"Lady Blake is much too kind." Geary looked past us with a frown. "Will you excuse me for just a moment? There are some things I would enjoy discussing with you, Lord Blake, if you can possibly spare the time, but first I need to make sure the evening is not a complete disaster."

"Of course," Aleister said. "By all means."

With a bow, Geary walked away, toward where the musicians sat, or had been sitting, since they looked like they were about to give up on the entire night. He hissed at them to take their seats in a way that made half of the guests still in the room cringe.

"He's not overly burdened with manners," Aleister murmured.

"Says the man who broke all of the crystal at a ball."

He gave me a sideways glance that held just enough amusement in it to reassure me that the unease between us, whatever its cause, had passed.

For now.

Geary turned to face his guests, lifting a hand to draw all eyes to him.

"Thank you all for coming tonight. And what a night it has already been! Please allow me to offer my sincerest apologies for all of this, though I am still not certain about what actually occurred. At any rate, we must not allow this unfortunate incident to ruin our enjoyment of the evening." He motioned around the room. "As you can see, my servants are already sweeping the glass away so that we may all continue dancing, and I've sent for new wineglasses as well as bottles of the finest champagne in the world which should arrive in the next half hour or so. I've also had my own personal physician fetched to care for all cuts and scratches. If there is anything else I can do to help put all of this unpleasantness behind us, I am all ears."

He pressed his hands to his chest and bowed his head. Beside me, Aleister snorted, and I breathed even easier.

There was a scatter of applause before Geary turned to the quartet of musicians and gestured for them to play. He waited for their first notes before he began to walk back toward us.

Aleister turned to me. "Second corridor on the right."

"I remember. Just keep him busy."

I offered Geary my brightest smile when he reached us. "If you'll both excuse me, gentlemen, I think I'll leave the two of you to your business while I get some fresh air. It's been such an exciting night and you know how we women need time to calm our nerves. A bit of quiet would be just the thing."

"But of course, Lady Blake. Ask any of the men in uniform for whatever you may require."

With an inclination of my head, I turned and walked back out into the refreshment room.

Aleister had not been exaggerating about the amount of damage it had suffered. Not only the wineglasses had shattered, but all the decanters as well, spilling wine, water, and lemonade down the tables to the floor. Servants were busy mopping up the largest puddles, most of which still had glass floating in them, and dabbing damp cloths on stained gowns and waistcoats.

It would be a long while before the mess was cleared up.

Right, no more dawdling.

As soon as I took a step into the room, ready to weave through the crystal that covered most of the floor in a sharp layer, I noticed the cleared path. It started at the ballroom's threshold, just inches from my feet, and led all the way to the door I needed to walk through. It wasn't like the rough tracks the servants left with their brooms, which only managed to scatter the larger shards, but a perfectly cleared path. The only one like it in the room. And it just happened to be the one that would allow me to walk right where I needed to go without slipping or cutting myself.

Aleister.

He had to have done this when he came searching for Geary. Even in the tense, unsettled state he'd been in when he walked away from me, he'd done what he could to keep me from harm. The same way he had shielded me from his own violent powers in the ballroom.

The strange flutter in my stomach returned, followed immediately by a flare of irritation.

There was no time for sentimentality. I had to get this done.

Pulling on my train to keep it lifted off the floor, I stepped onto Aleister's path and walked to the door half-hidden behind one of the silk trees. I turned my back to it, gazing out into the room bristling with activity. I reached behind me and tested the doorknob. It turned with ease in my hand.

Now came the most difficult part. If I'd been wearing trousers, I could have slipped through the doorway in less than a second, but with this dress it was bound to take me longer. Stealth and luxurious gowns were not a happy match.

I gazed around the room. Though most of the guests had left for the relative safety and order of the ballroom, there were servants everywhere. The majority of them had their eyes on the floor as they swept or soaked up the spills, and even the ones who didn't were more concerned with giving orders than with a stray guest hovering by a doorway, but any of them could look my way at the wrong time. And if they did, I had no reasonable excuse for my actions.

I would just have to risk it.

With one last look around me, I pushed open the door and hurried through it, yanking the gown in behind me. For half a heartbeat, an edge of lace caught on one of the silk tree's branches and I was sure I would bring the whole thing crashing down when I pulled, but it slid off without a sound.

I shut the door behind me and listened, waiting for voices to call after me.

Seconds ticked by and the same sounds of cleaning continued. No hurrying footsteps, no shouts. If the servants had seen me sneak into this wing, they didn't care enough to come after me.

Good.

Gathering my skirts and standing mostly on my toes to keep the heels from clicking against the floor, I walked down the hallway until I reached the second corridor. I turned into it.

It wasn't nearly as long as Aleister's wing, but it was still longer than I would have preferred. There were six rooms I had to check, six different doors to pick open if they were all locked.

Pulling the hairpins out of Long-Neck's intricate creation, I headed for the first door. I pressed my ear to the wood and listened for any sound that might reveal there was someone inside.

Nothing other than silence.

I tried the door. It wasn't locked but it also only opened into a room full of furniture covered in white sheets.

Five more to go.

I repeated the process as quickly as I was able, lifting the gown's skirts even higher to move faster, opening door after door to reveal a sitting room, a billiards room, and even a trophy room with stuffed animal heads on every wall.

Until I reached the second to last door. The handle clicked drily under my hand and refused to lower.

"Found you," I whispered with a smile.

I knelt—not an easy feat with all the layers I wore—and inserted the first pin into the lock. It was a four-tumbler one. Another two or three minutes and I would have the evidence of blackmail we needed in my hands. I wouldn't be able to lock the room behind me without the key but by the time Geary noticed, Aleister and I would be safely back in our—

A door opened somewhere behind me.

I froze.

From the noise that trickled in, the chattering voices and tinkling sounds, someone had walked in from the refreshment room.

Heavy footsteps started down the corridor and echoed throughout the wing. Not Aleister, then.

I yanked the pin out of the lock and slid it and its companion back into my hair as I leapt to my feet. A quick glance told me I wouldn't have time to hide in any of the other rooms before whoever was approaching saw me. Damn it!

I hurried away from the locked door a moment before Geary appeared.

"Lady Blake!"

"Oh, Mr. Geary, thank goodness!" I said, pressing my hands to my pounding chest. "I thought I'd never find my way out."

"What...?" His eyes trailed over me and down the corridor. The surprise and mild confusion on his face faded, slowly replaced by a narrowing of his eyes, a creasing of his forehead.

I had to keep talking. "I...I wanted to splash some water on my face," I started, "and one of your servants told me there was a bathroom this way, though I haven't been able to find it. Then I realized I didn't even know how to get back. Not very surprising, when you consider I'm likely to get lost in my own house!" I giggled, a shrill sound that could have scraped the paper off the walls. "But here you are, my savior once more."

Geary walked toward me and I had to resist the urge to retreat. Where the bloody hell was Aleister?

A crash resounded through the house.

I flinched in surprise at the same time that Geary reached out and grasped my arm. His hand tightened just beyond what would have been acceptable if he had meant the touch to be steadying or protective.

"Oh, Lady Blake, you should have mentioned it so that I could have had one of my servants escort you. We certainly don't want you getting lost."

His voice held no trace of friendliness. He knew I was lying.

The impulse to tug my arm away or land a knee to his groin was difficult to restrain. All that stopped me was the knowledge that if I did either one, there would be no going back. It would be as good as telling him why we were here.

The blackmailer's hand tightened on my arm.

"Nora?"

In all of human history, no one could have ever been as happy to hear the Devil's voice as I was at that moment.

"I'm here," I called out.

Geary loosened his grip and I took advantage of that moment, shifting away from him before starting toward Aleister's voice.

He stood at the doorway to the refreshment room, his eyes brightening unnaturally when I came into view.

"He knows," I mouthed.

Aleister's gaze moved sharply away from me, its shine taking on a hard edge as it landed on Geary.

"Lord Blake, it seems your wife got a bit lost on the way to the bathroom. I found her wandering the corridors."

"I am a silly thing," I said.

Aleister took as step forward. Energy rippled off him. "She does get flustered. Sometimes even in our own home."

"So Lady Blake has said." Geary turned to me. "But please, the room you are seeking is this way. Allow me to show you." He smiled tightly and motioned to the first corridor. "You just chose the wrong one."

"Oh, it's all right," I said. "I've been away from all of the beautiful waltz music long enough."

"I insist, Lady Blake." He took my arm again, fingers digging into me. "We wouldn't want you to feel ill from all of the excitement we've had this evening, would we?"

I could sense Aleister's rising anger, a coppery taste in the back of my throat. The same pressure had begun to build around us as I'd felt the day he'd pulled me out of his horrid room. Anger that enveloped, that overwhelmed. My skin prickled with it even though it was not directed at me.

Darkness began to pool around us, licking at our feet, the lights above us losing their strength.

Geary released his grip on me with a blink of confusion. He took a step back, but the darkness followed.

I glanced at Aleister and saw his eyes rapidly losing all expression. This wasn't going to end well.

The last thing I wanted to do was to protect Geary, but I'd be damned if we'd gone to all of this trouble to walk away without the answer we needed, losing the chance of freeing those girls and getting Aleister's wings back. There had to be a way to still salvage this opportunity.

I stepped in front of Geary, blocking him from the Devil's power. For this was that part of Aleister now.

"Our host is too kind. Isn't he, darling?"

I held his gaze.

Slowly, ever so slowly, like he was returning from an impossible distance away, the Aleister I recognized seeped back into those eyes. The pressure eased. The darkness grew wispy and thin before fading altogether.

"I wonder what the matter is with the lights tonight," I said, making my voice brighter than even I could stand. "Oh, all of this has left me so rattled that I do think I'll take your suggestion, Mr. Geary, and freshen up. If you'll excuse me."

Geary shook his head as if to clear it and took another step back. "Of course."

With one more glance at Aleister that I hoped was reassuring, I headed in the direction the blackmailer had pointed to.

"It's the last door," he said. His voice had the smallest of tremors in it.

I nodded and walked down the long hallway to it.

The bathroom contained just a ceramic sink and a large silk screen that most likely hid the toilet. It was nowhere near as overdone as the rest of the house, which led me to believe it wasn't meant for guests.

"I'll be just a moment," I said.

"Yes...yes, of course. Take all the time you need. Your husband and I will be waiting to guide you back to the festivities."

If he doesn't boil you from the inside out before I return.

I forced a smile and closed the door behind me.

Now what? It was obvious Geary knew something was not quite right with the two of us, perhaps even that we posed a danger to him. He was not nearly as idiotic as he looked.

Damn it! Had we lost this chance?

As I walked to the sink to turn the water on for Geary's benefit, my eyes caught a streak of unexpected color from behind the silk screen. For a moment, I feared that it was a person, that I'd walked in on someone using the toilet and would have to retreat in a flurry of apologies, but no one spoke out. Frowning, I stepped closer to the screen.

It was a window. A small square of stained-glass that dragged up flashing memories of those cold mornings in church with Peter. It had been constructed just a few inches above my head, so that I couldn't look out of it unless I hoisted myself up on its narrow ledge, but it did have a latch. Which meant it could be opened.

The idea had taken its shape by the time I walked back to the sink, turned on one of its faucets to mask any noise, and returned to the window.

The latch shifted easily in my hand. I gripped the window's frame and tugged it up. The wood didn't squeak or crack, but rose on well-oiled rails.

I opened it just an inch or so, just until I felt a breeze of fresh night air brush my face. That was all I would need for what I had in mind.

With a quick look to ensure that no one who stepped into the room would notice what I'd done, I turned the faucet off, and walked back out into the corridor.

"I hope you are feeling better now, Lady Blake," Geary said, having regained the kind of oily smile that deserved a fist through its center. The effects of Aleister's powers had apparently worn off completely. Pity, that.

"Oh, yes, thank you. A splash of water can work miracles."

He offered me his arm but I pretended not to see it, heading right past him toward Aleister who still watched everything from the door to the refreshment room.

"Lord Blake," Geary said from the middle of the corridor, "I just recalled I have some things to take care of that require my immediate attention. I think it best if we leave our business for some other time."

Aleister's smile could have covered the entire house with ice. "Of course. I am at your disposal."

The damage was done, we would gain nothing from talking with Geary anymore and Aleister knew it as well as I did. He offered me his arm.

In silence, he and I walked back out into the refreshment room still overrun with servants scurrying right and left to clear the damage.

"You couldn't keep him distracted for more than five minutes?" I said under my breath when we had made it past a large group of still dazed guests.

"He insisted he needed something from his study before we could discuss business and there was no dissuading him. Believe me, I made all manner of attempts. He even left his blasted sister behind to make sure I didn't go anywhere." His eyes flashed with irritation. "I had to bring an entire chandelier crashing down to distract her long enough to get away."

"So that's what that sound was, then."

He nodded. "And she was fortunate I didn't bring it down on *her*."

I snorted and looked at him. The anger I'd felt directed at Geary just seconds ago had already faded, but there was annoyance written on the crease of his forehead, on the tightness of his jaw.

"I suppose we've missed our chance," he said, returning a guest's bow with a sharp nod. "He won't leave his study unguarded now that he clearly suspects we're not who we say we are."

"No, you're right. He won't. Which is why I've thought of something else."

Aleister turned to me. "You have?"

"Yes, and I think it'll work. But I'm going to need to fetch something from the house."

He shrugged. "All right. What is it that you need?"

I gave him a sideways glance and a grin. "A pair of your trousers."

FIFTEEN

"YOU WOULD MAKE A lousy seamstress, Nora."

I looked down at the ragged, fraying hemlines on both trouser legs. "Can't say I disagree. Peter was always much better at sewing than I was."

I yanked loose a dangling bit of thread and moved my legs against the damp grass to find a more comfortable sitting position.

We'd left the ball immediately after I'd shared my new plan with Aleister, slipping out of Geary's estate without drawing any notice. I'd half expected people to chase after us on the blackmailer's order, but no one so much as looked our way as we grabbed our coats and hailed our carriage.

We headed straight back to the house. According to Aleister, most balls ended close to one or two in the morning, which meant we'd have plenty of time to prepare.

I'd taken a pair of scissors to the trousers he'd handed me and which I now wore, hacking at them until they no longer dragged on the floor when I stepped into them and tightening the suspenders that would keep them in place. I would have preferred my old trousers but if they still existed they were probably Sarah's now.

Wearing something of Aleister's felt odd, but there was no other option. I couldn't do what I needed to do in layers of skirts and a bustle, so unless we wanted to rob a clothes shop in the middle of the night, his trousers were the next best thing.

Around one, we hailed a regular cab and returned to Geary's estate. A number of carriages were starting to depart when we arrived, the confusion making it easier for us to walk into the grounds without drawing attention to our presence. We chose a spot from where we could see the stained-glass bathroom window and sat down to wait.

And then wait some more.

"This is rather dull, isn't it?" Aleister murmured, when about three-quarters of an hour had passed and people were still moving about in the house.

I shrugged. "I'm used to it. It's not very different from waiting for rats to return to their nests or to make a sound and reveal their presence."

"That sounds terrible."

I smiled. "Sometimes it was. In the summer, especially, when I had to sit still inside walls for hours at a time. On some days, I thought I would melt from the heat. Compared to that, this is much better. It's even better than still being in that ball with all of those people."

After a beat of silence, he spoke again. "I meant to apologize about what happened earlier. With Geary, I mean. I hope I didn't frighten you."

"You didn't."

He smiled. "I didn't think so, but I'm so used to humans reacting with fear that I can never be sure. Not many can claim not to be afraid of the Devil and honestly mean it."

"Ah, but that's because they haven't lived with you for weeks. You forget I've seen you mutter to yourself when you drop silverware and grimace when your coffee is not sweet enough."

His laughter was soft but bright. "That is true. Is that all it takes to make me less frightening? Seeing me in a more domestic setting?"

"Well, it doesn't hurt." I smiled and turned to look at him. "But would you have seriously harmed him? Geary?"

"Yes. If he hadn't released you I might have even killed him. As it was, the only reason Geary is not now in the care of physicians is because you stopped me."

His words created a flutter in my stomach that I couldn't identify. "You would have needed time to recover after using that kind of power on a human, and just when we could least afford it."

"It was impulsive, I know, but then that has gotten me into trouble now and then. I thank you for intervening."

I nodded.

Questions about what had happened even earlier, what had caused him to lose control of his own powers, once more sprouted. There was so much I wanted to ask now that we were alone and could speak without being overheard, but we had returned to our usual, comfortable companionship and I was hesitant to shatter it.

So I let the minutes pass in silence, Aleister's presence like a pulse against my skin, until the lights started to go out room by room in the house in front of us. First the top floor darkened, where Geary and whatever guests had stayed behind slept, like in most grand houses, and then the ground floor as the servants dragged themselves to bed.

We continued to wait until the house stilled, until we heard no sounds at all from inside.

Then it was time.

Kicking off my shoes, I slunk out of our hiding spot. Aleister made to do the same.

"What are you doing?" I asked.

He frowned. "Going with you, of course."

"Unless you can turn into a miniature version of yourself or into fog or something, I don't think you can fit through that window."

"Of course I can't—"

"So you're planning on doing what, then? Just stand by it in a casual manner?"

Aleister held my gaze for a moment before lifting an eyebrow and giving me a small, curled smile. "I suppose not."

"I can handle this," I said. "I've done this type of thing countless times."

"Don't you at least need help reaching the window? You are rather small."

I rolled my eyes and started to walk away. "Even my five-year-old self could have managed that."

He chuckled softly, leaning back against the tree again.

The truth was that I was looking forward to doing this. My heart raced as I walked to the window, not from fear or worry, but because it'd been too long since I'd stepped into a house that wasn't mine to take something that didn't belong to me. I'd forgotten how much I enjoyed doing what I wasn't supposed to.

The bathroom window was as I'd left it, open just enough to let me slide my fingers in and tug the whole thing up as much as I could from the ground, which I did quickly. I braced my arms against the sill and jumped, pulling myself up until my entire torso rested on the ledge. I winced as the movement placed pressure on the bruises the corset had left on my ribs. With a hand, I shoved the stained-glass panel farther up.

Trying to make as little noise as possible, I slid one leg up and then the other, until I was sitting on the windowsill. After a glance back at Aleister to let him know everything was fine, I leapt lightly onto the bathroom floor and smiled when I landed without a sound.

Hadn't lost the skill yet.

I padded on bare feet to the door and opened it. Had it made that loud a squeak a few hours ago?

I held my breath, listening for sounds. Except for the dry ticking of a clock, the house was silent.

Walking out of the bathroom into the dark corridor, I waited a second for my eyes to adjust. There wasn't any furniture in the way as far as I could remember, but I didn't want to run into a vase or statue and bring it crashing to the floor. Better to be safe.

Once I was confident I'd be able to make out the outline of objects in my path, I started down the corridor. With my bare feet as sure on the wooden floor as always, I turned away from the exit to what just hours ago had been the refreshment room, and started down the next hallway to the locked door I was sure was the study's.

I listened for sounds from inside but heard nothing beyond my own thumping heart.

My hands were steady when I reached into my hair for the ruby pins and inserted them into the lock. I'd never been one to lose my concentration or my skill when nerves made my blood rush, and I was glad to see that hadn't changed.

I started tapping tumblers up.

The lock lasted just a handful of seconds before submitting. It could have been faster, since it was only a four-tumbler lock, but then, I hadn't had a chance to practice. I would have to tell Aleister to buy me a set of padlocks or I might lose the agility that had taken me years to acquire.

There were no lights on in the room, but the moonlight easing in through the gap between the curtains was strong enough to reveal a large desk, bookcases on most of the walls, and a couple of armchairs. Definitely a study.

I walked over to the bulk that was the desk. As Aleister had said, it had truly hideous depictions of fat angels carved on its sides. The surface of it was bare, with not a single piece of paper on it, not even a fountain pen or an inkwell. If I'd had any doubts that Geary made his wealth by dishonorable means, this bareness would have ended them. A man with a legitimate business would have things on his desk, stacks of papers, letters to read, half-written answers to finish and mail. Especially if said desk was in his home, behind locked doors.

I parted the curtains and peered outside, but the window's angle was wrong and I couldn't see Aleister. I would have liked to at least seen his profile. The sudden realization of this made me frown and clench my jaw before I was able to shrug it away and turn back to the job at hand.

"Let's do this, then," I whispered, kneeling in front of the desk.

The drawers on the right side of it were unlocked, so I didn't bother with them yet. It wasn't likely Geary would keep something as important as what we needed just a tug of a handle away in a house full of servants.

The three locked drawers on the left were much more promising.

I picked open the first one.

It was full of thin cloth-bound ledgers, which themselves were stuffed with papers. Each ledger had a different name on the cover, most just a surname and some only initials. I flipped the one at the top of the pile open, squinting in the dim light to be able to read the tight script.

It was a record of a man's indiscretions with his mistress, a list of addresses and dates, along with a signed statement dated four years ago declaring Geary had been hired to make that mistress vanish for a sum of five hundred pounds.

The next ledger had the same kind of meticulous records of dates and locations, but this one had been signed by a woman who'd hired Geary to recover a forged painting she had sold off as the real thing. Scotland Yard was on the trail and she wanted all evidence that led back to her gone. It'd been signed almost three years ago.

On and on. Each ledger a binding contract between Geary and the idiots who had believed he could solve their problems. He had promised them theft, murder, revenge, and anything else they so desperately needed and they'd fallen for it.

How had he managed to get them to sign these papers, though? Didn't they know not to leave anything in writing if they could avoid it?

But no, perhaps they didn't. I'd stolen enough things from rich people to know they were much more naïve than they looked. Much more likely to take you at your word if you nodded enough times and listened to them without interrupting. And all of these people were rich, there was no doubt about that. Geary wouldn't have bothered with them, otherwise.

I glanced through the other ledgers, but none of them held the information I was looking for. Closing that drawer, I turned my attention to the next one.

It, too, was stuffed with papers that could unravel entire lives. Name after name, signature after signature. It was hardly a wonder that Geary was able to afford this luxurious house and his comfortable lifestyle. There had to be at least seventy different people he was blackmailing. Perhaps more.

But it wasn't just blackmail. Geary was involved in all manner of illegal activities, from the smuggling of antiquities out of locations I couldn't begin to pronounce to the rigging of the Ascot horse races.

From what I could see as I sifted through page after page, anything illicit occurring in London these days was tied to Geary in some form or other.

I started through this next pile of ledgers, a bit faster now, searching for that one name: *Pandemonium.*

The problem was that there was no order I could see to the files. It was just as if Geary had shuffled them like a deck of cards before storing them.

Just when I was reaching the bottom of the drawer and thought I would have to move on to the next one, a solitary initial caught my eyes.

P.

A flare of excitement rushed through me as I opened the ledger. I smiled.

"Found you," I whispered, flipping through the pages. There was the prime minister's signature on the inspection papers, as well as a few pages detailing the date, time, and location when the ship would dock.

I blinked. It was tomorrow night at midnight, at the East India Docks.

We'd done it! Now all we had to do was rescue the girls and the wings tomorrow night. We'd already toyed with some ideas about how we might do this, but we would have to see if we could put them into action once we got to the docks.

And then, when it was over, when Aleister had his wings back and the girls were safe, well, then we could do as we liked. Nothing stopped us, not now that I knew Peter was happy and that I would always be able to provide for him. I couldn't see him, but knowing he was safe, that he would go on to have a full life, had to be enough.

Perhaps it should have struck me as odd that that the idea of living the rest of my life with Aleister no longer bothered me, that the thought of it actually sent my heart beating faster. But, then, if I had any home at all now, it was with him.

Who knew? Perhaps he and I could even travel, visit places far beyond this city.

Imagine that, seeing the world with the Devil at my side.

I smiled as I replaced the other ledgers and closed the drawer.

I was almost at the door leading out of the study when something caught the attention of my magpie eyes. A twinkle. Whatever it was rested on top of a narrow table that I hadn't seen when I'd entered.

I headed directly for it.

The glitter came from a tie pin, still attached to a silk cravat.

Just a few weeks ago, I wouldn't have recognized what the object was at all. Peter had never needed to wear a tie pin and we wouldn't have been able to afford one even if he had, but Aleister had three or four of them that I'd noticed. They were meant to hold the cravat in place, keeping the folds perfectly crisp and unmoving while at the same time adding an ornament to the gentleman's outfit.

This pin was the prettiest one I'd seen yet. Made into the shape of a large bird in silver and with two green stones for its eyes that I would have bet my right hand were emeralds, it was much too majestic for someone as vile as Jonathan Geary.

I pulled it out of the fabric folds and looked at it closer.

In the second it took me to realize what kind of bird made up the head of the pin, I knew it would be leaving in my pocket.

It was a cormorant. The animal that Satan had turned into on his first visit to Eden to spy on Adam and Eve. Or at least it was according to *Paradise Lost*. Unlike the snake, which he had only possessed, Satan had become the cormorant. Transformed into it.

I knew very well it was a lie, for Aleister himself had told me he couldn't change shape, but it was a pretty lie. I could just picture him at the top of the Tree of Life, black wings glossy in the sun, his sharp eyes scanning the fields for those first two humans.

A creak from the floor above me made me clutch the ledger tighter and stuff the pin into one of the trouser pockets. I'd lingered long enough. It was time to leave.

I left the study with *Pandemonium's* information under my arm and started down the corridor, turning the corner toward the refreshment room's door a few seconds later.

At once, I came to an abrupt stop, my heart leaping into a gallop.

Before the door stood a shadowy figure a shade darker than the gloom around me.

It growled, a sound that was full of teeth.

A dog. Geary had a guard dog.

It wasn't an especially large animal, not nearly as large as some others I'd seen rummaging through garbage in the streets, but it was big enough to stop me. To make me consider a retreat. I knew, though, that if I turned and ran it would give chase and it would catch me easily. If I had learned anything after all of my years of scurrying after rats was that four legs always outran two.

I glanced around me for anything I could use as a weapon, but the corridor was as bare as it had been earlier. Unless I wanted to pelt the dog with the ledger, which would do nothing but anger it, I would have to deal with this animal in some other way.

Slowly, I began to bend down, ready to make myself smaller, less of a threat, but the dog's growls only intensified.

Bloody hell.

"It's all right," I murmured. "I'm not going to hurt you."

The dog took a step forward, a snarl ripping from its throat. It would never allow me to get to the corridor just a few steps to my left, let alone all the way down to the bathroom.

I heard the hissing first. A violent exhalation followed by high chittering that I recognized very well.

From the corridor I needed to enter leapt another dark figure, catapulting itself through the air and right onto the dog's head.

It was a rat, and I didn't need to look twice to know *which* rat.

The force with which the large, black rodent landed shifted the dog off balance, a whimper of surprise tangling in its growls. With agility that looked improbable in an animal of its size, the rat shimmied up to the top of the dog's head, far away from its gnashing teeth, and bit down right between its eyes.

The dog snarled, twisting about in an attempt to dislodge its attacker, but it was of no use. I'd been in that situation and I knew nothing short of a blow to the head would unclench the rat's jaws.

The growls warped into yelps as the dog turned in circles, contorting itself. Forgetting all about me.

This was my chance.

I ran the last few steps to the corridor on my left and raced down to the bathroom. I hesitated for only a moment, turning to look back in the direction of the growling and screeching, but I still had no viable weapon, nothing I could fight the dog with. I couldn't help. The only thing I could do was not waste the time the rat had bought me.

Stuffing the ledger between my teeth, I pulled myself up onto the windowsill again and swung my legs back out. With a whisper of sound, I landed on the moist grass and ran to Aleister, who had risen to his feet as soon as he'd seen me.

"What happened?"

"A dog," I said in between gasps. "Geary has a bloody guard dog."

Aleister frowned, his eyes traveling up and down my body in search of injuries.

I shook my head. "Your rat servant distracted it so I could get away. I'm fine."

Some of the tension eased out of him. "Good."

There wasn't even a trace of surprise in his face or voice at the mention of the rat. "I take it it's not a coincidence that it was here, then."

"No. I called him to me as soon as we settled down to wait and sent him in after you."

"Oh, so you assumed I wouldn't be able to do this on my own."

"What I *assumed*, Nora, was that I'd be much more comfortable while waiting here like an imbecile if I was certain you had help on hand should you need it. Which you did."

I nodded with a sigh. "Which I did. Fine. But what about the rat? It's still in there."

Aleister motioned back toward the house. I followed his eyes to the window I'd just climbed through.

A large black shape perched on the sill more gracefully that I could ever have done. It glanced in our direction for a moment before it jumped down to the grass and took off into the night.

A surprising ripple of relief coursed through me. What I felt for the rat wasn't exactly affection, but I was glad it hadn't had to sacrifice its life for me.

"He's under my protection," Aleister said. "Not very much can harm him. Certainly not a dog."

My grip on the ledger tightened as his words brought back a sudden memory of my last night at the Lantern, when that black rat had seemed to dart away from all danger, had seemed to be more than an ordinary rodent. But Aleister himself had denied that it was the same animal, and why would he lie? There was no reason for it, now.

No. The rat I'd seen had been killed by those dogs and then had either been tossed away or burnt to ashes. This one just happened to look similar to it, that was all.

Aleister glanced down at the ledger in my hands, bringing my mind back to the present. "Seems like you were successful despite the canine's intervention."

"Yes. This is everything we need. *Pandemonium* will dock tomorrow night."

Aleister's eyebrows rose.

"Just about missed it, didn't we?"

I held the ledger out to him but he shook his head. "I think we'd better leave the estate before anyone gets out of bed and catches us. We are quite visible."

He was right. We were both standing in front of the bushes that had hid us for the past few hours, in plain sight of anyone who might happen to peer out of the first or second story windows that looked out at this part of the grounds.

I turned, ready to walk toward the front of the house, but Aleister placed a hand lightly on my arm.

"We can't go that way. I heard the guards talking at the gate."

"They're still there?"

"I'm afraid so."

Damn it. One more complication. "Right. Well, we'll have to go over the wall, then."

Aleister groaned. "In these shoes?"

"You have your own self to blame," I said, heading toward the closest section of the stone wall surrounding the estate. "I did tell you to wear something more sensible."

Aleister chuckled. "Well, if you can't wear your finery to a robbery, just when can you?"

With a roll of my eyes, I walked the rest of the way to the wall and placed my hands on the grooves the stones in front of me created. Summoning all the energy I had left after this endless day, I pushed off the ground, and began to climb.

I was over the wall in a couple of minutes, jumping lightly to the ground in almost complete silence.

And from there I had a wonderful spot from which to watch Aleister struggle with his shoes' slippery soles, pressing a hand against my mouth to keep my laughter from waking up the entire house as he cursed under his breath with surprising creativity.

"Some of those I've never heard before," I said when he finally stood beside me.

He wiped at his trousers. "Yes, well, that's because they date back to the Dark Ages."

I laughed. "You'll have to teach them to me some day."

"I suppose that's fair." He smiled and looked at me. "Shall we head home, then?"

"Yes, please."

"We'll have to walk for a couple of streets to hail a cab, I think."

I nodded. "That's fine. It's a nice night to walk, at any rate."

In comfortable silence, we started down the steps and away from Geary's home. The sounds of the city, carriage wheels, harsh voices, and screeching laughter, were muffled here, as if they were occurring half a world away.

"The dog, he truly didn't manage to harm you?"

I shook my head. "Not one bit. It would have been worth a few bites, anyway, to finally get the information we wanted. And just in time, too."

"You do want to go to the docks with me tomorrow night, then?"

I glanced at him. What a strange thing to ask. After everything we'd gone through to learn the truth, he couldn't think I would sit by and not try to help when it counted most.

"Of course I want to go," I said.

He nodded, but there was a tightness to his face that hadn't been there before. As if he were hesitating to say something.

"Is anything wrong?" I asked.

That tightness disappeared in a blink. Wiped clean from his face. "Not at all. I was just thinking that if all of this ends tomorrow, we'll have to find something else with which to entertain our minds."

I smiled. "I was thinking that a few minutes ago, too. We'll find something, I've no doubt. We're nothing if not inventive."

"That, we are."

A horse whinnied not too far away, the sound echoing across the cobblestones and making both of us look toward it.

This peculiar peacefulness, this sensation that Aleister and I were apart from the rest of the world, would soon be over, then. At the next turn, we would start seeing carriages and people, even at this late hour, their movement and noise breaking this unexpected calm. It would have been nice to delay all of that just a bit longer.

I hadn't even given him the tie pin, yet. I could do it in the cab, I supposed, or even back at the house, but somehow that didn't seem right. It felt like something I should do now, while we were on our own, before we were caught up in the excitement of planning for tomorrow. Something to mark *this* evening.

With a breath that stirred up a surprising ripple of nerves, I reached into my pocket and brought the pin out.

"I...I saw this at Geary's house and thought you should have it," I said, stretching my hand toward Aleister. "A gift, I guess."

He stopped walking so abruptly, I went on for a couple of steps before I realized he wasn't moving anymore and had to turn around completely to see his face.

A frown creased his forehead as he watched me, but his expression was unreadable. He was encased in that unnatural immobility that always revealed his "otherness."

I swallowed the sudden dryness in my throat and stepped closer to him, holding the pin up. "It reminded me of you because it's a cormorant, see? The bird you supposedly turned into in *Paradi—*"

"*Paradise Lost*," he finished. His voice was soft, no more than a brush of air.

I nodded. "I know you can afford to buy countless more beautiful ones, but I saw it and wanted you to have it."

He lowered his eyes from me to the pin, his frown deepening as he broke his marble stillness to take it carefully from my hand. His fingertips brushed the bird's silver wings.

"I don't think..." he began, but stopped and shook his head. "No, I'm *sure*, no one has ever given me a gift before."

I frowned, his words heavy in my head. It hadn't even crossed my mind that someone who had lived so long in this world could go through it without being given something. Perhaps in theory it would have been obvious, because no one would willingly give the Devil a gift that wasn't part of a bribe or a bargain, but this wasn't theory. It was reality and it involved Aleister, who could be kinder, fairer, than many of the humans I'd met in my seventeen years. Did he deserve this kind of endless isolation and rejection? Did anyone?

"Never?" I finally said, blinking. "Not even when you had your wings?"

He shook his head.

"Oh, but it's not even a proper gift!" I said. "I just stole it. If I'd known, I would have gotten you something else. Something better."

Aleister looked up at me. "It's perfect, Nora. Truly."

He meant it. I knew him well enough now to see that in the soft, genuine smile on his lips, in the way it traveled up to his eyes. His expression made my heart beat just a bit faster.

He lifted his free hand to the deep green cravat that had replaced the bow tie he'd worn to the ball and pulled out the pin that held it in place with a sharp tug. He allowed it to clatter to the pavement without so much as a glance and bent his head to adjust the folds of the necktie again.

He'd have a hard time doing that without a mirror.

"Here," I said, reaching for the silver pin. "Let me."

He hesitated, but I didn't.

I plucked it from his palm and drew closer, bringing my hands up to the cravat. The silk was cool as it whispered under my fingers, soft as the night air. I tucked its folds in a similar manner to how they'd looked a moment ago and slid the pin in, catching the slippery layers with its sharp end. With a nod of satisfaction, I straightened the cormorant until it rested in the very center of the necktie and smoothed the fabric down.

It was only then, when my hands pressed against his chest, that I noticed how still Aleister had become under my touch. His whole body had stiffened. As if he didn't dare breathe.

I realized all at once how close together we stood. How quickly his heart was beating, much faster than any human's ever would, and how my own heart leapt to race with it.

Without more warning than the hairs on the back of my neck prickling up, the same energy I'd felt while we danced was suddenly rushing, swelling, over my skin.

My breath snagged as the power enveloped me. Warmth traveled up my legs, up my arms, making me feel as if all of me were glowing. The tips of my fingers, which were still resting against Aleister, vibrated with the force of the sensation.

I lowered my hands to my sides but I remained where I was. I knew I should step away, widen the distance between us until this rippling energy faded, but everything in me fought against that thought. I didn't want to obey it.

I wanted to draw closer still.

Lifting my head, I met Aleister's gaze.

The lights burst in the street, every lamp shattering at the same time. The night pressed against the two of us, the only brightness left in the entire world, it seemed, radiating out of Aleister's blazing eyes. Beneath us, the ground rumbled.

What is this? What is happening?

"I don't know," Aleister murmured, his voice ragged.

I swallowed. "You're reading my mind."

"I can't help it," he said with a breathless laugh. "Your thoughts fill my head. *You* fill my head."

He closed his eyes for a moment, as if trying to hold something back, as if trying to stop whatever this was. But there was no stopping it. His gaze was blinding when he looked at me again.

He touched my hand with his.

Without hesitation, our fingers enlaced.

A shiver raced up my spine, shaking me, waking every inch of my skin as though a current of electricity had shot into me.

The sensation spread through me and into Aleister, until he, too, shuddered with it. His fingers clasped me tighter.

The ground rumbled under our feet again.

My heart sped up as he brought his other hand to my face. He hesitated an instant before allowing himself to touch me, waiting for me to stop him, for me to take a step back, to flinch. But I didn't. I tightened my own grip on him, instead.

His fingertips finally brushed my forehead, his caress no more than the whisper of feathers.

I gasped at the immediate way my skin responded again to his slightest touch, becoming alive under it. Like this was what it had been waiting for all along.

Aleister's fingertips slid down the bridge of my nose to my lips, tracing their shape, their curves and ridges, as if he were memorizing them. His burning eyes returned to my own gaze with every move, always searching for fear or discomfort, for a sign that he should stop.

Aleister.

It was the only thing I could think, the strongest reassurance I could offer in my tangle of thoughts.

My rapid breath pressed against his fingers when I couldn't keep my lips closed against his caresses anymore.

The pavement beneath us shook like it would split in two, like it would destroy everything around us, but I only noticed it in a vague way, as if it were happening somewhere far away from where the two of us were. I felt no fear. I could feel nothing but Aleister's touch.

His thumb grazed my chin, down the length of my neck, his fingers then sweeping up to touch my cheek, leaving a tingling trail on my skin wherever they went.

How long? How long had I wanted this and had been too stubborn to allow myself to recognize it? Because I did want it. My body glowed under his every touch, it ached with the growing need to hold him, to feel his arms around me. It was as if a hunger I'd been ignoring had finally taken over.

A soft sound I didn't recognize escaped my throat when his fingers lingered on my cheek and I brought my own hand up, placing it over Aleister's and pressing it down until his palm cupped my face. I could hear, could feel, his heart beating, his blood rushing under his skin, pulsing against me. Closing my eyes with a shiver of pleasure, I leaned into his touch.

He sucked in a breath and the pavement beneath us ripped open with a savage tearing sound.

In an instant, the weight of his hand disappeared. My fingers suddenly clasped nothing but night air.

I opened my eyes, already knowing what I would see before I did. Already feeling the loss.

Aleister was gone.

Panting, the echo of his touch still on my skin, I turned around.

That was when I saw what we'd done.

Spanning the length of the entire street was the proof that we had been here together, that we had held each other so closely. That something we couldn't take back had just happened between us.

A wide, jagged rift like a scar had opened up in the pavement, revealing the ink-black depths of the earth. The ground on all sides of the opening had ripples of movement frozen through it from the force of the power that had made it, and these ripples reached up to the flanking homes, where they had cracked the stone steps, the white facades, the wooden doors. Where they had shattered windows.

I turned away from the destruction, lifting my gaze to the cold stars above me until my breathing slowed, allowing my heart to settle.

I had to make sense of all of this, of what I felt and of what Aleister felt.

I couldn't ignore it. Not after tonight. Not anymore.

SIXTEEN

"IS HE BACK YET?" I asked.

Long-Neck shook its head.

I sighed and closed the front door behind me. "All right. Don't bother with dinner for me, but could you put some food out for the rat waiting outside?"

The shadow nodded and hurried to do as I said.

The black rat had appeared just moments after Aleister left, ordered to my side, as always, to ensure I returned safely home. But I hadn't wanted to go back to the house yet. My mind had been too full of questions, too dark with confusion.

No, what I'd needed was to walk. And that was what I'd done, inviting the silent animal to my side.

The two of us must have been a strange sight as we made our way down one street swirling with fog after another, a young woman dressed in ragged trousers escorted through the lamp-lit night only by the large rat at her feet that hissed and chittered at anyone who got too close.

Onward and onward I'd led us, turning corners at random, crossing muddy streets for no other reason than the need of continuous movement while I pried my mind, my heart, open and looked inside.

Love. My experience with it was narrow. All of my life, it had applied only to my brother. It was the only context in which I understood it. I'd certainly never been *in* love, hadn't had so much as a flirtation with any of the young men I'd met at the Lantern or anywhere else in my other life.

Despite that, I did know what physical attraction and carnal love were. What they meant and what their consequences could be. Peter had attempted a clumsy explanation years ago, which had ended with his face turning the color of a beet and me having to search out one of the prostitutes that frequented the Lantern to get the answers I needed. And I had gotten them.

Which was why I knew that the easy-to-quench version of love I'd learned about sitting at the pub's bar was not what I felt.

Yes, Aleister was unnaturally handsome, and yes, my body had reacted strongly to his touch tonight, but it hadn't been his face that had first endeared him to me. That had allowed me to accept him and grow comfortable in his presence after he'd told me the truth. He had been handsome from the night we met, but I'd only grown fond of him when I'd gotten to know him. It had been his mind, the similarity of our sharp thoughts, the way our personalities fit together as perfectly, as naturally, as our hands had tonight that had done it. It had been the combination of all of what made him who he was.

I couldn't imagine now living without his dry irony, without hearing his real laughter, rare as it was, without seeing his instinctive flinch every time we walked into a small room as if he still had his wings to account for, without seeing him cock his head like a bird when I did or said something he found peculiar, without hearing the blade of intelligence in every word he spoke.

Finish that thought, then, Nora.

Yes, no more hiding.

I couldn't imagine living my life without him. I didn't *want* to imagine it.

And wasn't that love? In all of its forms?

I'd smiled into the night, then, my feelings suddenly so obvious I didn't know how I hadn't recognized them until now.

I loved Aleister.

The thought had lit an immediate warm glow inside me, a candle's flame of light, that I had carried all the way back to the house. That I still carried now as I walked into Aleister's study and sat down on the leather sofa.

But could the Devil return that love? Could he love at all?

I undid the laces on my shoes and kicked them off.

It had felt possible tonight, in the softness of his caresses and the way he'd responded to my own, in the way his powers had slipped his control. Even in his fleeing. But I couldn't be entirely sure. Not with him.

With a sigh, I leaned back, the movement allowing the lamp's light to fall on my left hand. On the wedding band I still wore.

The weight of the past few days suddenly fell on me, a wave of exhaustion tugging me down into the sofa. Not that surprising after everything the two of us had done. And then, of course, I'd just spent an hour walking and battling with my thoughts. I'd earned this exhaustion, inconvenient as it was.

I would fight it. I could rest later, after I'd seen and spoken with Aleister. Not now.

I would wait for him.

I would wait.

The sensation of falling woke me.

"It's all right, Nora," Aleister said softly, his voice so close to me I felt it thrum on my skin.

It took my tired mind a moment to wipe the confusion away and to remember, a moment for everything to rush back in.

His soft touch and blazing gaze. The cracking streets. The candle-flame glow I'd found within me.

I opened my eyes.

We were moving. But, no, that wasn't right. Aleister was moving, walking, and he was carrying me. The impossibly quick beating of his heart was in my ear, his strong arms cradling me as he took us down the familiar corridor. The one that led to my room.

My smile was soft with relief as I pressed myself against him, reveling in his nearness. Curling my fingers around his waistcoat, I closed my eyes again for just a moment more to try to slow time down, to keep this from ending. Trying to memorize what this felt like so that I could hold on to it if he vanished again.

Beneath us, the house rumbled, a continuous groan that had no beginning and no end.

He opened the door to my room and brought us inside. His eyes were the brightest thing in the darkness, brighter than the moon sifting in through the uncovered windows, brighter than the cormorant pin catching its light at his chest. Carefully, he ducked under the carved wooden frame and lowered me onto the bed.

The house's shaking dimmed under the growing noise of my own heart.

There was too much I wanted to ask him, too much I wanted to say, and now that he was right here, I didn't even know where to begin.

Aleister smoothed a curl away from my face, letting his fingertips brush my skin just for an instant. So many expressions and thoughts swept through his radiant eyes as he gazed down at me that I couldn't read them before he turned away, blinking rapidly and shifting to reach for the cufflinks on the night table. Gently, he placed them in my hand.

But they weren't what I wanted. Didn't he realize it?

With a sharp breath, I allowed them to fall, to tumble to the floor, and took his hand. The house shuddered.

"Aleister," I said. "Stay here with me. Please."

He exhaled harshly and sat down at the edge of the bed, his hand squeezing mine, grasping it as if I were about to be ripped away. He turned his head, so that I could only see his profile.

I sat up, drawing closer. "Aleister," I whispered.

He hesitated. I felt it, I saw it in the way his body tensed, in the way he closed his eyes. But why?

I touched his arm, wanting his voice and his silence at the same time.

He spoke again. Said two words in that twisting language I'd heard only once all those weeks before. They burned through me.

"What does that mean?"

His smile was the saddest one I'd ever seen. He turned toward me, untangling his fingers from mine before bringing my hand up to his lips. The simmer of movement and noise in the ground beneath us grew to a boil as he placed a lingering kiss on my palm.

Without a word, without giving me a chance to say anything else, to call him back and tell him what I'd only learned tonight, he rose and left the room.

The house seemed to splinter with his every step away from me.

Early as it was, Aleister had already left when I walked out of my room the following morning. My head pulsed with lack of sleep as I read the brief note he'd placed on the table by the door. He had duties to attend to but would be back as soon as he could.

This wasn't all that strange, I tried to tell myself when I began to feel a sinking sensation in my stomach. Many times during the past few weeks he'd been away during the day, after all.

But despite all of my self-reassurances, I couldn't stop a restlessness from growing as the minutes ticked by.

By noon, I couldn't sit still a moment longer.

Grabbing a handful of biscuits I had no real appetite for, I set off to walk the house, as I'd done when I was still trying to learn who Aleister was. How strange that day seemed. I'd been so frightened of him and of his house, something I couldn't even imagine now. I'd been so confused.

Well, I supposed *that* at least hadn't changed all that much.

I entered Aleister's bedroom and ran a hand along the carved wings that adorned his bed. Neither the pillows nor the sheets looked like they'd been touched. Did he even need to sleep? I hadn't ever thought to ask. There were a lot of things I hadn't thought to ask.

I walked down the corridor that led to the gate and the staircase that had almost crushed me, the hallway now much shorter than it had been, with just three or four rooms flanking it. They were empty. There was no longer any need to frighten me away from the second story.

For the briefest instant, I considered trying to climb over the gate to see if that would bring Aleister home. But I didn't. It would have been a childish thing to do.

When I could hardly stand the silence and stillness a moment longer, I left the house. I glanced up and down our street, knowing all too well I wouldn't see Aleister walking toward me. If he were traveling any streets at that instant, they wouldn't be human ones.

The rat was at my side after I'd taken only a few steps around the corner. It easily matched my pace, its eyes staring straight ahead, once again ready to fight off anything and anyone. It brought a surprising amount of comfort to have it beside me. How strange that was, to welcome the presence of a creature I had spent my entire life hunting, one I had only seen as a means to food and shelter.

I smiled at myself. Of all of this, I found *that* strange?

A carriage rumbled behind us, clattering closer at quite a quick pace. The rat chittered.

"Oh, it's all right," I said. "It's just a carr—"

A hand locked around my arm, yanking me backward. I opened my mouth to yelp in surprise but my voice disappeared against another hand and the wet cloth that covered it. It smelled sharp and biting, like alcohol. My stomach lurched at the scent, bile rising to my mouth.

I lunged forward with as much strength as I had, kicking out and tugging to get loose, but there was something funny happening to my limbs. They had lost consistency. My bones no longer felt like bones.

The street in front of me faded as I was lifted off my feet.

I screamed, or thought I did, but all I could hear was the sound of hooves against cobblestone, the creaking of the carriage as it started off again.

And then even that disappeared.

SEVENTEEN

PAIN TOOK ME BY the hand and yanked me out of the darkness.

The only thing I could register, at first, was the way my head throbbed. It felt like it had grown to twice its size, each of my heartbeats pounding against my skull like a clapper against a bell's bowl.

The voices came next. Male and distant. I couldn't hear what they were saying but I knew none of them was Aleister's.

I opened my eyes and flinched back from the lantern glowing in front of me, tears welling with the pain the light caused.

"My dear, how wonderful to have you back with us."

My breath caught, my head whipping towards\ the voice. The movement sent a spike of pain through my skull, making me groan under its power.

"I wouldn't try to move just yet," Jonathan Geary said. "Ether can have a nasty effect on the body."

Ether.

It all came back to me, then. The rat's hissing, the carriage, the vile cloth that had been pressed against my mouth. He had drugged me. He had taken me and brought me...where?

I jerked up to a sitting position and was almost ill. The dark room made a lazy turn around me, the lamp's burn cutting into my eyes until I had to close them. Saliva filled my mouth.

Geary chuckled. "I warned you, didn't I?"

Breathing slowly and carefully, I swallowed back the urge to vomit. The pain in my head receded enough to allow me to look again.

Wherever I was, it wasn't meant for human habitation. The walls were cracked and stained, the room cold and damp enough to have stiffened my limbs. The smell of mildew scratched at my throat each time I breathed. Underneath that odor, however, I thought I recognized a stronger, more pungent one. The smell of the Thames.

I looked down, and my breath knotted.

I saw the chains. I saw the cuffs around my wrists, the dark, soiled coils of metal that twisted like a serpent on the dirt floor in front of me, coils that led right to Geary's hands.

Noticing my gaze, he jerked his arm, making the chains rattle against the floor. "Do you like them? I think they look particularly lovely around your wrists, Nora. But then, you are a beautiful specimen. I thought so from the moment you first inserted yourself onto my path that day at the tobacco shop. I must congratulate you for that, actually." He chuckled. "Now that it's all over, I'm not ashamed to say you and your 'husband' had me fooled until the ball. I did have a few suspicions when I had you followed after our luncheon and learned you did not live at a Belgravia address as you had stated, but I didn't really know what you were after until that night. For that, I must applaud both of you."

He'd had me followed that time, too, then. I should have been more cautious. I should have known by then what kind of man he was.

"What do you want?" I hissed, my voice scraping against my dry and sore throat.

"Oh, nothing at all, my dear." He motioned to me with one hand at the same time that he rattled the chains with the other. "What I want, I already have."

"You don't know the mistake you've just made."

"You mean because of your companion? Aleister Blake or whoever he is?" He shook his head and smiled. "He is an odd man, I grant you that, but he'll be heading to the East India Docks, like the ledger you stole says. He and whatever authorities he's alerted about this special business of ours don't know that you and the rest of the cargo that will board *Pandemonium* are at the London Docks. We changed the location a week ago, as a precaution."

"But the inspection waiver—"

"When the prime minister is in your power, getting his signature on brand new papers is simple. What you stole from me is worthless."

A wave of fear swept through me, cutting through the rest of the ether's residue.

"So you see, my dear, you will be leaving our shores in chains. I will get the satisfaction of knowing you did not best me *and* you will be earning me a substantial sum, as well. A face like yours is worth quite a bit. It has actually been a very fortunate thing for me that you became involved in all of this."

I clenched my hands into fists to stop them from shaking. I'd be damned if I let Geary see my fear. Instead, I looked down at the cuffs that seemed to burn against my skin.

Come on, Nora. Think!

They were too small to be able to slip my hands through, I only had to look at them to realize that. They did have two keyholes to unlock them. If I could find something to pick them with—

"You can look at the cuffs for as long as you like, but you won't be unlocking them. I can assure you of that. I took the precaution of tossing the key into the Thames so you wouldn't pick it off me, and I will be watching you from now until you board the ship at midnight. Which," he said, and pulled out a pocket watch, "will be in just a few minutes."

Panic bloomed brightly. I'd been unconscious for that long, then, and Aleister hadn't found me. He didn't know where I was.

Unless I came up with a way to free myself, I would be boarding *Pandemonium*.

The thought launched me to my feet.

With a laugh, Geary yanked on the chains and brought me back down to my knees with a painful thud. I bit my lip to keep from groaning.

"You will get up when I tell you to do so."

I gathered as much saliva as I could and spat in his direction.

He gave the chains another yank. "You need to get used to this, Nora. This will be your life from now on."

The weight of his words was impossible to bear. My entire body, my entire being, began to tremble.

"Why do you do this?" I hissed.

Geary smiled. "For money, my dear. Lots and lots of money."

A man's booming yell made him flinch and turn to look at the only door in the room. Another voice shouted, the sound followed by a crash, and the thud of heavy footsteps began to race toward us.

"Geary!"

The door swung open, half-falling off its hinges, and a man ran in. On his heels came the dark smell of smoke.

"There's a fire!"

"What?" Geary turned his whole body away from me.

"A fire! In the building!" he said between gasps. "It just started on its own, leapin' up from one second to the next, and we can't put it out. It's growin' too strong, Geary."

I held my breath, my body tensing. Not daring to hope but doing so anyway.

A yell from the room beyond us was suddenly swallowed up by the crackle of flames.

"We need to get out of 'ere. The whole buildin' will burn."

Geary pointed to the door. "Go get the other girls and take them all outside."

The man nodded and did as he was told immediately, rushing out the door as Geary turned to me. He yanked on the chains.

"Get up."

I sat still, staring at him, the smallest of chances starting to take form in my mind.

"Get up!"

He grabbed more of the chains, wrapping the coils around his hand, before jerking me forward. I pulled with everything I had, only just managing to remain seated.

He stomped toward me and grabbed my arm as he had the night of the ball, tugging me to my feet.

If there was one thing I knew, one solitary thing, it was to always secure a wild animal by its head so it couldn't do what I was about to do now.

I leapt forward and sank my teeth right into his nose. I heard and felt a satisfying crunch.

He yelped, dropping the chains and staggering backward, his hands going to his face.

That was all I needed. Calling on the speed that had saved me from the monstrous spiral staircase, I darted down and grabbed as much of the chains as I could before taking off toward the door.

The next room was in flames, fire crawling up the walls and across crates and wooden boxes, as was the next room and the next, but I didn't stop, I didn't even slow down, running toward the opening in front of me that revealed night, cobblestone, and the glimmer of the Thames. With just that glance, I knew where I was. In one of the abandoned buildings near the London docks.

If Aleister wasn't out there, there were hundreds of spots in which I could hide. I could escape, I could—

I didn't see the man until it was too late.

He came out of a side door and slammed right into me, knocking me off balance. In an instant, he had a hold of me.

"Bitch," he said, his voice barely audible under the growing roar of flames.

He pulled me up by my hair and grabbed the chains before shoving me outside.

I turned to claw at him, to kick him where it could do the most damage, to do anything that might distract him enough to set me loose.

The blow, when it came, was swift and accurate. Fist connecting with my stomach, doubling me over. I saw Peter, his body as it collapsed that night in the alleyway, and I was unable to keep from echoing his movements with mine.

A deafening hiss filled the night.

I gasped.

As I watched, the cuffs around my wrists sizzled red, the metal bubbling up and separating from itself until it fell off me and morphed into flames.

Screams of pain and curses rose to join the hissing as the entire lengths of chains that had held me prisoner dissolved into fire.

"Nora, run!"

I was on my feet in a moment, ignoring the way my stomach ached, racing away from the men, past the black mass I barely registered as a ship, as *Pandemonium*, and toward Aleister's voice.

Heat rose behind me, the roar of fire becoming the sweetest sound I'd ever heard, and still I ran and ran.

Aleister was all at once in front of me, pulling me into his arms, holding on to me so tightly it was almost painful. Fury, the kind I had never felt before, radiated off him.

"You found me," I said into his chest.

"I should have found you sooner." His voice was tight, harsh. "The rat chased the carriage for as long as it could after you lost consciousness, but it couldn't keep up so I didn't know exactly where you were. I couldn't sense you, not until a few minutes ago when I heard your thoughts again. It's been hours..." Aleister tightened his grip on me. "I didn't know if you were even alive."

Somewhere behind us there were shouts and another sound, one that chilled me and brought back everything we needed to do: girls' screams.

I pulled away from Aleister, though it was the last thing I wanted to do. "I'm all right. They didn't do any lasting damage. Truly," I said when his eyes searched me for wounds. "But the other girls are not safe yet, and neither are your wings."

I looked behind me, past wall after wall of flames that Aleister had created to block us from the sailors that were pouring out of *Pandemonium*. At least two dozen men leaping off board to chase after us.

The ship itself loomed blacker than the night, than the water, its wide side pressed against the edge of the city. But this wasn't the actual dock. That was to the west of here. Had no one seen a ship this large just drop anchor where it pleased? Or was this the kind of power that the prime minister's signature could get you? The ability to do what you liked, where you liked?

"We have to get to those girls before they get them onboard," I said, because I could see why Geary had chosen this spot instead of the dock. It would be child's play to sail off from here. A matter of moments before the ship would be beyond reach.

Aleister nodded. "Come on. There may be a way."

He took my hand and we ran toward the end of the street, where a tall building I knew well separated this side of the Thames from the western docks. It was a building that had always caught my attention as a young girl because it was taller than all of the other ones around it, tall enough to compete with Big Ben, and because it had been constructed much too close to the water's edge. It wasn't even fully constructed, with disintegrating scaffolding that hadn't been used in years resting along some parts of its walls.

I knew what Aleister had in mind. To our right was a side passage, one that would take us back toward the ship using a street parallel to the riverline. From there, he might be able to use his powers to block off the men from the girls and from the ship. I would have preferred a more permanent solution for the kind of horrid beings who were happy to sell fellow humans for a few shillings, but that wasn't an option. Not without the risk of depleting Aleister's powers.

We started down this side passage but only made it a few steps before Aleister came to an abrupt stop. He placed a hand on my arm while he scanned the street.

"They're already heading this way," he said. "A large group of sailors. They'll cut us off in a few moments if we continue."

The flames behind us lit up the night enough to allow me to see a flicker of something I hadn't seen before in his eyes, not in all the weeks I'd known him. A spark of fear.

"What are we going to do?" I asked, hating the slight tremor in my voice.

"I might be able stop them, but—"

"No. You can't use up all of your powers now. We'll think of something else."

He locked his eyes on me for an instant before nodding and motioning me back with his arm. "Stand back."

Swallowing, I did as he said.

He moved his hand and another wall of flames rose in front of us, blocking the side street's entrance. Just in time, too, because no more than a few seconds later a man began shouting in frustration from behind the new burning barrier.

They couldn't reach us now, but we were also trapped among fire and stone. The river wasn't even an option, because setting aside my lack of swimming skills, the flames also blocked the water's edge.

"Come on," Aleister said, taking my hand and leading us back to the tall building's side.

The men now yelled and cursed at us from two different directions. I could hardly see them in the glare of the fires that kept them at bay, but the roar of the flames couldn't stop their voices, their obscenities, from reaching us. I forced myself to take a few steadying breaths. At least we knew *Pandemonium* wouldn't set sail yet. Not with all of the sailors still chasing after us.

I turned. "What are we going to d—?"

But Aleister was already doing it, running his hands up and down the brick walls that flanked us. "There's a thin ledge on the other side of this building," he said. "Pressed right against the water and hidden from view. It can get us back down past the sailors, but the only way to access it is by finding a way inside."

I joined him. I pressed my hands over the façade, but it was as solid as the cobblestones beneath me were. There were no weak spots.

Holding back the rising panic that wanted to flood out all reason from my mind, I ran in the opposite direction, back toward the side street. Sweat dripped down my forehead and down my legs, the heat of both fires surrounding me until it felt like my very blood would begin boiling. But there was scaffolding here, on this end, which the builders had used to reach higher up along the walls. Maybe there was a hastily patched up hole that would give way under my hand.

It was only when I drew nearer, when I looked closer at the collapsing wooden structures which hadn't been used in at least a decade, that I realized what I was seeing.

Stone steps cut right into the building's wall.

They'd been so covered in abandoned wooden planks, shredded canvas, mildew, and the shadows that always formed where the wall met the side street, that I had never noticed them in all of these years. I'd never had the need to until now.

I looked up. The steps went all the way to the top of the building, all the way to the flat cement roof. I couldn't remember if there was more scaffolding on the other side that we might use to climb down that way, but there might be a door on the roof that led into the building.

"Aleister! I've found stairs!"

He hurried to my side and glanced up.

"I don't know if there's a way down to the river bank," I said.

He took my hand once more. "It's the only chance we have to still do this. Let's go."

Ducking under the scaffolding and shoving aside a pail half-full of dried, cracking white paint, he led us up the seemingly endless steps. My legs burned with the effort of climbing and I was panting in seconds, but I didn't slow down.

Aleister halted me with a hand at the top and stepped onto the roof first to make sure it was sturdy and wouldn't collapse under our weight.

It was sturdy, but it also offered no solutions.

The narrow passage which pressed against the water was there below, as Aleister had said, but there wasn't any door to the inside or any scaffolding that would help us reach the ledge. Not so much as a rope. And the building was much too tall to attempt a jump, even into the water. It would be like diving into black stone.

Bloody hell.

Behind me, I heard the crackle of flames as Aleister created another wall of fire at the top of the stairs.

"I won't be able to sustain it for long," he said.

Frustration bit at me. We were losing our only chance of saving the girls. "There has to be a way down."

When he spoke, his voice was almost overwhelmed by the sound of the flames. "There is."

"I mean without using all of your powers."

He turned until I could only see his profile, his hands tightening into fists at his side. Something about his posture made my breath catch. "Yes. There is a way."

"Well, then, let's do it!"

He wouldn't look at me. A sudden chill raced down my spine despite the heat rising from the flames.

"Aleister, there's no time for this."

He stared at the fire, the fury of its power reflected in his eyes. His jaw tightened, as if trying to hold on to silence for a moment longer, to hold back the words I was asking for.

When he did finally begin, his voice was so low I had to draw even closer to hear him. "The only chance we have is if I get my wings, and my full powers, back now."

I frowned. "Yes, I'm sure that would be wonderful, but it's impossible to do from *up here* when your wings are all the way down there."

"No, it's not impossible."

I blinked, surprise taking my words from me for a moment. But only for a moment.

"If you can do it now, what the bloody hell are you waiting for?"

"I just...I haven't told you the truth, Nora. Not all of it, at least."

A bell-toll of fear echoed through me. "What do you mean? The truth about what?"

"About my wings." He exhaled and ran a hand through his hair. "Getting them back is much more complicated than I've made it seem."

"I don't understand."

"Even if I had them in my hands right now, I couldn't use them. I'm not allowed to unless I earn them, and I need one more thing to be able to do so."

He continued to stare into the flames, as if searching for the words within their light. His reluctance to look at me made my fear spread, knotting up my insides. Where was this leading? He could have told me all of this at the start, so why hadn't he? I knew him well enough now to realize there was a reason for it.

"What else do you need?"

His jaw tightened. "From the moment I was cast out of heaven, the only way I could get my wings back was if I found them and if I managed to obtain something that seemed so impossible it almost guaranteed I'd never get them back. And it did feel impossible until just a year ago, when I saw you for the first time. Because it is something that only you can grant me now."

His words brought back in a rush what he'd said the night of Geary's ball. "*You are not like any human I've ever known. You are unique.*"

And why was that? Come on, Nora. Why are you unique?

I felt the first stirrings of the truth within me.

The men below us had started flinging pieces of barrels against the building, curses and shouts chasing after them, adding to the noise of the fires. But I heard it all from a distance away because something had lodged itself in my throat, making it difficult to catch my breath. A doubt.

It wouldn't be. It couldn't.

I closed my eyes. "What, Aleister?"

"I had to get a human to love me."

With a shuddering exhale, I took a step away from him.

He ran a hand across his forehead and took a deep breath before starting again.

"Any human would do, but the person had to have full knowledge of who I was and still love me, still trust me. If I could find the wings and earn that love, they would be mine once again and I would have the power to return home."

He turned to me. A swift contraction of what looked like pain crossed his face as he met my gaze. "A year ago, I chose you, Nora."

"No," I said, and took another step away.

"Finding the wings themselves was no easy task. I spent centuries searching for them, with no success. It was only last year that I began to hear the first mutterings that sailors had found them, and I knew it was time to begin searching in earnest for the human who would make earning them possible. If that human even existed."

My teeth began to chatter together.

"When I saw you for the first time," Aleister said, looking away again, "you were dangling from a rooftop and shoving your arm into a hole that could have been filled with anything, and you were doing it all without a hint of fear. I saw your quick hands and even quicker mind, your ruthlessness, your fierce love for your brother. All of it in that one moment, and I knew you were the right one. So I waited for an opportunity to introduce myself into your life."

I winced, each word biting deeper into me. He had tricked me. Manipulated me. All of this time. Each gesture, each glance, each word, all of it had been a calculation. Even the fear and fury I'd seen in him tonight had been because I was something he needed, not someone he loved.

"The moment that blade sank into your brother's stomach, I decided it was time."

A streak of anger shot through me when I heard him speak with such ease of the worst thing that had ever happened to me. It pushed back the shock enough to allow me to find words again. "You used Peter, his death?"

"It hadn't been my plan, but yes, I did. It was an opportunity I couldn't allow to pass."

My stomach twisted. I could see the blood soaking my brother's shirt, I could feel it on my hands again.

I turned, bringing those hands up to my forehead to try to stop its unbearable pounding. This couldn't be happening. I would wake up at any moment, wouldn't I? And Aleister, the Aleister I knew and trusted and loved, the Aleister who would never have tricked or used me like this, would be with me.

"By then, I'd been watching you through the rat's eyes for months. Making sure you were safe," he continued softly, "learning what I could about you."

My mouth felt numb. All of me was numb. I couldn't feel my muscles as I turned again to face him. To face the stranger he'd become. "The rat, too, then. It *is* the same one I saw at the Lantern."

He met my eyes. "Yes."

It had really all been a lie, all of the past weeks. I'd been nothing more than a toy for him. The pain of that knowledge, of his betrayal, was staggering.

"You've lied to me from the very beginning."

"Yes, I have."

I pressed a hand against my torso to try to still a wave of nausea. "And what exactly did you expect from me? How was all of this going to end?"

The shouts of the men below us reached me as if from another world. They were still trying to get past the flames, which raged on.

Aleister looked over the edge. "Nora, we're running out of time—"

"Tell me." I turned my words into blades, wanting to hurt him as much as he had hurt me. "You owe me that much, Devil."

He flinched as if I'd struck him. He searched my face, though I couldn't imagine what he expected to find there. I held his eyes until he looked away with a sharp exhale.

"Once I was in the vicinity of the wings, you had to declare your love for me and they would be just as they were before I fell. I would have them back, as well as the rest of my powers."

"And what would happen to me in your perfect little plan?"

He shook his head.

"Tell me!"

"The instant I had my wings back, your soul would belong to hell."

I laughed, a sound that scraped my throat. "Of course. You would get everything you wanted, and I would be left to pay the price for all eternity."

The cormorant pin glittered in the flames as he moved closer. Another wave of nausea overtook me when I remembered last night, everything I'd realized I felt for him, everything I'd imagined he felt for me when he was just using me.

"And I thought...I *actually* thought..."

"What? You thought what?"

There was no point in holding anything back now, was there? "That you cared for me. That you could even love me." I scoffed. "I'm so stupid, oh, so, so stupid."

"That was all real, Nora." He reached for my hand but I yanked it away, the light from the fire dancing across the wedding ring I still wore. "That wasn't part of the plan. I wasn't pretending or lying. It might have started that way, but you've seen the effect you have on me with your own eyes, you've seen my lack of control when I'm near you. I've never felt anything like it."

I tried to laugh again, but it sounded more like a sob. "Do you expect me to believe you now?" With a jerk, I tugged the golden band off my finger and flung it with all the strength I had into the water. "You're a liar. All you do is lie."

A sucking sound drew my eyes to the ground so far below us. The glow of the flames had disappeared, the fire itself vanishing as quickly as it had started. The men hesitated for only a moment before launching toward the stairs that would lead them right to where we were.

"Nora," he said, the urgency in his voice like a warning light, "I know what you feel for me because it is the same thing I feel for you. If you just say the words I can get my wings back and get you safely off this rooftop."

I turned away but he grabbed my arms firmly, making me look at him again.

"You *need* to listen. There's only one barrier left and that won't hold for very long. I can't protect you against all of these men without my full powers."

"Let me go!"

"They'll take you. They'll put you on that ship. You have to choose me; you have to let me save you. With my wings, we could even help the girls."

"Choose *you*, someone who has betrayed me so entirely that there are no words for it, in the hopes that there is the least bit of decency in you to actually help me or them?" Laughter burst out of my throat, ripping through it and twisting into a scream of rage as it reached the air. "How could you do this to me?"

My heart hammered against my ribs. Fear knotted up my thoughts, muddled them, and there wasn't time. I was cornered. I would be forced to choose between chains while I lived and chains throughout eternity. Either way, I'd be a prisoner.

My whole being reared away from that as it would from flames.

No. Aleister wouldn't manipulate me anymore. I refused. He wasn't going to help me or the girls; he was just saying anything at all to convince me. Well, he had chosen the wrong person, then, because I wouldn't accept chains.

There was freedom in that thought. And, nestled within it, a third option.

As if sensing the course my mind traveled, Aleister reached for me again but I backed away.

He closed his eyes tightly for a moment. "Nora, I wanted to tell you. I started to so many times. I wasn't going to let you come tonight. I was going to stop you somehow. Lock you in the house to keep you from this, if needed—"

I shook my head. "And then what? Get me to declare my love for you when you got back with the wings? Trick me into it and then leave?"

"No—"

"You used me and you were going to continue to use me."

"This is who I am. I'm not a hero; you knew that."

My lips trembled as I tried to smile. "Well, who you are has just sentenced me to death."

I turned away from him and started toward the edge of the building.

He sucked in a breath when he realized what I meant to do, the sound mixed with a growl of pure fear, and his hand locked around my arm to hold me back. "No, stop it! Stop! I'll do everything I can to protect you, just stop."

"I don't need or want help. Not from you," I said, without turning around. My rage had condensed into a tight pressure in my very center that seemed to burn with its force. "Get your hand off me."

I felt him recoil as if I'd struck him, and he let go of my arm.

I didn't wait. With legs that shook fiercely and threatened to give under me, I stepped right up to the edge of the building. The black water tossed far beneath me, so dark it could have been a mirror for all it revealed of its depths. But it didn't matter. I knew what was waiting for me within it.

I almost laughed as it struck me that this was the nightmare than had haunted me for weeks. I was in it. I'd known from the very first night that Aleister would bring me to this, that I'd always been in danger, even when my waking mind didn't believe so any longer.

"Nora, please, the last barrier is breaking down," Aleister said, appearing by my side again. His hands reached out to me but stopped just short of touching me. "Please."

"I don't want anything more to do with you." I hated my voice for shaking, for being so fragile the night wind seemed to scatter it into nothing. "You don't have to stay and watch if you don't want to. Go get your precious wings. Then you can start your search for another bloody stupid human to seduce."

"Stop it!"

The men's shouts were drawing close enough that I could feel their voices against my skin. My entire body shook, my heart's pounding making it difficult to even think. Panic was taking over.

"There she is!" one of the men yelled behind us.

Aleister let out a hiss and turned.

And I waited no more.

I leapt into the night.

"No!" Aleister shouted, but it was too late.

The world went still and silent. For an instant, I hovered between the starless sky and the water, suspended between their opposing glassy depths. The only thing I could hear was my heart, beating furiously.

And then another of Aleister's yells cracked through that silence and brought back all of the noise and the movement.

I gasped, the sound echoing across the entire world, it seemed, and I was plunging, my limbs grasping for anything that would stop me.

But of course there was nothing. I was just falling and falling, the wind whipping through my hair, stealing the tears from my eyes with its power.

I felt the rumbling deep in my bones before I heard it. The monstrous surge of water that was woven through with Aleister's shouts, his voice twisted in the terrible language of angels.

A ship's prow suddenly pierced through the churning waves below me, rising and rising, wood creaking and snapping, splintering and shedding water as it was violently wrenched from the center of the river where it had once sunk and dragged to the very edge of the building I'd leapt from.

Its masts, like hands, reached up to me.

My screams tangled with Aleister's voice and the groans of the ship until the whole world was burning with sound.

And all I could do was fall and fall.

EIGHTEEN

SOAKED ROPES SCRAPED MY skin and jerked my left shoulder back as they caught my fall.

I gasped when pain bloomed as bright as fire, but I forced my arms and legs to wrap tightly around the half-rotten mast, my hands clutching at the ragged pieces of rigging.

Thoughts crashed against thoughts and I couldn't catch my breath. Blood dripped down my cheeks from a wound in my forehead, but I didn't wipe it off. I couldn't do anything but repeat to myself that I was alive. That the men hadn't gotten to me.

That Aleister—

No. Now was not the time to think about him or what he'd done.

As if confirming that, a crack resounded throughout the ship and the mast shook enough to make my heart lurch. I glanced down and saw water flooding the splintering deck, the dark waves starting to reclaim what had been stolen from them. Once Aleister's powers were exhausted, the ship would sink quickly, and I had to get back on shore. This wasn't over yet.

Because there was one thought that latched on to me now and focused my mind, sharpening it like a whetstone: I had to get to those girls. If there was one thing I could do to make this entire nightmare worthwhile, it was saving them. Damn everything else.

Wincing at the pain, I unwound my arm from the rigging, steadying myself against the cross where the mast would have met the sail if it hadn't disintegrated in the water, and cast my eyes about for a way off the ship.

It took only a glance to see that sinking was not the only problem. The force that had pulled this wreckage out of the Thames' floor in seconds was now propelling it headlong into *Pandemonium*. Even if I could get down to the deck on time, I wouldn't know how to begin steering this half-floating carcass away from the other ship before they collided.

But perhaps I didn't need to.

The idea had formed in an instant. Ignoring the sounds of splitting wood and rushing water, I looked for the girls.

They were huddled together on shore. The men hadn't been smart enough, then, to drag them onto the ship before launching after Aleister and me. Good.

That I could make out, there was only one man left to watch over them and *Pandemonium*: Jonathan Geary. His gaze remained locked in the direction of the building I had just leapt from, his whole body turned away from me. I resisted the urge to look back and see if Aleister was still there on the rooftop. He wouldn't be. He'd be trying to get his wings back.

I waited until I could almost reach out and touch one of *Pandemonium*'s sails and then, timing it as carefully as my tangled, frantic mind allowed me to, I propelled myself off the rigging, off the mast, and into the darkness once again.

Pandemonium's deck rose to meet me faster than I was prepared for, robbing me of all breath as my limbs connected with the wood. Around me, I felt the ship shudder as hull connected with hull. For a moment, my vision darkened, night crowding around it until only a pinpoint of light remained. I latched on to that light. If I lost consciousness now, it would all have been for nothing.

"She's here! She's on board!" Geary shouted. His voice swelled and receded like the water that shifted this blasted ship. Soon, the rest of the sailors would return and I would have no options left. I had to get up.

Biting down on my lips and calling on all the strength I had ever had, I forced myself to stand. My legs trembled and blood trickled from wounds too numerous to count but I walked forward.

"You little bitch," Geary yelled at me from shore. "I don't know how you managed to escape, but you won't do it again."

I ignored him and searched out for anything I could defend myself with. I didn't have a plan, nothing more concrete than to provide a distraction so that as many of the girls as possible could escape. Until I neared the open door that led into the ship's hold.

An oil lamp burned inside, dangling above piles of sacks and crates. Straw took up one entire side of the space, covering the floor until the wooden boards were completely hidden. What I had to do rushed at me all at once.

"You and that blasted man of yours. I'll make you both regret you ever came near me," Geary said.

I looked up and waved my hand sharply to catch one of the chained girls' attention, one of the older girls who had her arms wrapped around as many of the younger ones as she could manage.

"You can stop him," I shouted. "All of you can stop him if you're quick."

With a shaking hand, I pointed at her chains and at the only man who stood between them and freedom at the moment. I mimed a noose and even from the deck I saw her eyes flare to life. In an instant she was on her feet, her hoarse voice spreading the seeds of my plan among the rest. A wall of girls rose behind Geary amid the thunder of chains, the power behind the sound forcing him to turn around.

"Scotland Yard!" I called out. "Get rid of him and go to Scotland Yard!"

I didn't know if that would do any good, if the coppers would do anything for them when even members of Parliament were involved in these atrocities, but I couldn't think of anywhere else where they might have a chance of getting help.

Now for my part.

I half-climbed, half-leapt into the hold. The warm smell of wood and straw brought a tight smile to my lips. This would be easy and it would create a large enough distraction to allow the girls time to escape. They could take care of Geary, but if all of the sailors tried to corral them again...

Grasping a handful of dry straw, I pulled the lamp down and removed the glass that caged the flame.

No hesitation, now.

The straw caught easily. I blew on it gently to give it more life and lowered the flaming handful to the floor, creating another patch of fire. And another and another.

Fire as a shield, once again.

Crackling rose around me rapidly, heat once again lapping at my heels as I hurried deeper into the hold, the lamp and straw in my hands. I slammed the glass that held the oil against one of the ceiling's beams and smiled as the dark liquid splashed onto the wooden boards. Even onto my clothes. Forcing my hands steady, I held the lit straw to the ceiling.

A sky of fire spread above me.

The sailors, the captain, everyone, would be too concerned with saving their ship now, this costly nightmare made of wood, to pay attention to its intended cargo.

Pandemonium would never again transport anyone into a life of slavery.

This was all I could offer.

Smoke bit into my eyes and throat with teeth as sharp as those I'd felt in Aleister's horrid room. It was time to go.

I turned to walk back to the ladder I'd used to climb down and a glint of silver among the flames caught my eyes.

A small sound escaped my throat as every part of me recognized what I was seeing. *No. Oh, no.*

I ran toward that glint, shoving aside crates that had already caught fire, blinking smoldering ash from my eyes, fighting back the smoke that was already making it difficult to draw breath.

With a moan, I pushed away the last sacks. I took a shaking step back.

"No."

Aleister's wings lay flat on the floor. He hadn't been able to get them.

As I watched, flames licked at the feathers, leaving trails of black wherever they touched. The crackling sound of destruction sent a wave of icy horror through me.

"No. No!" Even now, after everything, I couldn't bear to watch them burn.

I lunged forward and wrapped my arms around the wings, but they were so large, so heavy it was impossible to lift them. Coughing, I grabbed hold of one end and began to pull. They shifted but only a little. I kicked aside crates and pulled again but managed only a few tugs before my vision darkened.

Exhaustion and pain joined into a mantle that dropped onto me with little warning, so heavy I couldn't fight it off any longer. My knees buckled and I fell.

Each breath I took burned my throat and I found I couldn't stop coughing. It became hard to draw breath at all.

I dug my fingers into the feathers but I didn't have any more strength.

Darkness pulled on me and I let it. As if it were happening to someone else, I felt my body collapse against the straw. Heat embraced me. Distantly, like a muffled scream, I felt the first lick of flames against my skin.

I closed my eyes. Just for a moment.

"Nora!"

The fire was calling my name. Peculiar. I didn't know fire could speak.

"Nora!"

Was it the fire, though? The voice was so familiar...I tried to open my eyes but I couldn't remember how.

Something strong slid under me and I was floating, flying. I'd grown wings! But they weren't mine, they couldn't be, no, not mine. They were Aleister's. Yes, they had to be his. I had to tell him that they were here...that I had them...I had to...

NINETEEN

"DO YOU WANT IT or not?" I said, turning my hand so that the light danced across the gold pocket watch.

The man shrugged. "I'll give you ten pounds for it."

"You know very well it's worth at least twice that." I closed my hand and made to tuck the watch into one of my skirt's pockets. "I'll go somewhere else."

"Wait. Thirteen pounds."

I looked up. "Seventeen."

The man shook his head. "Fifteen. That's the highest I can go."

"Deal."

I watched him as he counted out the money, keeping a close eye on his fingers to make sure he didn't trick me. It was known to happen, even in some of the higher class pawn shops like this one.

He handed me the bundle of bills and coins and I placed the watch in his palm.

"I suppose there's no point asking where you got it?" he asked, holding it up by its chain.

Tucking the money away, I turned and headed for the door. "I'm sure you know the answer to that already."

The door jingled behind me as I stepped out into the London morning. The sun, bright and warm, brought a smile to my lips. It was turning into a beautiful day.

"Come on, Milton," I said.

The black rat stood at once from where I'd told him to wait and scurried to my side, his fur glittering in the light. We set off down the street side by side.

Almost three weeks had passed since I'd woken back at Aleister's home, in my bed. He had pulled me out of the burning ship and had watched over me for the two days I'd been unconscious. The strain of worrying, of not being able to help me without my permission, had been clearly written in his tired eyes and in the way his hands had reached out to me the moment I'd stirred. But just one of my glances, a single look full of the pain of his betrayal, and he'd retreated with a soft nod, leaving me alone.

It'd been two more days before the many aches and burns spread throughout my body had allowed me to leave the house. I carried nothing away with me, not even the cufflinks I'd arrived with. Certainly not the purses of money Aleister urged me to take in the note he'd left next to the door. He'd known me well enough, then, to realize I wouldn't stay.

The first thing I'd done was pick a man's pocket. I rented a room at a boardinghouse with that money and allowed myself to sleep, to finally rest, my dreams blank and silent.

When I'd woken and ventured out for food, the rat had been sitting by the door, waiting. It had followed me to the first newspaper boy I saw where I'd read of the girls' escape and of the mysterious young man who'd led them right to Scotland Yard's door and refused to give his name.

It had also taken time for me to be able to look at the rat without wanting to fling something at it. Time for the anger at everything and everyone to die down. Then, and only then, could I really think of Aleister and what he'd done.

I forced myself to look at his actions when all I wanted to do was turn away. I'd thought and thought, deep into the nights, some days waking up in a rage that urged me to walk the streets for hours at a time, the rat running beside me, while other days only managing to feel a deep hole in my center that nothing seemed to be able to fill.

Because there were no simple answers I could hold on to when I began to examine that night.

Once my mind was clear enough to gaze at Aleister's actions through his eyes, it was easy, too easy, to understand them. Not to forgive them, but to understand them. Wouldn't I have done everything he had and more if it meant being able to return home? If it meant getting Peter back? Wouldn't I have lied and used anything and anyone to get my way?

Aleister and I were too alike for me not to understand. Not to recognize that type of selfishness.

And yes, of course he had betrayed me, lied to me, but as much as I resisted admitting it those first few days, he had also saved me. He could have let me die when I jumped. He could have used his powers to fetch his wings while my lifeless body sank into the Thames, but he hadn't.

And the struggle in my mind went even deeper.

I could have dealt with Aleister's betrayal much more easily if I could have hated him. If my love for him had been seared away with the fury that consumed me those first days. But it hadn't been. It had only burned itself down to its core, to the hot coals that refused to die out. Even when I couldn't think of him without wanting to scream until I was hoarse, I was hungry to see him. My need to lunge at him and hurt him as much as he had hurt me alternated with my wish to demand explanations and apologies.

I knew hate. It was simple. What I felt for Aleister was anything but.

I began to allow the rat into the room I was renting. Since I lived on the ground floor, all I needed to do was open the window and hoist the animal up. It was a male, a buck, and I gave him the most appropriate name I could come up with: Milton. He insisted on following me about and I couldn't very well just keep calling him "rat." Not when he was all I had left.

"Are you hungry, Milton?" I asked now as we turned toward Trafalgar Square. "I am, rather. There's bound to be something to buy around here."

Or steal, if there was an opportunity, because without Peter to give me one of his looks and to steer me toward honest work, I saw no reason to make my life more difficult. Stealing was something I was good at and I would make use of it for as long as I was able to. The fifteen pounds I'd made today were more than even I could have made catching rats, not that I *would* do that anymore. I'd had enough of it, of its cruelty. Let the animals live in peace.

We crossed the street and walked past Nelson's Column. There wasn't anyone else in the Square, not a single person even feeding pigeons.

I knew he was behind me before he spoke.

"Nora," he said.

I turned. Aleister stood just a few feet away, a pale, tired smile on his lips. He watched me carefully, looking for any signs that I might bolt or lunge at him as I might have done when I woke at his home, my throat still raw from the smoke. But I felt no fear and no anger now, just a deep sadness.

"You look well," he said.

"I'm better than I was. I no longer want to burn everything to the ground, so I would call that progress."

He looked away, his hands clenching into fists. The cormorant pin glittered when he moved, as it had that night on the rooftop. "I don't know how to apologize for what I did to you."

I'd planned and planned what I would say to Aleister if I saw him again. But now that he was here, now that I heard the same grief I felt in his voice, all of those words deserted me. It didn't appear like he'd had a much easier time of all of this than I'd had.

"I would take it all back, if I could," he said.

I shrugged. "But it's done, Aleister. There's no point in wishing things were different. I've thought about this a lot once I got through my initial shock and fury and I...I understand why you did all of this. It still hurts, and I don't think I can forgive you, but I do understand."

He looked at me again, a hint of surprise on his face.

I swallowed. "I read that you helped the girls."

"I just led them to the police. You were the one who helped them."

"What will happen to them now?"

"Most of them have already been returned to their homes."

I gave him a small smile. "Good."

But there was something else I needed to know, the question I'd woken with after that terrible night and that had chased me until this moment. I feared the answer, but I needed to hear it, nonetheless.

"And your wings? What happened to them?"

"It doesn't matter."

"Of course it does, Aleister."

He took a deep breath. "They burned with the ship. I couldn't get them out in time."

I winced and closed my eyes. He had saved me, then, and left them behind. He had lost what he'd wanted most in this world. "I'm sorry. I tried—"

"You never have to apologize to me, Nora. Not ever. You know that."

"But they meant so much to you."

He cocked his head lightly to one side and watched me for a moment. "Yes, but I realized that night that you meant more."

I looked away to keep him from seeing the deep pain his words caused. Because as much as I loved him, as much as I wanted his arms around me, I couldn't forgive his betrayal. He already knew that, of course. We *were* too alike for him not to.

"I named the rat Milton," I said, forcing my mind away from the sting. "I know he's your servant, but he needed a name."

Aleister's obvious relief at my lighter tone made his eyes shine in the sun. "It's a good name." He glanced past me, to where the rat sat, waiting. "You don't mind him, then?"

"No. He's pleasant company."

We stood in silence for a moment, listening to birds scuffling nearby. How long ago the day we'd sat here together, the day we'd gone into the National Gallery, seemed now.

"Here," he said, breaking the silence and walking the few steps that separated us. "This belongs to you, to do with as you wish."

It was the wedding band I'd tossed into the river. It looked just as bright as it'd been the day he'd given it to me.

I took it from his hand.

"You had no trouble finding this tiny thing in the depths of the Thames, but you couldn't find my old hairpin in that horrible room of yours?"

He smiled. "I did find it, but I'm afraid I kept it." He was about to say something else, but stopped himself.

"What?"

He cleared his throat. "I wanted something of yours, though I didn't understand why at the time. I didn't know what I was feeling. I didn't know that I *could* feel that."

His words made my heart beat faster. I gazed down at the ring in my hand for an instant before making the decision and sliding it onto the finger on which I'd worn it for weeks. It was more than just a prop, I realized. It meant more to me than that. That was why I had tossed it into the river and why I chose to wear it again now.

We were bound to each other, whether I liked it or not, whether I could forgive him or not.

A coil of Aleister's power wrapped around me, making me tremble. I looked up at him.

The ground beneath us gave a rumble.

He drew closer and touched my hand with his. It was an unsure touch, one that ached with longing. With the same need thrumming through me.

I took his hand, holding on to it as tightly as I could.

Somewhere nearby, glass shattered.

"I wish...I wish so many things were different," he said, his voice a murmur that sent shivers down my back. "Because I love you, Nora. In my awful, destructive, selfish way, I love you. I have for some time."

The ground shook with more violence, his power making the pavement ripple like water.

I had to finally say it. This might be my last chance. "And I love you, Aleister. In a way I've never loved anyone else, despite everything. But I can't..." My throat tightened, the words refusing to come out.

"I know." He brushed a curl from my face. Softly, he said the same two words in his native tongue that he'd said that night in my room.

"What does that mean?" I asked again when they'd burned through me.

He traced my face with his eyes. "It means 'my love.'"

I couldn't hold the tears back anymore. They brimmed over, spilling down my cheeks. It felt as if someone were squeezing my chest, making it impossible to draw breath. How could this hurt so much?

Aleister brushed my tears away with his fingertips. "Oh, Nora."

The rain began then, all at once, a warm drizzle that was like a curtain of crystals. We both looked up at the same time in surprise. There were no clouds, no darkness, nothing but the bluest of skies and the undimmed sun.

We smiled at the strange rain and at each other and Aleister pulled me into his arms. I wrapped myself around him, my face pressed against his chest, my eyes shut tightly. This would be the last time I would hold him. The last time I would see him. I knew it as well as I knew my name.

We stayed like that, his racing heartbeat in my ear, his hand gently stroking my hair, until we were soaked through. Then I felt Aleister breathe deeply and I knew he was going to release me. It was time to let go.

I unwound myself from him and he stepped away.

His lips trembled for a second when he smiled again. "Things will be all right, Nora. You'll see."

Without waiting for an answer, for me to say anything else or to attempt to memorize the way he looked right there, caught in the rain and sunlight, he turned and disappeared.

I pressed a hand against my mouth to hold back the immediate sob that demanded to tear itself free.

We were both alone again. Both Aleister and I. Each one of us on our own.

Milton's quick feet brought him to my side, his dark face turned up to look at me, to make sure I was all right. Offering what comfort he could.

I bent down, my entire body trembling, and stroked his head.

It was over.

Slowly, ever so slowly, soothed by the repetitive motion of my hand passing over fur, by Milton's steady, even breaths, by the gentle depths of his dark eyes, I stopped shaking, the tears stopped falling. And with them, the rain.

"We should get going," I finally said, wiping my face with my skirt. "I promised you food."

"Nora, what in God's name are you doing?"

The voice surprised me so much I flinched. I looked up.

Peter was staring at me, mouth slightly open, surprise and confusion written on all of his features. "What are you doing petting a rat?"

Of course. I was an upper-class lady to him still. I stood up. "Oh, just being silly, that's all." I cleared my throat. "Where's Sarah?"

"Sarah? Who's Sarah?"

I frowned. "Sarah, you know, your—" And then it all struck me. Peter's casual tone, his lack of deference, his confusion at seeing me pet a rat.

I swallowed. It couldn't be.

"Your sister, Sarah," I said, watching him carefully.

Peter's eyebrows rose. "Have you hit your head or something, Nora? As far as I know, you're the only sister I have. And let me tell you, that's plenty."

No, but Aleister had said...he'd said...Oh, that liar. That absolute liar!

I let out a screech and propelled myself at my brother, leaping into his arms with such force we almost toppled over.

"What's gotten into you?" Peter said in my ear.

I just squeezed him tighter. He was here, he was really here and he knew me! Aleister had returned him to me!

"You're soaked through. You're going to catch cold."

"I don't care."

"Well, I care! You're insufferable when you're sick."

I laughed through the new tears that had sprung up.

"Are you crying?" Peter pulled me away from him and frowned. "Why are you crying?"

"It doesn't matter. Nothing matters now." I wanted to hug him again, to latch myself on to him like a vine.

"Wait, wait, wait!" Peter said when he saw I was about to squeeze him once more. "The strangest thing just happened. Well, apart from seeing you pet a rat."

He showed me a large, leather envelope he'd been holding all of this time. I hadn't even seen it.

"Someone delivered this to our room earlier. You won't believe what it says. I'm still not sure it's not a joke of some sort."

"What is it?"

"Well, apparently, some distant relative has left us a house. I didn't know we had relatives of *any* sort, let alone someone this rich. All the legal documents are here, and signed. There's even a key to the house! Oh, and this."

He reached into the envelope and pulled out a feather.

Aleister's glittering gray feather.

"Strange, isn't it?"

Feeling that tightness in my throat again, I took it from my brother's hand. It would be safe with me. For as long as I lived, it would have its home wherever I was.

"None of it makes any sense to me," Peter continued, "but we're rich, Nora. If this is real, we never have to work another day of our lives. We can do anything we want." Peter shook his head. "All because of some man named Aleister Blake. That's the name on the papers, anyway. He left us everything he owned."

I wiped at my tears and pressed the feather to my chest. "It looks like we've been very lucky."

"Lucky? I don't know. More like someone is finally making up for everything that has happened to us, all the terrible things we've been through." He frowned. "Do you know what I mean?"

Smiling softly, I took my brother's hand and motioned to Milton.

"Oh, I know exactly what you mean, but it doesn't matter now, Peter. Let's just go home. Please, I just want to go home."

Acknowledgments

Books are tricky beasts and none can be wrangled without help. I want to thank agent extraordinaire, Christopher Schelling, for loving Aleister and Nora from the start and for his "this is fixable" attitude. It keeps my dramatic soul from leaping off its own tall buildings every other day.

Thank you to Scarlett R. Algee and the whole team at Trepidatio Publishing for having faith in the novel.

My family deserves a round of thanks, as well. Thank you for making room for me to work, even through the structural disaster that was our home at that time. Thank you to my sister for listening to me sputter about the first inklings of this story over lunch oh so many years ago, to Mom, for putting up with my tangled ramblings about plot points, and to Dad for lowering the volume.

And, of course, thank you to Rory, for lending me his wings.

ABOUT THE AUTHOR

Valentina Cano is a writer and singer who lives in a secluded Victorian watermill in Italy that is ripe with history. She is the author of *The Rose Master* and its sequel, and she runs a page dedicated to exploring the folklore of the devil across different countries and eras. You can find her on Twitter at @valca85 and @adversaryand.

www.ingramcontent.com/pod-product-compliance
Lightning Source LLC
Chambersburg PA
CBHW021008260626
47169CB00006B/2000